MARMALADY

by Wendy Evans

Marmalady

Published: 10th Mar 2014
ISBN: 978-0-9924784-0-7
Print Edition

Chapter 1

Golden-orange fruit pulp blurped and bubbled on the stove. The air was filled with the pungent aroma, sharp and tingly. Molly Anstruther, who'd never known romance and knew precious little of love, was making marmalade because she was unhappy. The cupboards were full of jars of four-fruit, tangelo and lemon, grapefruit and mandarin. The misery had become worse in the past six months. The old refrigerator in the garage was stacked with rough-cut.

The superabundance hadn't stopped her getting up at first light to make another batch. She stirred vigorously but jumped when Dot Langford, her next door neighbour, came in with arms laden with bags of sugar. Dot's hair was in curlers and her face plastered with a red-brown mud pack. She wore her dressing gown and pink fluffy bedroom slippers with rabbit ears.

"I know, I know. I look like hell," said Dot. "Why on earth you had to start boiling fruit at this time in the morning I'll never know. I'm sorry I forgot the sugar yesterday."

"I wanted to get the school's fruit done before Frank woke up. He hates the smell. Says it puts him off his breakfast."

"He'd better not see me then, or he'll not eat lunch or supper. Here, can I rinse this stuff off my face before I shock Bud out of his socks?"

"Be my guest. You look like the negative of a panda. Coffee?"

"Mm!" There was a lot of splashing going on in the sink. Dot emerged from the gunk, her skin looking taut and shiny. "Oh, what one suffers!"

"This in aid of the wind-up party for the pickle factory?"

"Sure is. Maybe I'll meet a handsome prince tomorrow."

Molly raised her eyebrows. "But what about Bud?"

"Oh, I know already that he says grubbit when I kiss him. I'd just like to find a man who doesn't want to make tadpoles every night! I want one who's romantic."

"Fat chance," said Molly. "You're lucky to have Bud. He's worth a hundred princes. Anyway, who on earth is there on the staff who'd turn you on? Not Peter Piper?"

"The boss? No way. I don't go for short and fat, even with a goatee beard. I'd go for someone like David, the delivery truck driver, or young Nigel from labelling, or Jake Morgan from security."

"David is eighteen, Nigel is gay and Jake Morgan has a wife and kid. We went to the party to wet the baby's head, remember?"

"Jake wasn't married to Jen, Molly. And it's all bust up, from what Bud says. He met Jake in the pub last week, drowning his sorrows."

Molly tipped sugar into the preserving pan and sighed. "Poor lad. He was besotted with that baby. Over the moon. He's a nice guy, Jake. Polite and friendly. A smashing smile."

"And those pecs, Molly. He's no Brad Pitt, but he's got a body to die for."

Molly laughed. "I've never noticed. I just enjoy his company."

"I've seen you chatting him up. I may be only an office girl, but I see what you get up to. You fancy him, don't you?"

"Dot, he's young enough to be my son!"

"He is not so! He's more than thirty. Unless you started when you were nine years old, you're talking rubbish. You just feel safer, pretending you're only mothering him."

Molly went red. "I mean, I'd have liked a son like Jake."

Dot blew a raspberry. For two years Jake had been with the company for which she and Molly worked. She knew there was a different quality about Molly when she talked to the security guard. She was about to have another dig when Molly changed the subject.

"Did you get the numbers for last night's lottery?"

Dot handed her a strip of paper, torn from the top of the previous day's West Australian.

"Cross fingers," Molly said. "I could do with some luck. Haven't had more than four numbers in a line for a year or more."

"Hang on, Molly. You've had your share. You won that car in a raffle six years ago."

"Much good it did me. Frank traded it in for a BMW and got me a second-hand Barina."

"You said you didn't mind."

"Well, the prize car was too big for me, but I would have liked to have been asked before Frank steam-rollered me."

"Yeah. Well, your luck ran out with him. If he was a winning ticket in the game of life, how come you got stuck?"

"I was too young to know better."

The hot pipes started banging. They could hear Frank singing in the shower.

"He thinks he's Australia's answer to Placido Domingo," said Molly.

Dot frowned. "What? With a gut like Pavarotti's?"

"In his dreams! Pity mine turned into a nightmare." She grabbed a wooden spoon and stirred the mixture again to ensure it didn't stick to the bottom of the pan.

Dot giggled. "You know, you look like a witch hovering over a cauldron

Molly popped a knob of butter into the bubbling pan and gave it another powerful mix. "O Great Genie of the Magic Preserving Pan, send me a hot young lover!"

"Frank will think you barmy if he hears you carrying on like that," said Dot. "Is that ready to jell yet? I'll pick it up later and run it down to the school fete organisers. Thanks for helping out. Must go."

"No sweat," said Molly. She smiled ruefully and tucked a strand of faded blond hair into the neat bun she wore at the nape of her neck. Frank allowed no money in the budget for fancy haircuts and she rarely had time to tint her shoulder-length locks back to the golden sheen they'd had when she first married. Still, the steam from the preserving pan kept her skin as soft as it had been when she was a girl and had thought Frank a demi-god. More than twenty-five years later she thought he was a slob. She turned the gas off and, skimming the pan, burnt her finger. She pinched the hot spot to her ear to cool it and kissed herself better.

"I've no one else to do it," Molly muttered, with a rueful smile, recognising the absurdity of her action. She got back to the task in hand, putting five kilos of the latest recipe, rhubarb and orange, into jars already warming in the oven. She hummed contentedly as she placed the cellophane covers on top, snapped them tight with rubber bands. No, making marmalade didn't make Molly feel happy. It made her feel needed, appreciated, useful.

It hadn't been easy to find the time when she was at work but, since the pickle factory closed down, she found the hours dragging. It had been a good job. She'd had free sugar; the boss had given her all the bags which had been split or gone lumpy. Now she had to buy it, or get Dot to do so on her behalf. She dreaded Frank finding out how much she'd spent. Luckily community groups provided all the ingredients when they asked for her services.

The man of the house was now gargling. The hot pipes had stopped banging and she could hear his rinse and spit routine. Time to get his breakfast. She switched on the extractor fan on to clear the air and covered the pan with a thick cloth.

Frank hated her hobby. He hated the tang of lemon, the zing of grapefruit, the sweet sharpness of oranges. He hated the fact that Molly had an interest and one which made her popular with the locals. "Common, that's what it is," he said, whenever he was in a grouchy temper. "It's nearly as bad as frying fish down at the chip-shop. Trouble with you, Molly, is you've got no class. Why don't you try to better yourself? How do you think I feel, having to tell my colleagues my wife is a pickle-packer?"

Molly sighed and sprayed air-freshener around. She slapped the frying pan on the stove. Frank was a bacon and two eggs man. Muesli first, as it was good for his health, he claimed, sousing it with cream and a couple of spoonfuls of sugar, and following up the daily cholesterol fix with two slices of toast, lashing of butter and vegemite. Never marmalade; jam, maybe. The diet was making him fat and jowly. He'd always been big. Now he was turning into a six-foot tall, three-foot wide pig of a man. It had taken her five years to realise her husband was a male chauvinist, long before the women's libbers had coined the phrase, but now he was more oink than any man she'd met.

"Have you any idea how much our gas bill has gone up since you started going crazy making marmalade?" he barked, waving a power bill in front of her face. "You need a shrink. You're obsessed with those bloody jam jars. My mother says you're probably on the change of life. She says some women go queer when they've passed forty."

Molly ignored him. She didn't like Frank any more. The sooner he'd go off and broke stock, or sell insurance, or peddle mortgage finance, the sooner she would be free of his bullying, his haranguing. His words were like lemon juice rubbed into a cut. She sucked her burnt finger. That wound was physical but the words and attitude hurt more.

"You meeting Peter Piper this morning?" Frank asked. "Mind you ask him for redundancy money. He owes you, after all the years you spent working for his company."

"I'll get my holiday pay," Molly muttered. "That's more than I expected."

"When you do, hand it over. You can have it back each week as housekeeping until you get another job. Can't have you wasting it on fripperies, now can we?"

She didn't argue. She watched him stuffing his face with toast and thought of pig-swill. Molly had tried standing up for herself when they first married but he'd sweet-talked her into letting him handle their finances. He'd made her feel stupid, him with his accounting diploma and a good job at the rural bank and she forced to drop-out from a high school in the bush. At first she was adrift. Marriage was not what she expected. Soon Frank was promoted and there was the move to the city and the wrench of leaving Dancer's Creek. She no longer had her parents close at hand, nor her godmother, Aunty Flo, for advice. She'd faced trouble alone.

"Don't you worry your pretty little head about the finances," Frank had said. "Money's my business, Molly. I'm trained to handle investments. You can work until the baby comes and put aside a little nest egg. Then I'll look after the two of you, or however many we have. You can go find another job when the youngest goes to school."

Well, there hadn't been any family, had there? She lost the first and nearly her own life. The doctor had drawn a pint of blood from Frank by direct transfusion, such was the emergency. Since then, however often she tried, could never carry beyond the fourth month. The doctor had suggested she stay in bed for the whole of her pregnancy but Frank had laughed at the very idea. They needed her wages; he'd set up an investment strategy and having to pay housekeeping out of his commission would play hell with his portfolio.

When she got a rise, he bought a bigger house in Wintergully, on the river south of Perth, suitable for an up-and-coming stockbroker. It wasn't new. It was post-war with high ceilings and polished floor boards, big open fire places and many-paned windows. Molly loved it, despite it being a dust trap. The house stood on a large block, almost an acre, sloping down to the Canning, a tributary of the Swan River. It had been on the outskirts of the city when they'd moved in. It was part of an old orange orchard. The ready supply of fruit had started her interest in preserves but it was not that which had first attracted her.

"Room for the children to play," Molly had said. She was

then still hopeful of having a parcel of kids. She still idolised her husband and hoped to gentle him.

"Good investment," Frank had replied. "We'll fence off the trees and keep a tidy bit of lawn for entertainment; then, in twenty years or so, we'll subdivide the land and sell the back to a developer."

Frank spent no more than was necessary, apart from having the grass in the orchard slashed once or twice a year, to make sure snakes hadn't come up from the wetlands fringing the river. Now suburbia was all around them and the view was spoiled by rooftops.

The kitchen had been remodelled before they bought. There was an upright gas stove and a dishwasher, plenty of bench space but a lack of power points. The laundry was in a separate building, with its own wood stove for heating water. The old boiler, still operational, had been replaced by a gas-fired system to take care of domestic needs. The drawback was that the pipes were built for a kinder era. They went crazy when the high pressure hot taps were turned on. As things turned out, the wood stove proved a blessing for large runs of marmalade and Christmas puddings. In the height of an Australian summer it was good to be able to cook outside the house.

The only other concession Frank had made was reverse cycle air-conditioning, which was turned on only when he judged the weather too hot or bitterly cold, as it often was in mid-winter. Except during heatwaves the high ceilings and fans had to keep the bedrooms cool. In winter they were freezing. Luckily the kitchen was warm, despite sudden flurries of rain carried by winds straight off the southern ocean. The bite in the morning air had driven Molly's marmalading into the house.

Frank still kept tight control of the bank account. Their first big row had come over a production bonus when Peter Piper landed an export order to Indonesia. Molly had wanted to buy a new rug for the lounge but Frank had slapped her face and twisted her arm behind her back until she dropped the wages envelope He had enjoyed that. It had set a pattern. If she spent anything he defined as wasteful he'd make her pay for it. She'd got used to covering up the bruises so her workmates would not see them.

"You don't have to put up with that sort of behaviour," her mother had said, more than ten years earlier. She'd been on a visit to have chemotherapy in the city, treatment that had only delayed the end for her. "Come back and live on the farm. Look after your father when I'm gone."

Molly had shaken her head. "I made a commitment to marriage. I married Frank for better or for worse," she'd said. "He needs me."

"Well, that's a load of old claptrap if I ever heard one," Mrs Grayson had said. "Your Frank needs someone to feed his gut, iron his shirts, polish his shoes and let him rut like the big mallee bull he always has been. The fact that you also earn the money to run this house is just another bonus. What does he do with the money he earns? Plays the stock-market! He must be rolling in it."

"I shouldn't complain, Mum. He doesn't gamble, he doesn't drink much, except socially. He spends time and money playing golf, but he writes that off as a tax deduction because he's entertaining clients. There's lots worse off than I am."

"And his other women? He's the sort that would have other women."

Molly had turned her head away. "I don't know. Mum, I don't care. If it means he'll leave me alone, I don't care."

Her mother had pursed her lips. Poor Molly. She'd guessed that the bedroom had given her girl little joy. If the big brute had interests on the side, at least he didn't flaunt them in front of his wife. The worst she suspected of Frank Anstruther was that he was turning into a regular abuser and a mean, miserly son of a polecat. He'd claw the very life out of her daughter if he could. It was no use trying to tell Molly to leave Frank. He'd stood by when he got her in the family way. That one act of loyalty had locked her into a relationship that was, by any standards, rotten.

"It's time you got smart, Molly," Mrs Grayson had said. Six months later she was dead.

*

Molly wished the past would not keep unrolling in her mind like a repeat soap-opera on the TV. She'd had thirteen years action replay to realise her mother had been right. There was no time to reflect on that, despite the nagging ache in her heart. She cleared the table and made the beds.

She had an appointment to keep and it was not in her nature to be late. Peter Piper's Pickles was deserted, the gates padlocked. She knew the boss was there, because his car was outside the offices. She tooted. Jake Morgan ran out with keys to let her in. He was, as always, immaculately dressed in security uniform, a thick reefer jacket, light blue shirt and navy strides. His hair, dark and curling, was cut short. He looked fit and tanned, but infinitely miserable.

She beamed to cheer him up. "You still here, Jake? I thought you'd got a new job as a council ranger?"

"I start on Monday, Molly. The boss asked me to stay on until the new company took over the premises. I don't know what to do."

"When do they move in?"

"God knows, but it will be months before they start making alterations."

"You'd hate it, Jake, guarding an empty building. You need people around you. Here, all you'd have are ghosts."

"I know. I'd be thinking of all of you and the great times we had. End of an era, Molly."

"I'll miss you."

He smiled as if his teeth were hurting. She guessed he hadn't been smiling too much in recent weeks. He was out of practice.

"I mean that, Jake. You've been a good friend, a pleasure to work with."

"You too, Molly. Save a dance for me at the party, won't you?"

She nodded as he swung the gate aside.

"Leave the back of the car open, Moll. The boss found boxes of jars and big bags of sugar in the stores. I'll load them for you. What I can't get in, I'll bring round tonight."

"Your blood's worth bottling, Jake."

The big multinational grocery chain that was buying the factory planned to convert it into a warehouse. They had their own label for preserves and had no desire to stock Peter Piper's Pickles. Molly was deeply saddened by the situation. She'd been part of a team, respected, useful, creative. She'd been fulfilled, interested in her work, so wrapped up in the day-to-day lives of the staff that she'd not seen the flaws in her own relationship. When she had time to think about it she realised her marriage had more holes in it than a jelly-bag. She was neither understood nor appreciated by Frank or his mother. It was not surprising. Frank thought little further than what suited Frank. Hermione thought only of who had done her wrong.

Peter Piper, the Pickle King, in contrast, thought the world of Molly. He knew what strife she faced at home. She'd been his trouble-shooter, a reliable assistant who knew almost as much about running the factory as he did. She'd refused every offer to give her a grand title, preferring to be known as the gopher. As circumstances required, she'd go for this or go for that. For fifteen years her take-home pay packet had remained about the same, given cost of living increases, but a monthly bonus went straight into the account of Molly Grayson, not Molly Anstruther.

The boss gave her a kiss on the cheek and showed her into his office.

"You're the last and the best," he said. "I've seen every member of the staff and thanked them. But I wanted to meet my gopher for a serious talk. Me advising you, not you advising me."

She bowed her head and smiled shyly. Molly didn't know how to take praise. It was rare in her life.

"Molly, you know I can't stand that pig of a man you married," said Peter Piper. "You know I think you ought to divorce the big hunk."

"I daren't," Molly said. "My mother left me some money that she'd inherited from her grandmother. I was so upset when she died from breast cancer that I let Frank talk me into investing it through him."

"Did he lose it on the stock exchange?"

"No, he turned it into a small fortune, but he won't let me touch it. I've asked and asked, but he's put it into a property development now. That's what the new broking company specialises in."

"Well, you watch what Frank's up to. You tell him your tax accountant needs an investment statement. Start reading what you sign, Moll, or he'll move the whole lot off-shore and you can kiss goodbye to your share of the family estate."

"Can he do that?"

"Easy peasy. Have you got a joint account? Can you draw on it? You could but you don't? No cheque book? I thought not. Well, young lady, make sure that mortgage account with your mother's money is paid out and put in your name only. Tell Frank that, with the way the economy is going, he'd also be wise to put the house in your name only."

"He did that last year, boss. I couldn't think why."

"Hmm. Tax fiddle. Now take a tip from me, Molly. You and I will take a little trip down town next week and see my lawyers. Do you know what we're going to do? We're going to put a caveat on your house to stop him borrowing against it."

Molly grew a worried frown. "What are you trying to tell me, boss? Frank must be loaded by now. He's always been into investing in a big way."

"But has he always invested wisely, Molly? Would he admit it if he'd lost money? I hear things, down at the Settlers' Club. The brokers talk. There's some of them have got into very leery deals lately. Your Frank's associates into mortgage broking?"

"I think so."

"Well, Molly, my dear, be careful. There are some projects where sharks buy land cheaply, inflate its value to investors and suggest the profits will be huge. The brokers sell mortgages and, when the whole deal goes sour, the people who trusted them find the kitty is empty. It was fine while the market was booming, but the bubble's burst. So you just do what I tell you. Yes?"

She nodded. If Flatterjohn and Associates could do it to others, what was stopping Frank's firm doing the dirty on her?

"Right. Oh, and don't let him see your redundancy cheque. I made it out to M Grayson, as per our agreement."

Molly looked at the cheque with wide eyes. "That's too much!"

"No, it's not. Your taste-buds were the company's greatest asset. Don't blush, Molly. Many a time you've got us out of a right pickle. You're the only person who could tell what was in a batch by sipping and sniffing. If there was a worry about the colour of a run of mustard pickle, one taste and you could tell immediately what was missing and how much of this spice or that had to be added. And half the new recipes were developed in your test kitchen. Molly, do you know what skills like that were worth to the company?"

"It wasn't something I thought about," said Molly. "It was sort of natural."

"Pshaw! Don't put yourself down, girl. I've written you a reference. I liked the way you got on with the staff. They liked you because you listened to their problems but stood no nonsense. You got on well with the foremen because you made sure each section ran like clockwork. You should have let me make you assistant manager."

"No. It wouldn't have been proper. I liked things the way they were."

"Your Frank never showed an interest in your work, did he? I bet he didn't realise how good you were or how well-thought of. I never told him. No one would have told him. We couldn't stand the pompous git. The couple of times he came to company functions, he just talked about himself. He still thinks you're just a pickle-packer, doesn't he?"

Molly nodded. "Well, I was."

Peter Piper sighed. "Oh, Molly, in your own way, you're a creative genius. Wake up. And don't trust the big hunk."

Molly certainly didn't trust Frank, now now. It wasn't the other women that had soured Molly's perception of her relationship with Frank. It was the one, the big, the unforgivable betrayal that was turning her guts inside out. She had just learned that Frank had had a vasectomy. Probably years ago. He'd never told her. He'd never asked her. He'd let her think she was sterile. He'd let her take the blame for not giving him a family. No wonder there'd been no children. She had been cheated. There was a white hot anger in her heart, so hot that she had not dared talk about it to anyone, not even Dot.

But damn, it was hard to carry on as normal, to smile, to joke, to make bloody marmalade, when all she wanted to do was to boil Frank's balls in hot oil.

Chapter 2

Frank was in a foul mood when he got home. Maybe it wasn't the best time to broach money matters with him, but with Peter Piper's words ringing in her ears, Molly tried.

"I want my mother's money." she said.

"Why?" he yelled. "I know what I'm doing. Trust me."

He rabbited on about the East Timor crisis and how Indonesian investors were going cold on Australia. He reminded her the Indonesian economy, once roaring like a tiger, had collapsed with a change of government. The new president had agreed with a United Nations proposal that East Timor, a small island nation to the north of Australia, should be allowed to vote for independence. The East Timorese hadn't had much choice earlier. It had been invaded by Indonesia when Portugal abandoned its colonial role. Only Australia had given tacit recognition to the situation.

Jakarta had taken it as a given that it had a right to rule the predominantly Christian country. That didn't go down too well with freedom fighters, as Indonesia was run by Islamic powers. After years of conflict, Australia was now in favour of the islanders' right of self-determination.

"Read the papers, Molly! Watch the news. Don't you realise this is playing hell with the market? I'm supposed to find rich investors for the schemes we're promoting. For three months I've been trying to din it into your thick head that our foreign policy is giving me headaches."

"It's not my fault that you don't like the government. I'm sick of you walking all over me. I am not your damn doormat. I want my mother's money!"

"You can't touch it. I've invested it for another three years. It's showing a growth of 15 per cent per annum. It's doing nicely."

"And what exactly does that mean? How much is it worth?"

He told her. She gasped. Why, she could buy a small house with that amount. Added to her other savings, her hidden savings, she'd be quite comfortably off if she sought a divorce. She'd still have to work but she'd get by. She was glad she'd taken Peter Piper's advice years ago. Long before the banks made it hard to open accounts, requesting proof of identity in twenty different ways, she'd opened an account at Dancer's Creek, where they knew her as George Grayson's girl.

Molly clenched her fists and tried to control her temper. "Frank, I want to take control of my own affairs."

He sneered. "You been talking to Dot again? Bloody women's libber! Won't even shave her armpits! God knows why Bud puts up with her. I can't stand dominant females."

"Only your mother!"

"You leave her out of this!"

"How can I leave Hermione out of this? You're the one who talked her into selling her retirement unit and moved her in with us."

"Well, why not? I can put her money to better use than she can. She trusts me! What's the point in having the granny flat standing empty?"

"That was built by my father with his money for his use. Not for your mother!"

"It's not my fault your father died last year. And without a cent to his name. Rich farmer! Huh! Mortgaged the property up to the hilt. Damn fool."

"It was your investment advice that drove him to it!"

"I didn't tell him to sell when the market crashed. If he'd hung on like I did, he'd have come out laughing."

Molly pursed her lips. Having Frank's mother living next door was a penance but what could she say? Frank had, after all, allowed Molly's father to build on their block. After her mother died, George Grayson said he found farming damned lonely. Those had been good years. Molly had enjoyed her father's company and Frank had kept his fists to himself.

"But surely the granny flat has added to the value of our house," Molly protested. "Dad spent about $50,000 building it."

"More fool he. It's probably worth more than this dump. Face it Molly, it's the land value that's important here. The house is crap."

"That's how you see everything, isn't it, Frank? You don't value relationships. Everything has to have a monetary value. I suppose that's why you tolerated me, because of my so-called expectations."

Her husband gave her a black look. "George Grayson cheated me," he growled. "And you're not much bloody use, either, now you've lost your job at the pickle factory. You know the game plan. We live off your income so I can invest my commission."

"But what for, Frank?"

He looked at her in astonishment. "So we can get rich, of course."

"But what use is all that money? I don't get any joy out of it. What does it get me?"

He blustered. "I bought you a mink coat for Christmas. You never wear it."

"It was 46 degrees on Christmas Day. We were sweltering. What I needed at the time was a new vacuum cleaner."

"So it could suck your brains out? You're an empty-headed cow, Molly. You're not fit to handle money. I'm sick of your nagging. I'm going to the casino." He stormed out, churning up the drive with the BMW, gunning the engine. Big car, big man, big deal! Casino, indeed. Only if it was spelt Nina.

Moments later there was the sound of a car outside. Why the devil was he back, Molly wondered. There was a dull knock on the door, as if it had been tapped with a foot.

"It's me, Jake. I've got your gear."

The security officer's face was obscured by two huge boxes. "Where'd you want these pickle jars, Molly? Quick, before I drop them."

Molly took the top box and laughed at her workmate. "You idiot, Jake. You trying to impress me, or what?"

He grinned. "It seemed a good idea at the time."

"We'll put them in the shower in the laundry." She pointed and he went ahead of her.

"Heck, Molly, the recess is full of oranges."

"Lord, I forgot about them. Rest the jars on the washing machine while I move the buckets into the dunny. There's room alongside the toilet."

It took Jake a good ten minutes to carry in all the supplies. "The boss says you can have what you want. Pans, mixers, anything. It's all going for auction in a few months."

Molly nodded. "That's a thought. Fancy a beer?"

"Lead me to it."

"I don't suppose you'd like to have supper with me? Frank rushed off without eating a meal."

"Wouldn't say no."

It was warm and cosy in the kitchen. There was a good smell of steak and kidney pie. Jake tucked in eagerly.

"That was good. My big sister's the only other person who can make pastry like that."

"I didn't know you had a sister."

"She's in California. Lives near Mom and Pop. She's ten years older than me. Married with kids."

"You don't have an American accent."

"I do when I go back. I pick it up like a dog picks up fleas. But I was born here. My Pop was with the US Navy communications base on your north-west coast. We came back ten years later on a repeat assignment."

"I envy you, growing up in Exmouth."

"I wasn't there much. They sent me to Guildford Grammar School as a boarder. Sis went back when Pop retired from the navy. I didn't."

"Why not?"

He grinned. "The Americans don't play Aussie Rules football, do they?"

"And you did?"

"Loved it. Got picked for a Colts team and played a few seasons with Geelong."

"I didn't know. You're not exactly my idea of a footballer."

"I wasn't Geelong's either in the end. Too short, too slow, couldn't kick straight enough."

"What did you do afterwards?" Molly placed a slice of apple-cake on a plate and handed him the cream.

"I was in the Army cadets at boarding school. Great fun, so I joined the Australian Defence Force. I'm still in the Reserves."

"Do you like working in security?"

"Similar job, I suppose. A couple of my Army buddies joined the police force. I didn't want to work in an office either. I like to be out and about."

"But the shift work! It couldn't have been easy with a family." Molly regretted her words as she had obviously touched a raw spot with Jake. His smile faded.

"No. It wasn't. Jen got fed up trying to keep Morris quiet when I was sleeping during the day. Not right, trying to bring up a baby in an apartment. We only had the balcony where she could put the pram. It got on her nerves."

"Is that why she left? Surely not."

He raised a stricken face to hers. "She says Morris isn't my baby, Molly. I thought he was. Jen and I had a bit of a fling after a beach-volleyball carnival. You know, that was Jen, all muscle and sun and sand. She told me I'd got her preggers so she moved in on me. I didn't mind. Not bad company, Jen, but she couldn't cook a worth a damn."

"It's not everything, Jake."

"No, it's not. Hey, no regrets. She was a great gal but...strewth, Molly, she was twelve years younger than me. She was just a kid, really. I loved the idea of being a father. Hell, I loved Jen. I was that proud of Morris. Then Jen started going cold on me. I couldn't work out what was wrong. Figured that twenty didn't have much to say to thirty plus...you know. One day this big Maori who'd been working on the oil rigs in the Gulf just came strolling in, looked Jen in the eye, picked up Morris and told me to piss off before he smashed my face in for playing around with his bird."

"And Jen took it?"

"Hell, Molly, she was drooling. Went off with Te Pongarani, smiling from her toes to the roots of her hair. I felt helpless. Like a caterpillar someone had put their foot on. All my guts hanging out with the misery."

She took his hand and squeezed it in sympathy.

"I loved her, Molly, and I adored the kid. I was up there, high with happiness and, well, feeling that I was somebody, that I'd done something worthwhile with my life, having a cool chick and a smashing kid then, crash, they were gone. The apartment was empty."

"Where were they?"

"They'd gone to Kiwiland. I'm left here, feeling as useless as a smear of grease on a carpet."

"Maybe she'll come back."

He frowned. "Maybe I don't want her back. She lied to me, Molly. She made a total fool of me. You don't know what it's like."

"Oh, don't I just."

Jake's brown eyes, flecked with amber and gold, met hers. He read the deep trouble in her gaze, watched a tear slide down her cheek. His finger wiped it off her face, tenderly.

"Come on. Telling time. What's wrong? You shouldn't bottle things up."

"Oh, it'll sound silly to you. Frank's been having an affair. Don't get me wrong, Jake. Frank's always having affairs. I can tell, you see. He buys me expensive and useless gifts when he's unfaithful. I mean, he bought me a mink coat. I guessed it was a guilt gift."

"You'd look good in mink!"

"Bah!" Molly dashed away another tear. "Look, we went to an office dinner last week. An awards presentation. Broker of the Year or something. He flirted all night with this flashy red-head, Nina Lavell. You know the sort, all plunging neckline and deep cleavage."

"Tart?"

"No! Predator. Tiger woman. Used to be Gary Flatterjohn's mistress until his wife found out. Now she's got her claws into Frank. I saw them slip into a store room. Oh, I knew what was going on. Frank's noisy. I didn't know what to do, my face was that red with embarrassment. You know, people were avoiding my eye. They all turned a blind eye to his fun and games. I felt like the outcast, as if I was in the wrong! So I locked myself in a toilet for a little weep."

"Good move."

"No, it was a terrible move. A couple of tiddly secretaries came in to do their makeup. By the time they'd giggled and gossiped I'd got no more illusions about Frank and his floozies. One of them said Franky boy was a safe root. She said he'd had a snip job and told her not to worry her pretty little head about having a quickie. She said he went some for an old fart and paid up handsomely!"

"Oh. You know, Molly, you're mad if you put up with that sort of thing, especially with HIV around."

"I never let him near me without a condom once I realised what he was like. I went and got myself tested six months ago and made sure we had safe sex from there on in."

"Wise lady. I had to do the same thing once I discovered Jen had been two-timing me."

"Yes, but it wasn't the affair with Nina that was upsetting. Apparently she's a rich bitch and he likes her money. But he likes her kinky ways better, the girls said. Well, Jake, I honestly don't care about that because I think Frank's a lousy lover. He's rough. He hurts me. The less he comes on to me, the better I like it."

"Shit, Molly, why do you put up with it?"

She put her head in her hands and let the tears come. "I knew you'd think me stupid. I wanted a family, you see. I thought he'd be different if I could give him a child."

Jake got up and put his arm round her shoulders, comforting.

"Oh, it was just mindless chit-chat but it made me feel sick and angry, Jake." She turned her face to his. "Years and years, hoping for a baby, putting up with his petty ways and his temper, growing older, sadder and...oh, Jake. I'm sorry to be such a misery."

"You never show the world this side of yourself. You always seem so calm, so contented, so very, well, so very Molly."

She sniffed. "I have my pride, you know. But how would you like it if you'd spent a lifetime trying to get pregnant and you found out your partner had had a vasectomy without even telling you?"

Jake pulled her to her feet and put his arms around her. He hugged her and he kissed her cheek. He laughed softly. "Oh, Molly, if I'd spent a lifetime trying to get pregnant, I'd feel very peculiar indeed!"

Her eyes opened wide as she caught his meaning and she started to giggle. And Jake, squeezing her even tighter, gave her a smacking kiss.

Frank's mother, Hermione Anstruther, who never knocked, burst into the kitchen, her face dark with indignation.

"So! So this is what goes on when my son's back is turned! You, Molly Grayson, are a slut! You, young man, put my daughter-in-law down and get out of here before I call the police!"

"Police?" said Jake. "Police? Whatever for?"

"You are an intruder."

"He's here by invitation," Molly snapped.

"He's kissing you!"

"Yes, and it's very nice," said Jake. "So I'm going to do it again!"

Mrs Anstruther screamed. She shouted and yelled all the way to the back door.

Bud and Dot ran up the drive. "What's wrong? What's happened?" cried Bud. "Are you all right?"

"Molly, Molly, what's the matter?" said Dot, bursting into the kitchen, to find Jake and her friend in fits of giggles.

"Nothing's wrong," said Molly. "Oh, go home, do. You too, Jake. I'll see you tomorrow."

"You wait until Frank hears about this," the old lady hollered.

Dot's eyes were popping with curiosity but Bud tactfully steered her back to their own house.

Molly wiped her eyes and shouted Goodnight to Frank's mother, then locked and bolted the back door. If Frank came home he could whistle Dixie. Bugger waiting to see if he turned up smelling of Nina's perfume, bugger looking for lipstick on his shirts, observing the scratch marks on his back. Bugger doing her wifely duty if Frank hadn't been worn out by his extramarital adventures.

Molly, still chuckling, turned off the lights and went to bed in the spare room. She pushed a chest of drawers in front of the door. If Frank worked out that he could get in the house with his front door key so be it, but she had no wish to have him pawing her again. It was already light when she heard him stumbling around, but he didn't try the knob to her room. He just woke her by taking a hot shower. Bang, crash, shudder, wobble, went the pipes. Molly pulled her pillow over her head and went back to sleep, in a strange land where a man with a prickly chin was kissing a jar of marmalade.

*

She woke up with a start. Marmalade! Oh, Lord. There were four buckets of fruit behind the dunny door waiting to be boiled. She got dressed in a hurry and went out to the laundry

- 24 -

to light the boiler. Soon the largest preserving pan was nearly full and simmering nicely. She wanted to wash her hair and was darned if she would risk waking Frank by using the inside taps.

"Good morning," said Dot, impatient for all the details of the scene the previous night. "Your Frank didn't come home until sparrow's fart. I heard the taxi in the drive. Did he prang the BMW?"

"I expect he was too drunk to drive it from the casino, if that's where he really was."

"Womanising again? Why don't you get smart and give him the boot? Oh, come on, Molly, let's get your shampoo done so I can put this lightener through your hair."

"You sure I won't look silly?"

"No way. This will take you down a shade or so and fill in the grey, take my word for it. Then I'll set your hair on big rollers."

"The steam will take out the curl."

"No, it won't. I'll use a lotion to give it body. Anyway, why are you boiling stuff out here?"

"If Frank's had a winning streak, he's impossible, all boisterous and boastful; if he's lost, he'll let fly."

"Trouble with your Frank and money is that he just likes having it. He's a real Scrooge. If it came in gold coins, he'd sit there counting it. The only reason you got that coat is so that he can boast about having bought it to his friends at the club. And I bet he got it at cut price."

Molly grinned. "I'm going to wear it tonight just for the hell of it."

She fetched a garden chair and sat near the laundry trough, letting her friend run her fingers across her scalp, massaging the conditioner into the clean tresses. Molly relaxed and thought about life. She didn't want the trappings of wealth, the fancy house, the imported car, the yacht, the box at the races. She had just wanted Frank to love her, to appreciate who she was and what she had to offer, but the passing years had shown her only that he was a dead loss to her ambitions. He got rich and they lived poor.

She leaned over the trough so that Dot could give her a rinse then sat back while her head was given a brisk towelling.

"What did you do to upset the old lady last night?"

"Kissed Jake."

"Shit oh dear!"

"Ooh! Language!"

"Mind my own business, you mean. Molly, whatever made your Frank think you and his mother could live in the same house?"

"She pays him rent. And he says I've got the time to look after her because the pickle-packing's finished."

"Doesn't he know you and his mother don't like one another?"

"He doesn't want to know. I'm sick of her. She's more than capable of doing things like making her own meals and keeping the granny flat clean and tidy. My father could do it; so can she, but she treats me as a skivvy."

"Frank says she's not a well woman."

"Rubbish. There's nothing wrong with his mother's health. She only pretends to be sick. But Frank says she has malignant hypertension and needs proper care. What she has is a long sticky beak and a malignant personality."

"She's a big lady."

"Sure is. I couldn't handle her if she really took sick. She's too tall and too heavy. If she fell, I'd never get her back on her feet."

"Tell Frank."

"I did. His face went red, just like his mother's when she's in one of her 'moods'. He slammed his fists on the table. He'd have belted me if I hadn't warned him he could burst a blood vessel if he didn't calm down. He said he was perfectly calm but I was stupid. He said I could call an ambulance if she fell."

"Then I bet he said, 'Can't you think of a thing for yourself, woman?' He always says that when he's running you down. To hear him talk anyone would think you were a complete doozy. He doesn't know you, does he?"

"Oh, I can think for myself all right, Dot. I've had weeks to think about the situation. I think it's either she goes or I go."

Dot stuck the last pin through a roller and tied a scarf round Molly's head. "Talking about going, I'd better dash home to get Bud off to work. There go your pipes again. Frank must be up."

Frank, a sullen, surly Frank, refused to speak to her at the breakfast table, except to comment that for once the house didn't smell of marmalade.

"Worse than cat's pee, boiling oranges are. Disgusting stuff."

"Yes, Frank."

"You look bloody horrible with your hair in curlers. What's this for?"

"The Peter Piper party."

"I'm not going. I've got a Mortgage Brokers' dinner. You should be with me. The other wives will be there. Mrs Flatterjohn expects it. Looks respectable."

"Frank, you know how it will be. You'll get me one drink and then ignore me. I'm not standing round watching you flirting with Nina Lavell."

"I don't flirt with her. She's my associate. She works under me!"

Molly's cheeks puffed out with the effort of stifling an indecent remark, merely muttering, "I'll bet she does!" Frank didn't hear her.

"Oh, have it your own way," her husband said, pushing back his chair. "Go off and play with the pickle-packers. They're your kind of people."

As soon as he'd gone Molly fetched the boiled fruit from the laundry and fixed the mincer to her old food processor. It was a large industrial model, battered and with enamel chipped from the stand.

She started to feed the softened skins through it, steadying it as she did so because the machine was cranky and very, very noisy. It was rather like Frank. She gave a rueful grin She'd had him more than twenty-five years as well. Both were usually well-oiled but no amount of sugar was going to turn her husband into a sweet delight.

"I detest you, Frank Anstruther," Molly yelled, confident that the noise of the mincer would drown out her wrath. "You are a pig and a fat pig at that." She deftly pushed six quarters of lemon into the feeder spout. "You are a cheat and a liar and a mean, miserly bastard!"

She found there was a great deal of frustration that could be let out while mincing five kilos of mixed citrus fruit.

"God knows why I married you. If I hadn't been seventeen and pregnant I wouldn't have. You're the one who made me drunk and forced me. I didn't like what you did then and I never liked what you did since. You're rough and you're cruel and you've never given a damn about what I'd like. But it wasn't my fault I lost the baby. And it wasn't my fault we never had a family. Four miscarriages weren't my fault. And even when the doctor told you there should be no more pregnancies, would you take precautions? No, you bloody well wouldn't. You forced me, time and again you forced me. And I put up with it, hoping I'd catch again. And all the time you were making a fool of me!"

She didn't see the back door opening. She didn't notice Frank's mother standing in the kitchen until the old woman slashed at her legs with her heavy walking stick. Molly yelped and turned the mincer off.

"Wicked! Wicked, that's what you are, Molly. Screaming out your lies about my son. I knew how it would be, the minute he brought you home. Little frit of a thing, no hips, no bosoms worth mentioning. A little brown mouse, squeak, squeak, squeak. And my boy so tall and strong, a real sportsman, a clever, smart boy and you, well, I could see you were not built for breeding." Hermione sneered. Molly thought she looked as if she'd smelt her own feet. "God knows why he fancied you."

"He fancied me because I was a little mouse and he was a

big, randy tom cat!" Molly protested. "He fancied me because I said no. And he's been playing games with me ever since."

"Pshaw!" Hermione had the sort of lip that could curl and the sort of eyes that could curdle cream. "You didn't have to marry him."

"I did. I was expecting his child." Molly braced herself. She knew what was coming.

"And that I'll never believe. A monster, that was what you had. Tricked him, you did, rushing him off to the registry office instead of having a decent wedding. Then later trying to tell us you'd lost the baby. Tricked him I said then, and that's what I'll say until I go to my grave. There's no abnormalities in our family!"

"Nor in ours!"

"Your mother died of breast cancer. What's that, if not an abnormality?"

"I'll not argue with you, Mother. What do you want?"

"I want my breakfast. And you'll have to wash my sheets. I came over all peculiar in the night."

"I've been lumbered," Molly muttered, washing her hands and putting bread in the toaster. "Have you run out of bread next door?" she asked. "Is your toaster broken?"

"I fancied white for a change. And I wanted to know why you were shouting."

"Well, you found out. And much good may it do you. You want marmalade on your toast?"

"Can't stand it. Vegemite, girl. I thought Frank said you weren't to make any more jam?"

"Mind yours," said Molly, mashing a pot of tea and putting it on a tray with the rest of the breakfast things. "I'll carry this into your flat and collect your washing at the same time. I'm too busy to sit here gossiping."

"I do not gossip," the old lady snapped. "I was giving you the benefit of a life of experience!"

"Gee, thanks."

Molly slammed the tray down on the dining room table, made up her mother-in-law's bed and took the soiled linen to the laundry. She rinsed the sheets and left them to sterilise in nappy solution. She scrubbed her hands clean and finished mincing, voicing her frustration into the grinding rumble of the metallic maw. Was she never to be free of Frank's mother goading her about her failure to have babies?

Molly sat at the kitchen table with a cup of coffee and wondered what to do with the rest of her life. She took the slip of newspaper on which Bud had written the lottery numbers and checked her entry. Two on a line, three, four. My God! Five and yes, the sixth was there. The lottery ticket felt hot against her fingers as she rechecked it. Molly grinned. She felt like turning cartwheels and shouting "Yippee" but she contained her euphoria. If she yahooed Hermione would come nosing around. And if Frank got so much as a sniff of good fortune he'd have the money out of her by stealth or force.

She had a year in which to claim the prize. She had a year in which to get free of Frank. She kissed the ticket and sealed it in an envelope. It meant freedom. She would post it to Aunty Flo by certified mail and ask her to put it in a safe deposit box at the bank in Dancer's Creek. She would put it out of her mind, she decided. Relying on good luck to make a difference was not the way to go. She needed a purpose, not an escape route.

Chapter 3

Dot Langford wiggled her fingers over the top of Bud's morning paper until he put it down and looked her in the eye.

"No," he said. "Don't even ask me. No. I am not going to interfere with Frank and Molly's lives."

"But she's been shouting again."

"Molly doesn't shout. Molly's a lady. If she gets excited she mutters. She doesn't shout."

"She does these days."

"Can't say I blame her, but she'd better not let Frank hear her. He'll get her locked up in a psychiatric ward if he has half a chance."

"It's not fair, Bud. She's a kind, good-natured person. She's not stupid. He makes her seem that way. She's like a rabbit under attack from a weasel."

"Bloody big weasel. But you're right. She was a different sort of person at work. A proper pickle, she was. You know, funny and happy. Not bossy, just competent, if that's the word."

"She's been damned unlucky having Frank's mother move in on her. Drama queen, that's what Molly calls Hermione. All that fuss because she gave Jake Morgan a goodnight kiss."

Bud chortled. "Is that what it was about? I thought someone was being murdered when the old lady started screeching."

"Molly's asked me to look after Hermione when she and Frank go down south to Albany for the annual company conference. Could you put up with the old lady under your feet some of the time?"

"Don't do it, Dot. You don't like the old cow any more than Molly does. I'll tell Frank to put his mother in a nursing home for the week. She's a vicious old biddy. I saw the bruises on Moll's legs yesterday. Frank ought to have her put away, not his wife."

"The trouble is that he'll probably make Molly stay home to look after her and she does so like getting away once a year. It's the only holiday she gets, except when she goes to stay with her Aunty Flo."

"Heavens knows why she'd want to spend more time with Frank than she has to. He's a big bully."

"But she doesn't. He's off playing golf when he isn't in training sessions or getting motivated. They lay on bus trips for the wives and the secretarial staff. They go sight-seeing and shopping, and visit the wineries. She enjoys it."

Dot wondered if Molly would find the trip as pleasant this year, knowing the tension there'd been next door.

"I'll talk to Frank tonight," said Bud. "It will be good to see the other guys and find out who's doing what since the factory closed."

Dot shook her head. "Frank's not going. He's got a dinner for the Mortgage Brokers' Association. He blew his stack when Molly said she had a prior engagement."

"What a way to live, eh? Shall we give her a lift to the party?"

"Yes. Then she can have a drink or two and let her hair down."

*

Molly had to stand on tip-toe to knot Frank's bow-tie. He refused to wear the self-adjustable one she'd bought him. It was a minor matter, but one of his power ploys. When younger he'd said he liked her doing it because it gave him the chance to perve down her cleavage. He'd even been known to clasp her by the buttocks, lift her skirts, ram her against the wall and have his way with her while she struggled to get his tie fixed. She'd long passed the stage of giggling at such dalliance. It was hurtful and had ruined too many dresses for her to regard it as amusing. She'd learned to go limp and submissive. This bored him, so he was quick about it. If she fought him, it made him rougher and this made what had become a torture last even longer. She'd wondered what would happen if she kneed him in the crotch, but had never dared to find out.

"I may not be home tonight," he said. "If it's a late session, I'll stay at the club."

"I may not be home tonight, either," Molly snapped, knowing he meant he'd be with his woman. "I may find a young stud and go night-clubbing."

Frank looked down at her and roared with laughter. "You? You with a young stud? About the only thing you could get off with at your work party is a pickled gherkin!"

He turned her to face the mirror. Hair in curlers, face cream thick on her cheeks, dressed in an old track suit, Molly admitted that she looked a fright. Her huge blue eyes filled with tears as he thrust her from him and went off, chuckling.

"Oh, hell," she said. "I haven't put the last batch of marmalade in jars. I'll put it in the laundry overnight." She put cling-wrap over the big pot to keep out hungry insects, carried it outside and slid it inside the door.

She'd showered earlier and now went to the bathroom to wash her face and clean her teeth. An oatmeal beauty pack had left her skin extra soft and clear. She sat before the dressing table and eased her track top off over her curlers. She rarely wore makeup but now applied it with skill, brushing violet onto her lids to enhance the periwinkle of her eyes, darkening lashes and brows with subtle strokes of colour. She smoothed the foundation cream down her neck, pleased that it showed no sign of crepe nor flabbiness along the jaw.

She hesitated before taking the turban off her head, worried that Dot's boldness would prove a disaster. It had taken some courage to ask her to buy that pack of hair lightener and half a nail-biting hour to let her leave it on for the maximum period recommended. It was hard to judge the effect while it was wet. While Dot rolled her damp locks, Molly had closed her eyes and prayed for the best.

The mouse was gone. The setting lotion had given her fine tresses body and they unwound from the rollers in loose curls of honey-gold. It needed no more than a light brushing to transform her into a stunning blonde. It was an old-fashioned style, but it suited her.

"Wow!" said Molly, impressed. She slid the fashion-house box from under the bed and lifted out the creation she had chosen for the night. She usually haunted the better op-shops for Frank did not approve of her spending on herself. But, just for once, she'd gone crazy, knowing that, in less than a year, she'd never have to worry about money again.

The little black dress was iridescent, shot with deep blue and peacock green, the shoulder line trimmed with long black feathers and the neck plunging over her breasts. Her bra showed so she took it off, thankful that she'd never had to suckle a child and that her bosoms were nearly as high and pert as they'd been when she was a new bride. The nipples stuck out, but that was Frank's doing. They showed, hard and knubbly against the silky fabric. Molly frowned and then thought, what the hell, and left them to their own devices.

Sheer pantyhose and a lacy bikini brief completed her preparations, before she slid her feet into black strappy sandals studded with diamante. There were sparkling droplets in her ears and a single crystal pendant on a silver chain around her neck. A swish of Tabu at neck and wrists then Molly looked at herself in the long mirror inside the wardrobe door.

She said, "Wow!" again, and turned back to the dressing table. She pressed her soft pink lips against a tissue and unscrewed the top of a different lipstick, a deeper, vibrant shade.

"Well, double Wow!" she murmured, picking up her evening bag. She slipped the mink coat over her shoulders, locked the door and waited on the porch until Bud had backed the car down his drive and pulled up outside her home.

"Hell, you look good," he said, as she slid into the back seat.

"Good job you're here to chaperone me, Dot, or I might drag Molly off into the bushes and prune roses, or something!"

"It's the coat, Molly. He just wants to feel something that smells of rich."

"No, I don't. I just want to feel her up."

Dot smacked him on the cheek playfully. "Watch it, lover boy!"

The party was in Peter Piper's house, a sprawling mansion overlooking the Swan River. The boss saw them coming up the steps to his front door but didn't immediately recognise his gopher.

"By Golly, Miss Molly!" he cried. "You look a million dollars! Pardon me, dear," he said to his wife. "I really must take this delectable morsel and give her a whirl around the dance floor before I have a heart attack!"

His wife smiled. Rita liked Molly. She knew her to be loyal, steadfast, supportive of her husband without making sheep's eyes at him. "How anyone so bright could marry a pompous bore like Frank Anstruther beats me," she'd said many times.

"He's her blind spot, dear. It's hard to admit you've landed a blowfish!"

The transformation of Molly Anstruther was the talk of the night. She wasn't the prettiest thing there, not by a long chalk, nor did she have the best legs, the shortest skirt, the most pinchable bottom or the deepest cleavage. Her nose was too tip-tilted and her lips not full enough to be called luscious, but they smiled enchantingly. There was such friendship in the laughter lines around her eyes that the staff from Peter Piper's Pickles remembered that, not only had they always liked the boss's assistant, but also that they had loved her in the nicest sense of the word.

The men vied for her to partner them on the dance floor on the terrace, and in the breaks she talked to the wives and caught up on family news while sipping a little champagne and eating delectable food brought round by an army of waiters.

She heard about the love lives of the typists and packers, the engagements and the travel plans, the new jobs and the changes of address. She talked to the old boys about their retirement and what pastimes they'd taken up, and she even let a few of her oldest mates give her a kiss behind the bushes. Bud took advantage but in front of Dot, who saw, and winked at Molly.

"Go on, ginger him up for me, Molly."

The only one not enjoying the party seemed to be Jake. Molly found him sitting morosely in a corner of the conservatory, surrounded by tropical vegetation, gazing sadly into a beer.

"It's like being in the jungle," he said. "Reminds me of being in the Army on Bougainville."

Molly flopped down beside him on a bench and shivered.

"It's cold out here."

"I'll get your coat."

He held the mink so she could slide her bare arms into the sleeves. He looked at her consideringly. "Now you're a wild, furry animal in the jungle. Come here and let me give you a bear hug."

It was a gentle, passive embrace. "You didn't get into trouble over last night, did you?"

"No. Frank went out this morning before his mother had a chance to drip poison in his ears. What's up, Jake? You promised me a dance and I've seen nothing of you."

"Sorry, Molly. Too many beers and a letter from Jen. She sent pictures of Morris. Made me feel sad again."

"Did you bring them?"

He reached into his jacket and handed her six snapshots. The child was cute, with big brown eyes and a mop of dark curls. Molly smiled. No wonder Jake adored the child. He looked a little darling.

"Jen doesn't like it in New Zealand," he said, stumbling on his words. "She's told Te Pongo, Puto, Pogo, whatever his name is, that she wants to come back to Australia, to be near her family. She says she misses me. Oh hell, Molly, it's such a mess. I'm drunk. I feel howling drunk. I'm such a mess."

It was the most natural thing in the world for Molly to open her arms to him, and the second most natural thing for him to cry a few tears on her shoulder. She smoothed the short-cropped dark hair on the back of his tanned, muscular neck, kissed his cheek and ran comforting hands across the rippled muscles of his back. When his stifled misery quietened he breathed deeply of the perfume in her cleavage and he kissed her there, between her breasts.

Molly gasped but made no gesture of resistance when his mouth was on hers, his tongue thrusting deep into her throat and his arms hugging her tightly to his chest.

"Take me home, Molly," he whispered. "Take me home."

She saw he was not fit to drive and knew herself to be well under the limit. After all, she didn't much like champagne. They went quietly through a side gate to where his car was parked and left without farewells. Molly dared not face the throng. Had she done so, she knew she would never have thrown her courage into the ring and made good her threat to Frank. It might not come to that but Molly's lottery luck had made her feel liberated. For once, Molly was willing to take a risk.

Jake might not be a stud, but Molly was certainly a sleeper, although he had pierced her heart, not her ears. Yes, she'd throw caution to wind and her wedding ring into the sand-dunes. Just for once. Just to be needed, really needed. Just to be genuinely wanted.

Jake's place was an apartment overlooking the beach. Molly helped him out of the car and up in the lift, as he was unsteady on his feet. The sitting-room was untidy in the way that only a bachelor or an idle housewife could make it. He'd made no attempt to turn it into a home again. The knick-knacks that make a space personal had gone with Jen. All he had on show was a snapshot of the baby and a picture of a couple who were probably his parents. Molly eased him onto the bed but, in doing so, he pulled her down beside him and rolled half on top of her.

"You are so pretty, Molly," he murmured, feather-kissing her nose and her brows and the tender places between ear and neck. Molly giggled. It was a spot that always made her tingle with laughter. Jake's tongue tasted the inner lobe of an ear and probed deeper into its concavities.

"I want you," he said.

There was a large tear in one corner of Molly's eye and it ran down her cheek and past her nose. Jake licked it off with great tenderness.

"And I want you," Molly admitted, a note of wonder in her voice.

"You're sure?"

"Yes, please." She smiled, purring, as she leaned back on an elbow and watched Jake struggling to remove his jeans.

"Take your boots off first," she suggested.

He did so and eased the denim from lithe, wiry-haired limbs. She helped him unbutton his shirt. His chest was dark with a thin vee of hair from throat to waist, tapering off under the band of his jocks. He knelt beside her and she eased the elastic out and over, pushing him back against the pillows while she slipped her little black number off her shoulders and her little black lacy pants from around her hips and ankles.

He was a gentle and accomplished lover. Accustomed only to bite and rasp, to prod and claw and thrust, Molly was amazed by his roving tongue and nibbling teeth, so white and even on her breasts. Her skin was charged like static electricity as he kissed her under her arms, under her ribs, his tongue circling her navel and tracing its way downwards, soft fingers parting and breath heavy on her inner flesh. His lips whispered soft endearments, his tongue probed and set her most sensitive point on fire.

It was a long and lingering loving. She fell asleep in his arms, his body still within her as he drew her back hard into his loins and felt her buttocks nestle against his pelvis. They awoke with the pink shimmer of dawn and the cry of an insomniac seagull. And then they did it all over again, slowly, languorously, deliciously until Molly felt as sweet and melting as a marshmallow. Jake made coffee and they sipped it with honeyed smiles and, thirst quenched, went vigorously to the ritual with passion unassuaged.

"Wow!" said Molly.

"Thank you, lovely lady," Jake replied, and kissed her deep and true.

Molly looked ruefully at the discarded mink, at the iridescent fabric lying among its feathers like a broken bird. "I can't wear those home at this time of day," she muttered. "I'd look like a tart. Do you realise its gone nine, Jake?"

"I'll drive you."

"And what would the neighbours say to that? No, love, I'll get a bus. Just lend me an old shirt and a pair of jeans. I can roll up the legs and tie a belt round the waist."

"We can do better than that. Jen left a bag of clothes behind. I've hung on to it, hoping she'd be back some day. It's about the only thing she didn't take. She stripped the place bare on her way."

Molly riffled through the old clothes. "There's not much good stuff here. It's a charity bin job, I think. Chuck them, Jake. She'll not want these," said Molly, pulling on a bright pink track suit with a large blue stain down one leg. "I can stuff some toilet tissue in the toes of these trainers to make them fit. Have you got a beanie, by any chance?"

He nodded and pulled a knitted cap from a drawer.

"Yes, it'll do fine. Can't have my husband seeing the colour of my hair until I tone it down a bit."

"But Molly, it's beautiful. And so are you."

"Thank you, kind sir. How does it feel to have spent the night with an old lady?"

"Very bloody nice, but you're not old. Lord, not much older than me, anyway. I'm thirty five."

"Nine years. Big gap."

"My sister's that age but you feel like a mere girl in my arms. Honestly. But Moll, I'm sorry. We took no precautions. Are you on the pill?"

"Jake, at my age we don't worry about such things."

His face brightened. "I've not got anything, in case you worry."

"You told me that before. And nor have I, except a feeling that I've been very thoroughly romped. Very stiff, a little sore, but tingly happy all over."

He grinned. "And when would you like to romp again?" he asked, catching her in his arms and swinging her off her feet. "I'm on afternoon shift next week. Come and have breakfast with me on Monday morning, please?"

"Will I wake you up?"

"Lady, just hugging you wakes me up." He enfolded her in his arms and nuzzled the nape of her neck.

She melted under his kiss and, feeling the strength of his arousal, was tempted to stay for another hour or so. She had never dreamed intercourse could be so enjoyable, so moreish.

"Come on, Molly, my love. I'll drive you as far as the shops down your road and you can walk home from there. Tell Fatso you've been to fetch some bacon."

They took the scenic route along the river and parked to watch a young angler reeling in a silver bream. Molly walked down to the jetty and returned with the rod and the catch. "He struck a hard bargain. Cost me twenty dollars," she said, grinning.

Jake looked puzzled. "Why'd you do that?" he asked.

"It's called camouflage, soldier. I have to have some excuse for being out so early. And coming back in such a state."

"Well, lovely lady, I'm glad you like fishing. You're the best catch I've ever landed."

"Tug on my line, any time, Jake. I'm hooked on you."

They kissed passionately in the car. Molly, emboldened, slid her hand over his trousers and stroked him.

"Save yourself for me," she whispered.

Jake grinned and tooted as he drove past her, admiring the rise and fall of her tight buttocks as she jogged, the fishing rod in one hand, the fish in the other. What a bird! He'd always respected Molly Anstruther. Now he lusted for her. No. A smile twitched his lips. She deserved more than lust. She was appreciative, she was welcoming. She made him feel needed, wanted, loved. The very thought made his heart lurch. What a damn fool time to be falling in love, when he could be called up at any time. Jake was going to war, but had first to face a war with his emotions.

Chapter 4

There was an ambulance in the drive of Molly's home and a cluster of neighbours round the gateway, sticky-beaking. Frank, still in his dinner jacket but with his bow-tie loose around his neck, was watching as the paramedics lifted a stretcher into the back of the vehicle.

Molly came through the crowd with a leaden feeling of disaster in her stomach. The neighbours looked at her with hooded eyes and drew away from her. She felt like a leper, her with a fishing rod and scruffy old clothes, hangdog, grovelling to Frank's side.

"What's happened? What's the matter?"

"Where have you been?" he hissed, grabbing her arm until pain made her drop the fish. "Fishing? Don't tell me you've been fishing?"

Her chin came up and she met his eye with a blaze of anger. "No. I've been out all night shagging with a young stud!"

"Bull-dust!" he spat. "What man would look at you twice? Why weren't you home to look after my mother? I told you I was staying at the club!"

Molly sighed deeply. "What's the old lady done, then? How come whatever it is, is my fault?"

"It is your fault. She wet her bed and went to the laundry to put her sheets in the washing machine. She tripped over that damned pan of marmalade you put there last night and fell. She's broken her hip. She was lying there unconscious for hours, all covered in jam and ants."

"I'm sorry."

"I'm going with her in the ambulance. That's it, Molly. If there's one jar of bloody marmalade left in this house when I get back, I'll smash it to smithereens, you hear me?

"But how was I to know your mother would got there first

- 42 -

thing in the morning?"

"No more!" Frank shouted. "It's finished! Caput! No more bloody marmalade!"

She bowed her head, tears streaming down her face, fighting to silence her sobbing. He let go her arm at last and got in the back of the wagon. His angry puce features glared at her from the rear window as the emergency vehicle drove off.

"You need a cuppa," Dot suggested, leading her into the house. "I'll put the kettle on. You shower and change. You smell like something the cat's brought in. And I don't mean fish. I mean man!"

Red flushed Molly's cheeks and she ran for to the bathroom, washing herself with vigour, scrubbing away at the tell-tale marks of passion but only making them worse. The pipes banged and rattled in fury. There was a bottle of the hair-colour restorer that Frank used to darken his grey. She rubbed that into her honey-blond and prayed it would dull the colour.

Nothing could hide the signs on her neck where Jake had bit in ecstasy so she pulled on a sleeveless but roll-top sweater, feeling it rough against her still sensitive nipples. A crisp pleated skirt and a pair of scuffs completed her ensemble. She went out to the kitchen still rubbing her hair to dry it. Frank's dye came off onto the towel and she cursed in annoyance.

"Pity," said Dot. "It was a wicked colour, but I think you're wise." She pushed a steaming mug towards her friend and cupped her own brew, her head cocked on one side like a cheeky robin. "Well? How was it? I saw you sneaking off."

Molly blushed again and raised her eyes to meet Dot's. "It was flamin' fantastic," she said. "I never knew..."

"No. I thought you didn't. If you'd known, you wouldn't have put up with Frank all these years. Will you see Jake again?"

"Sure will, as long as he needs me."

"Or until Frank finds out!"

Molly shuddered. "At least I won't have his mother spying on me for a few weeks. It takes ages for a broken hip to mend, especially in older folk. I know, because the nurses at the old people's home tell me about the patients when I bring them marmalade. Some of the oldies are really good friends."

"I'll cover for you if I can. I don't like Frank and nor does Bud."

"Was there much talk after we left?"

"Who knew? Bud saw you drive away, but he didn't tell anyone. The boss saw as well. We said, 'Good on you, Molly, go for it!' Why don't you just leave the bastard?"

"He's got my mother's money tied up in one of his hair-brained schemes."

"Well, get it back. Ask Peter Piper what to do. He's full of ideas."

"Couldn't save the factory, could he?"

"Bud says he didn't really want to. He'd paid out his creditors and there'll be enough left over from the sale of the premises to settle the debts. The old boy's banked the profits for years and didn't want any more worry. He found jobs for nearly everyone, did you know that?"

"Not for me, he didn't."

"He told me it was time Frank looked after you for a change. He said Molly's at that time of life when a woman has a lot to put up with and he knew all about it because his wife was going through the menopause as well. He said he'll get you set up when your body settles down. Or when you get shot of the big hunk."

"Oh, really. Did he say all this before I went off with Jake, or afterwards?"

Dot grinned. "Before."

"And what did he say after?"

"Well, I never!"

To her surprise, Molly started to laugh. "Well, he never did, but I reckon the old boy would have liked to. The furthest he ever went was to pinch my bottom." She sighed and took her mug to rinse it. "I'd better go and start cleaning up the mess in the laundry."

"I'll send Bud down to the supermarket to get some apple boxes. Then we'll come over and help you move that marmalade into our garage."

Molly looked startled. "You think Frank means it? He'd really smash every jar?"

"Molly, he was ranting about it for a good ten minutes before you got home. And you're not going to be able to lift much with your arm like that. Lord, you're black and blue already."

"Frank doesn't know his own strength!"

"The hell he doesn't. He enjoys hurting you! He's a sadistic bugger."

The laundry was like a scene from a horror movie, marmalade oozing from under the door like an alien invasion. There was the grate of broken glass stuck under the weather-seal as Molly pushed it open. Mrs Anstruther senior had knocked over a tray of jars as she slid and had cut herself on the shards. There was blood among the jelly and dead ants around the edges. The smell of insecticide made Molly choke. There'd been blow-flies at the blood and on the soiled sheets. It took her a good hour to scoop up the debris, bag it, bin it and mop away every trace of stickiness. By then the washing cycle was finished and she pegged out the bed-linen, thankful that it was a warm day.

She had to shower again to get the sweet, tacky remains from her skin and to cool off from the sweat the task had caused. She used the cold tap, unwilling to face the noise of the hot. It was going to be a balmy winter's afternoon. She settled for shorts and a shirt, pulled her dull blond hair into a pony tail and tied a scarf around her neck. It wasn't as good a cover-up as the sweater, but would have to do.

She fetched the wheelbarrow and filled it with preserving pans, her mincer and a batch of grapefruit and lemon.

"I'll do the garage," said Bud, arriving with his brick trolley and a load of boxes. "Dot will help you clear the kitchen cupboards. You've got enough stock for an army. You know, Molly, you could sell most of this gear."

She blinked at him. "How?"

"Down the markets. There'd be plenty of buyers. They know your name. They always make a bee-line for the bring and buy stall at the fetes and it's your marmalade that goes fastest."

"Great. Put it on my gravestone. Molly, the Marmalady!"

Bud chuckled. "Don't sell yourself short. You never know what you can do until you try. For instance, all the years I've known you, I never knew you were a little beauty!"

Dot came up behind him and smacked his butt. "None of that, Bud. You only need one of us to tickle your fancy!"

It was mid-afternoon before the last box was safely stowed at the Langford's.

"Nearly five hundred jars all up," Bud said, pouring lager for the ladies. "Dot will finish making the last batch for you."

"I'll give you a hand."

"No, you won't. If Frank guesses you're round our place making more preserves he'll give you a hard time. He can't grumble at me doing it."

"Damn," Molly exclaimed. "I should have moved my cookery books. He'll probably tear those up as well."

Bud fished in his pocket and handed her a ten dollar note. "No, he won't. I've bought them from you as a present for Dot. Right?"

Molly nodded. "Then finish your beer and we'll go and get your property."

She was startled by the sound of a car door slamming. Dot ran to peek through the front curtains.

"He's come by taxi," she yelled. "And he looks in a hell of a temper."

"Aw, let him yell," said Bud. "Over here, Frank. Come and have a beer!"

"Is Molly there? Tell her I want to talk to her."

"She ain't coming, Frank. You quit your hollering and come round quiet and neighbourly." Bud patted Molly on the shoulder reassuringly. "He'll be all right, you'll see. I'll calm him down."

Bud met Frank at the gate and pressed a tinny into his hand.

Dot plumped up the cushion on a garden lounger and eased him into it. She adjusted the big umbrella in the centre of the table so that it shaded him. "Take your jacket off, Frank. It's hot in the sunshine."

"How's Mother?" asked Molly. "I'm so sorry."

"Sleeping off the anaesthetic. Had to put steel pins in her hip. She's not good."

"You must be worried sick," said Bud. "My aunty never walked again after she did her hip. Had to put her in a nursing home. She was a big lady, like your mother. No flesh on her, but she had the bones of an ox. Weighed a tonne."

Dot shook her head. "Molly couldn't handle nursing your mother. You'd need a trained carer."

"She's not coming home," said Frank. "She says she doesn't feel safe. Thinks Molly's trying to do away with her. Oh, don't look so panic stricken, Molly. I know you meant no harm. It's just the knock on the head that made her get paranoid. But you can't cope, that's clear. You'll just have to go out to work."

"I don't mind working," said Molly. "I prefer to work."

"Then I'll find a tenant for the flat. You could do night-fill at the supermarket. If you can pack pickles, I suppose you could manage to unpack jars and stack them on shelves. You should be smart enough to do a job like that."

"Yes, Frank."

Bud glared at his neighbour but Molly caught his eye and put her finger to her lips. She didn't want Bud standing up for her abilities. He turned the conversation to test cricket. It wasn't long before talk drifted to politics and Frank waxed loud on the impact on financial markets of the East Timor crisis.

"We'll have to go in there to stop the Indonesian-backed

militia massacring the independence fighters," he said. "You mark my words. And what will that do to Indonesian investment in Australia, Bud? Property values will crash. It's grim, Bud. Grim."

"Wouldn't know, Frank. We've only got the house and there's only one foreign owner in this deal. Dotty here comes from Queensland! A real blow-in."

Frank laughed uneasily. He didn't seem sure of the point of the joke but everyone else was chuckling. He nodded over his beer and was soon sound asleep.

"Lord, what a mess he's in. Come on, Molly, let's go and get Bud's cookery books. We'll send your bundle of joy home when he wakes up."

Molly spent the early evening preparing a supper of salad to go with a quiche she'd defrosted. It was too warm for a cooked meal. Frank came in, took a shower, and came to the table in pyjamas and a dressing gown. He ate silently, left the table without so much as a thanks, and turned on the television.

"I'll sleep in the spare room," Molly said. "Let you have an undisturbed night, after what you've been through today."

"Suit yourself. I'm watching the cricket. I may not go to bed."

Molly shrugged. Daft bugger, she thought. She cleared up the kitchen and mopped the floors. She took a cool drink to the bedroom and put clean sheets on the single divan. After showering, she slipped into a cotton nightshirt and brushed her hair. There was no bedside light so she could not read a book. She smiled. She needed no book. She lay in the dark and smoothed her hands across her body, feeling the memories that Jake's fingers had written on her skin. She grew moist just from the thinking of it and she groaned as her hands rekindled sensation. She fell asleep with Monday on her lips.

*

It went wrong from the outset. Frank demanded that she visit his mother first thing, taking toiletries Hermione needed.

He gave her money for flowers and a large box of chocolates. He had a meeting with a client from Jakarta which he could not postpone.

"Can't I go this afternoon?" Molly was hopeful but he said no way. He'd arranged for her to speak to a social worker about finding a nursing home for Mrs Anstruther.

"If you don't go as soon as I leave, you'll be late for the appointment," he growled. "Don't pull the stupid bitch act on me, Molly. Just do what you're told."

It took her ages to find a parking spot near the hospital and ten minutes to find out from reception that her mother-in-law was out of intensive care and had been transferred to an annexe on the far side of the main building. Molly ran to the geriatric unit but it was mid-morning before she got there, only to find the old lady had been given a sedative and was fast asleep. Sister shook her head when Molly asked to see the community nursing director.

"She had to go, dear. She had a meeting in the city. But she said there was no hurry to discuss things. It will be weeks before Mrs Anstruther will be ready to leave here. Plenty of time."

Molly could have stamped with frustration. It would be gone noon before she could get to Jake's and she had no way of letting him know why she was late. She hadn't even thought to get his telephone number. He'd be getting ready for work, not nibbling toast and Molly for breakfast.

"What will he think of me? He'll think I chickened out! He'll think I didn't want him. Oh, dear heavens, how I want him! But what's the point if he's rushing around, trying to shave and find his work boots and ironing his shirt?" Molly sighed. "Well, at least I can do the ironing, even if I can't press sheets as we'd planned!"

She parked the Barina all askew and ran up the stairs. The lift was on the top floor and she felt too impatient to wait for it to come down. She put her finger on the bell and stood there, panting, red in the face, full of apologies. Jake dragged her through the door, hugging her, kissing her, laughing at her bedraggled state. He left her gasping for breath and hungry for his touch. She pressed herself eagerly to his body and begged him to satisfy her. She felt shameless, wanton, wicked. Oh yes, oh yes. It was as she remembered, wonderful, powerful, sensual, drawing a great whoop and crow of ecstasy from her throat as she responded to his body.

Her hands roved over his chest as she settled down into the peaceful sensations that followed relief, into the afterplay that replaced the preliminaries she had not needed, moist with desire as she'd been. He kissed and nuzzled and stroked, and she cupped him in her hands and tasted herself on him. There was a cool breeze from the ocean on their bodies and the curtains billowed in its caress.

Jake looked down at her and glanced at his wristwatch. He grinned cheekily and enfolded her breasts in his hands, rolling them against his palms. "That was a superb breakfast," he murmured. "How do you fancy a lazy lunch?"

"But you've got to go to work!"

"I'm not on duty until three, lovely lady. Plenty of time for main course and we may even get in a quick dessert!"

He smoothed back stray tendrils from her forehead and pulled the band from the chignon in the nape of her neck. Her curls fell free and he pulled them forward around her shoulders.

"I like the honey better, but you still look good enough to eat, Miss Molly."

"Then do something about it," she whispered boldly, and he did. And when he'd done so he pulled her on top of him.

"Oh, ooh, ooh!" cried Molly, eager to learn how to pleasure a man, finding muscles she never knew she had, feeling for the first time the power of being in control, not merely a passive partner in the game of love. Looking down at Jake, watching the expression of pleasure on his face, seeing how her movement brought his eyes wide open and hearing his gasps of delight, was a new experience. He cried aloud and rolled her onto her back, to finish their joining in a crescendo of feeling.

Dessert was a shower, the fresh feeling of soap-satinned limbs and of water pouring over heated flesh.

"I have to go, Molly. I don't want to, but I have to go."

"Tomorrow?"

He shook his head. "I can't, love. I have to go to the barracks. You know I'm in the Army Reserves?"

She nodded and straightened his tie, studying the serious expression on his face.

"Molly, it looks as if we're going to be called up for duty in East Timor. They'll call ex-Regulars before the weekend soldiers. I have to report in for a medical check and shots for tropical diseases."

There was a heavy sadness in the pit of her stomach. "How soon will you know when you're to leave?"

"Not sure. Maybe we'll get an idea today. Maybe we'll not be needed at all. I just want you to know where we stand. You're more woman than I've ever known, Molly, but we may not have much time together."

She swallowed the lump in her throat. "I understand. I've no claim on you. I'd just like to make the most of what's possible. Then you can go off and do your duty and leave me with some very happy memories."

"That's not enough," he said, kissing her under her ear. "I want more than that!"

Molly put her hands under his buttocks and squeezed him to her hips. "Me too, Jake, but in this life we take what we can get. I never knew that until I met you. I was fooled into taking the crumbs that were given me. No longer."

"What now?" he whispered against her lips.

She smiled. "Oh, now I want to have my cake and eat it too."

Jake kissed her long and deep. "Until Wednesday, then, my dear delight!"

Chapter 5

The clock hands crept round on Tuesday, leaving Molly with endless hours to reflect on what had happened between her and Jake. She had plunged into behaviour which she would previously have castigated as highly improper and, on consideration, lacking common sense. There was no pretence that Jake regarded her as anything other than what men called 'a good lay' nor was there any justification for thinking that his heart was not still yearning for Jen and Morris. She had, Molly decided, simply been the means by which he had forgotten his unhappiness for a while.

That her little adventure had brought with it such physical satisfaction, such a sense of joy and freedom, was a bonus. She felt as giddy as a young girl and knew that, sense or nonsense, she was going to seek Jake's company until he cast her off for a woman closer to his own age. She could anticipate the sort of sad hunger he would leave in her life, but was determined to suck every possible happy memory from the affair. If nothing else came her way, she would have this brief passion to look back on and savour.

"You can start sorting through mother's things," Frank said, breaking into her reverie. "If she's going to a nursing home there will be a great deal of expense. We need to get a tenant for the granny flat as soon as possible."

"Shall I put a notice on the board at the supermarket?"

"No. I've got someone lined up already but their lease has another month to run. You could have a word with the human resources person about nightfill while you're there. We'll need the money."

"Frank, don't you earn any commission these days? How come it's money, money, money all the time? I know you took a battering in 1987 but I thought you'd recouped your losses.

Have you made some bad investments?"

He glared at her. "You wouldn't understand. I earn plenty but there's a special two for one scrip issue coming up next month in a major holding and I've the chance to get a big slice of the action in a resort development. I keep telling you, Molly, money is not for spending. It is there to work for us and idle capital earns no interest."

"Good. I'm glad you've no financial worries because I haven't changed my mind. I'd still like my mother's money, Frank."

He laughed in mockery. "What on earth would you do with it? Put it under the bed? Is that where you put the deeds to the house when I put it into your name? That's where you put the mink coat I gave you, isn't it? It shows how much you appreciate things of value!"

"You can't say I'm not looking after it. It's too good to wear to the shops!"

"I suppose I should be grateful you didn't put the mink on to make marmalade. It would be just like you to spill grot all down the front!"

"That's unfair. I'm a clean cook!"

"You're an airhead, Molly. Why don't you accept it? You did put the deeds in the bank like I told you?"

"Yes, I did. Mr Piper said it was a good tax move. He said you were a sensible man."

"Sensible? I didn't do it because I was sensible. I did it because I was fed up with your yammering. God, I can't even have an intelligent conversation with you."

"Frank, I want to buy another house with my mother's money. Mr Piper said bricks and mortar are a solid investment."

There was a roar of indignation from her husband, who proceeded to lecture her on the relative value of the house market, mortgage investments and shares. Her head was buzzing with statistics and taxation benefits and dividends. Her ears hurt with his pressure selling. But her chin came up and her blue eyes did not leave his face.

"Maybe a tax audit would establish just what our net worth is," she said.

Frank went very quiet.

"I've been looking into things, Frank. I know what you've done with mother's money and I'm not impressed. I want no part of that scheme. I mean it, Frank!"

"You haven't listened to a word I've said, have you? You, Molly Anstruther, are a dumb, stupid, useless bitch." The doorframe shuddered with the force of his departure.

Molly smiled softly. The big hunk never thought to ask which bank the deeds were in. Lord, he'd have a fit if he knew about the caveat she was about to put on them. She wanted her share of their joint estate sitting safely in Dancer's Creek. Her husband still didn't have a clue about the Grayson account. She even filed tax returns under two names. She wasn't keen to defraud the government. Only Frank. He was going to get his, just as soon as she could make sure she got hers. The crunch was coming.

*

"You know, Dot, if I had a conscience, I might admit I'd lied, cheated and played Frank false. But when I think about what he's done to me, you know, I don't feel guilty at all," she said to her friend, pouring water onto the coffee granules.

"Molly, Bud and I aren't playing the violins for him. We try to be polite, for your sake, but we can't think how you've stood it, all these years. We didn't realise how he'd tied up your money."

"How could you? I've only just realised what a barrel he's got me over. The boss guessed, but it isn't the sort of thing you bandy round the workplace, is it?"

The morning passed swiftly in packing Frank's mother's clothes into cases. Dot suggested they put winter clothes in one and summer gear in the other. Molly would swap them as the seasons changed for there was little storage space in most nursing homes. Books, ornaments and other fripperies would have to wait for more cardboard boxes.

A trip to the supermarket gave her the chance to buy fresh flowers for the old lady, scrounge banana boxes and, if possible, see the manager, Bert Welcome, whom she knew quite well.

"Nightfill? Molly, are you sure you're strong enough for nightfill? Some of the cartons are very heavy and we make no allowances for women. You're only a slip of a thing."

"But I'm tough. I could handle cartons of pickles, you know."

"I'd like to help, but I don't really need another shelf-stacker right now. I don't suppose you can do stocktake? Or night audit? The administration's getting me down, what with Goods and Services Tax and business activity statements for the government."

Molly grinned and handed him the reference from Peter Piper. His eyebrows shot up in surprise. "Personal assistant? I didn't know. I thought you were just a pickle-packer. That's what your husband told me at Rotary."

"That's what he thinks," she said. "I can see I need to explain it all to you."

Half an hour later she walked out with a done deal, accompanied by a new and smiling employer. "Promise, now, Mr Welcome. Not a word to Frank about what I'll be doing."

He chuckled. "Not a word. I can't stand your old man, Molly. It will be a pleasure to do business with you. See you next week, then. Nightfill, indeed!"

Frank's mother was awake when she visited and in as cranky a mood as she'd ever been.

"Cat got the cream," she snapped. "What are you looking so pleased about? Glad to be rid of me, are you?"

"No." Molly lied in her teeth. "It's just that I've got a new job, stocking shelves in the shop down the road."

"All you're good for! Don't give me those carnations. Can't stand them. They give me hay fever. Roses. That's what I like. Roses."

"Frank brought you carnations for your birthday. You liked

them well enough, then."

"Frank's were different. They were special, non-allergenic blooms. He ordered them specially for me, knowing my sensitivity!"

Molly stifled a giggle. She'd bought them herself because Frank had phoned to say he'd forgotten his mother's present. They'd come from the same florist from whom Molly had bought the present bunch.

"If you don't want them, I'll take them home and give them to Dot, to thank her for helping me move the marmalade."

"So it's gone, is it? Nearly killed me you did with that nasty, smelly old stuff. Cut me to ribbons, those jars. I can still smell it on my skin. Horrible. Leave the flowers. I'll put up with them, for Frank's sake. But I could sue you, for leaving that death trap outside."

"I didn't know you'd need to go into the laundry," Molly protested. "I meant no harm."

"Thoughtless, that's what you are. Thoughtless and careless. And a liar. Don't try to tell me you went fishing that morning. That was a right old load of cobblers. You were out all night, I know. Drunk in a gutter, I expect."

"No, I wasn't. I was out with a man, fornicating!"

The old lady gave a great howl of laughter and gasped for breath. "Go away! Go away, Molly, before I choke. You with a man? You can't keep one decent man happy, let alone two. All you can do is kiss a delivery man!"

A nurse came bustling in and shooed Molly out. "Mrs Anstruther mustn't get excited," the woman said. "Her heart's been playing up since the operation."

"Like mine, like mine," whispered Jake's lover to herself. "Mine's been playing up like you wouldn't believe!"

She nodded obediently and said Frank would be in later. When he didn't come home for dinner she assumed he had gone straight to the hospital. There was no sign of him at 9pm, 10pm and, when the hospital rang at 11pm to say the old lady had taken a turn for the worse and perhaps Mr Anstruther would like to be with her, Molly didn't know where to turn. He wasn't at the club and his mobile phone was turned off. In desperation she rang the chairman of the broking company. Gary Flatterjohn, of Flatterjohn and Associates, promised to hunt Frank down. Within half-an-hour he'd found Frank's appointment secretary who thought Mr Anstruther was dining at Mizendum, in Subiaco.

"I'm sorry," the maitre d' replied. "There's no booking under that name."

"Maybe a client booked the table. You can't mistake Frank. He's very tall, dark hair greying at the temples, quite plump. He'll be wearing a business suit and...let me think...a green tie. Yes, he wears a green tie on Tuesdays."

"Oh, yes. Nina Lavell's partner. I'll see if he'll take your message."

Frank was pretty irate at being disturbed by her call but calmed down when she relayed the news.

"I'll see you there!" he snapped, and hung up before she could tell him she had no intention of keeping a vigil at his mother's bedside. She made herself a whisky toddy, took a sleeping tablet, and went to bed. She was asleep almost at once but was woken by the phone at 2am.

"Where are you?" Frank growled. "I told you to be here. I took a taxi from the restaurant because I'd had too much to drink."

"Why didn't your fancy woman drive you there?"

"Nina is a colleague, not my fancy woman. I work with her, Molly. We were talking business. Anyway, she couldn't. She's lost her licence."

"Frank, stop blathering. You always blather when you're up to something."

"Leave Nina out of this. You'll have to come and get me after the operation's over."

"How is your mother?"

"I told you. Not good. It's an emergency, Molly. She's got a blood clot near her heart. She could die, Molly. Don't you care?" He sounded very squiffy. His speech was slurred. He sounded as if he was choking back tears.

"When does she go down to theatre?"

"They've taken her already. I'm just sitting here, waiting for news."

"Then you call again when you're ready to come home. There's no point in both of us being fagged out." Molly slammed the phone down and fumbled for the switch of the bedside light. Bugger Frank. He never took her out to dinner at swish restaurants, even in the days when she'd thought he loved her.

Despite her agitation, she slept soundly. It was daybreak before she heard the back door slam and the sound of a car backing out of the drive. Frank looked down at her, his face white and drawn.

"Thanks for nothing, Molly. I rang and rang but the phone was engaged. I had to get another taxi."

Conscience-stricken, Molly looked at the extension by the bed. She'd knocked the handpiece from its cradle during the night.

"I'm sorry," she whispered. "How did the operation go?"

"It didn't. She died in theatre."

"Oh, no! That's terrible." She tried to put her arms round him but he thrust her away.

"I don't want to talk about it. The doctor's given me a sedative. I just want to sleep the clock round. There'll be arrangements to make, but they can wait. There's no hurry now." He threw his clothes onto the floor and tumbled into bed. Five minutes later he was sound asleep, his thumb in his mouth, comforting himself like a small boy.

Molly put the answering machine on so that no phone calls would disturb him. She got dressed quietly then let herself out of the house. She let the car roll down the drive with the door ajar, waiting until she was on the road before closing it and starting the engine. She picked up bacon, eggs and fresh croissants at an all-night deli. She doubted whether Jake would have the makings of breakfast in his apartment. At least she would be on time for her date with a toaster on this occasion.

He opened the door to her sleepily, rubbing his eyes and scratching his chest.

"Hell, Moll, it's only 6am. I haven't even shaved."

"I wanted to see what you looked like with a beard!"

"Damn awful."

"Go back to bed. I'll wake you when food's ready."

"No way. I'm only going back to bed if you're coming with me."

"Right. But only for holding, Jake. I need to be held. I don't need more than that right now."

"What's wrong, Molly? Tell me."

She did. "Not good," he whispered, pulling the blankets over her shoulders and enfolding her in comforting arms. They slept. Molly felt safer than she had done at any time since her childhood.

Sunshine streaming across the bed woke Molly. She blinked into the shimmering light. How odd to be in bed, fully-clothed, with a naked man pressed close to her back. She lifted Jake's arm from her hip and eased out of his embrace. She looked down at his finely muscled shoulders and ribcage, at the taut belly and the readiness of him. She sighed. It would have been disrespectful to have done anything about that, under the circumstances. She gently replaced the doona and left him.

She went out onto the balcony and stretched in the sunshine like a little cat, breathing the cold salt air and listening to the sound of the breakers on the shore. She had much to think about but seemed trapped in a timeless zone where there was no room for anything other than appreciation of the moment. She didn't hear Jake come out to join her. He put his arms around her and kissed the back of her neck.

"I've got your mink coat on," he said, rubbing it against her skin.

"Mmm. That's nice," she murmured.

He pulled her track pants down and laid his hardness against her buttocks, not doing anything, just letting her feel his need for her. When she made no responsive movement he kissed her again and his eagerness faded away.

"I'm starving," he said. "Shall you cook or I?"

"You get dressed, standing out here with your interesting bits stark bollocky naked. What will the neighbours say?"

"They'll say I'm damned lucky! I'll shower and dress."

"One egg or two?"

It was strange being in another woman's kitchen. Jen may have taken all her ornaments and pictures, but there was still infant formula in the cupboard and tins of baby food. There were jars of spices that Molly never used and coffee in a brand name she detested. Jen was a buyer of ready-mix sauces and meals-in-a-can. There were packs of steak in the freezer, probably destined for the barbecue on the balcony. Molly put the bacon under the grill, glad to find aluminium foil to cover the baked-on grease. Jen might be good at volleyball, but she was no housewife. Molly poached the eggs because the frying pan was filthy.

She found a cloth to cover the table from which she had swept Jake's piles of old newspapers and empty beer cans. There was a tea-pot with mould on the old tea-leaves but it scrubbed up well. She put the buttered croissants in a dish and covered them with a napkin to keep them warm. Jake, looking fresh and young, took his place at the table as she placed bacon and eggs on hot plates. He smiled his appreciation.

"Four star service. Thank you."

It was a quiet meal. They talked about Jake's interview with the Army Reserves.

"I'll be called up early," he said. "I was in a special unit in the regulars and it looks as if we'll be needed to flush out the pro-

Indonesian militia. It's not so much a matter of 'if' now, but of 'when'. The referendum's at the end of the month. If there's trouble we may have to go in to protect the citizens until the United Nations can set up a peace-keeping force."

"I'll be sorry when you go," she whispered.

"Hey, Molly, not so miserable, please. I'll be back. We'll soon sort this problem out."

"You could be killed."

"Would you care? Really care?"

She nodded. "You're a pretty special sort of man, Jake Morgan. You'll never know how much you've meant to me, how much you've changed my life."

He took her hand and kissed her knuckles. "You, too, Molly. I was shattered when Jen went. You've made me feel whole again. I don't want to leave you, my darling girl!"

The pink started in Molly's neck and rushed up to her cheeks. A fine time to have a hot flush, she said to herself. Darling girl, indeed!

"I'm sorry I didn't want sex this morning," she said.

"Hey, there are more things in a relationship than getting it away. I've got a lot more to learn about you than how your body responds. I want to know what goes on in your head, what you think about things, how the world looks to you. I'd like to know about your family and your childhood and your favourite books. What's your favourite hobby, Molly?"

She grinned. "You know I make marmalade. I make marmalade like you couldn't imagine! And lemon curd. I make enough to feed the whole of the battalion if it goes to East Timor!"

"I know. I brought the jars, remember? Why didn't you bring me some?"

"Because there isn't a jar left in the house. It's all next door. I could hardly wake Dot and Bud to get some out of their garage, now could I. What excuse could I have given?"

"That's Bud from despatch? You could have told him you

needed it to have breakfast with your lover. Your randy, handy lover!"

"If you look at me like that, with those hot eyes, I'll be shucking you out of your jeans faster than you can say croissant," Molly chuckled. "But we mustn't, Jake. I must be there when Frank wakes up or there'll be hell to pay. I just wanted to see you, to talk to you, to be held by you. I just wanted to know if there was more to us than hot sex. I wasn't sure if there was even an 'us'. I thought maybe you'd just been being kind to me."

"Hey, Molly, I'm not a sleep-around guy. I don't give out without commitment. I've known you ever since I got out of the Army and I've always thought you were a cool lady. I just hadn't realised how hot you were inside. You, Mrs Anstruther, are well worth knowing. We've got a lot of exploring to do, you and I."

She dimpled. "But when? That's the question. It won't be easy while we're busy with funeral arrangements and I start work next week, at nights."

"So do I. The council's running security patrols round the suburbs. Here's a key to the flat. Come and cuddle up with me when you finish. And ring me if you can get away at the weekend."

"You're sure?"

"I wouldn't lie to you, Moll. Come on, leave the washing up to me. I'll walk you down to the car."

He drew her into his arms for a breath-taking embrace as she left, holding her so closely that she could feel his erection growing against her body.

"Heck, Molly, I just can't seem to control myself when I'm near you," he gasped. "No other woman has ever had this effect on me."

Molly, nipples tingling, belly burning and rippling, pushed him gently from her and opened the door of her car. She was nearly sobbing with the need for him but damped down the fire as best she could.

"Just one thing, Jake. Please. Never call me Mrs Anstruther again. I don't want to be Mrs Anstruther. I want to be me, Molly, Jake Morgan's lover. Kiss me, kiss me, you wonderful man." Deep, deep, tonguing, probing, teeth-grating, lips burning, hands clutching and clinging until sheer lack of breath drew them apart. Molly gave a little mew of sadness and slid into the car, slamming the door on the moment of passionate abandonment. And drove away, unfulfilled.

Chapter 6

When Frank snored, he did so with a vengeance. Molly could hear him from outside the bedroom window, which she checked after parking in Dot's drive, not her own. Bud had left for work so there was a chance to bring her friend up to date with the news. They sat at the kitchen table, drinking coffee with a slug of brandy in it.

"You told Jake?" Dot asked.

"Yes. Of course. He was pretty sweet about it all. He's been around death, serving in Bougainville. A friend of his was killed in a helicopter crash during an SAS training exercise. Left a wife and two kids. He said Frank would be a mess for a couple of weeks."

"What about you? You're not going to pretend you're sorry."

"No. I'm not, not to you. You know how much I loved Frank's mother, but she doted on him and I think he was genuinely fond of her."

"As much as he could be, perhaps. I think Frank only loves Frank."

"Oh Dot, maybe. But I'd better go so I'm there when he comes round. We'll have to make the arrangements for the funeral. I expect we'll have the same firm that handled my father's death."

"You make sure Frank gets caterers in for the wake. Don't you try baking for the mourners."

"We'll see."

Molly's first task was to go through the messages on the answering machine and make notes of who had called. Then she rang Aunty Flo, in Dancer's Creek, and broke the news.

"I'll catch the Greyhound coach tomorrow," the old lady said. "Got to pay my respects, Molly. You got a spare bed for an old biddy? You'll be glad of my help, I expect."

"Yes, of course. But are you sure it won't be too much for you?"

Aunty Flo gave a chuckle as rich as honeycomb crunch. "I'm not an antique, Molly, even if I'm showing a few cracks in the veneer. Nothing like a good funeral to make me glad to be alive!"

Frank, still heavy-eyed from the sedative, woke up like a bear coming out of hibernation. He was sullen, grumpy and scratched a lot because he'd not showered before taking to the sheets. He sat over coffee, gazing miserably at two headache tablets. Molly didn't talk to him. She cooked his breakfast as usual but he waved it away.

"Not hungry."

"Just some toast?"

The grizzly grunted.

"I'll go and get the papers, shall I?"

"Leave it. I'll write a death notice first, then you can pay to have it put in."

She placed a pad and pen in front of him and left him to it. She changed the linen on the spare bed and made the room pretty for Aunty Flo. He handed her his choice of words and started making a list of people to ring. Molly walked down to the newsagents and placed the advertisement. She dropped in to see Mr Welcome to explain what had happened.

"It won't stop you coming in as arranged?" the manager said. "I need to get these tax papers sorted."

"As long as you realise this will only be temporary," Molly replied. "I'll straighten you out, but there'll be big changes at home, I expect."

Frank was not ecstatic to hear that Aunty Flo was riding in like the cavalry. "She needn't think she's moving into the granny flat," he snapped. "I told you, I've found a tenant. I'm not having that old busybody under my feet. The new tenant will give you no trouble at all." He smirked.

"Heavens, Frank, nothing would get Aunty Flo out of

Dancer's Creek. She hates the city. She likes country life. She said it was the worst mistake my father ever made, moving in with us, leaving his old friends from farming days."

"Well, if he hadn't let the farm go to rack and ruin, the bank wouldn't have foreclosed on him."

"If he hadn't made some unwise investments on your say-so, he wouldn't have needed to take a mortgage."

"If your mother had left her family money to him instead of to you, it would all have gone down the gurgler. I didn't tell him to sell out when the market crashed. Buy when it's low, sell when the market's high. If he'd taken my advice, he'd have been back in profit within a year. Damn cockies think they know everything."

"You haven't forgotten that I want my mother's money, have you?"

"God, woman, my mother's just died. Do you really think this is the time to start nagging at me again? I'm going to start making arrangements. Don't you try to use the phone." Frank slammed the door of his office.

Never had such a feeling of uselessness enveloped Molly. She begged the use of Dot's mobile and called the hospital. Yes, she could drop past and pick up Mrs Anstruther's effects. They were in a plastic bag; her sponge-bag, talcum powder, bag of lollies, eau de cologne, nightwear, slippers, dressing gown. The Sister urged Molly to take the carnations she had brought for the old lady.

"She got no joy out of them," said Molly. "She wanted roses, but the only ones they had were very miserable."

"Good gracious, she told me they were just what she liked best and that her son had chosen them. She was quite besotted with Mr Anstruther, wasn't she?"

"Oh, a devoted mother!" Molly bit her tongue. Never speak ill of the dead, they said, but she couldn't help thinking it was a good job the miserable old girl had gone quickly instead of making the lives of the nurses a nightmare during a long convalescence. How was it that Frank's mother could not see him for what he was? She pulled herself together and faced facts.

"She couldn't see any fault in Frank because she loved him," she said to her inner self. "And I, having been a good, faithful wife, listening to his pontificating for years, thinking him wise, tolerating his domination because my acceptance made him strong, I fell out of love with him. And," said Molly Anstruther to the newborn rebel in her heart, "if I'm honest about it, I don't blame myself one little bit."

She was, she decided, like her own marmalade. She'd been chopped up, minced, simmered, brought to the boil, sweetened and stirred. And all the while her nature was changing until setting point was reached. Now, at last, her determination was jelling. Once set, marmalade was quite firm. And very tasty...at least, Jake found her so.

There was no hope of seeing him again that day. Molly made up a savoury hot-pot that could be eaten whenever Frank felt like a meal. He turned up his nose at it and said he'd eat at the club. Molly protested. It would be disrespectful to go out the night his mother died, she said. The other club members would think him very unfeeling.

"Damn it, woman, I need a drink."

"Well, eat here and go down the pub for an hour or so," she said. "They don't know you at the local. The walk will do you good and I won't disturb you with idle chatter when you come home. I'm going to bed after the news."

Frank was roaring drunk when he staggered home. He switched on the bedroom light, undressed clumsily, throwing his clothes all over the floor, and forced himself on Molly. He greeted her protests and her attempt to hand him a condom with a whack on the face.

"You killed my mother," he snarled, pushing her back against the pillows. He had started her nose bleeding. When she gagged from it, he gave her a backhander that landed on her cheekbone. He went at her savagely and, when he had done, started howling for his Mummy. Molly, sickened, staunched the flow of blood with a towel, grabbed her dressing gown and a pillow, and took refuge in her car. She locked the doors and huddled under a travel rug on the back seat, snuffling through her tears.

She was shivering with cold by the time the grey light of day pushed back the veil of night. Winter was back in charge. Molly left her refuge and went to the outside laundry. She filled her preserving pan with water and lit the old wood fire. The only place to sit was on the lavatory seat, so she perched there as warmth filled the small outhouse. When the water was hot enough she bathed herself from head to toe, washing the stink of Frank from her body. There was no way she would risk taking a shower and having the pipes wake the brute.

There was beer in the bar refrigerator and, while what she really wanted was a hot coffee, anything that would take the taste of blood from her mouth was welcome. There was a chest freezer in the corner. Scrabbling in its depths, she discovered a bag of frozen peas. She wrapped them in a cloth and pressed them to her cheek and eyelid. There would be a massive bruise, she suspected.

When the first rays of the sun stole through the dark clouds, she decided to venture into the house. Like a mouse, she crept into the bedroom to get clean clothes. Frank was snoring. He had vomited in the bed and was lying in his own filth and the stains from her nose-bleed.

"Pig," whispered Molly. "Stinking fat animal! May you rot!"

She took her makeup bag from the bathroom and tried to cover the injury to her face. It was not a good attempt. The foundation cream did little. She brushed her hair, cleaned her teeth and found her handbag. As soon as the shops opened she'd buy a proper cover-stick from a pharmacy. There was little traffic on the road to Jake's place. She took his key from her purse and let herself quietly into the silent apartment.

Jake was not there. On the coffee table was an envelope bearing her name. MOLLY. "Sorry, doll, but I've got to go to a weekend camp with the Reserves. Special training for you know what. Tried to call you but the answering machine was on. See you next week. Love, Jake."

There was even a string of kisses. Molly smiled gently. She made herself a coffee and sat on the balcony, watching the early morning surfers, in their wetsuits, braving the icy morning sea. A band of drizzle drifted in from the Indian Ocean and forced her inside. She lay down on Jake's bed and fell asleep, waking with a start two hours later. Panic-stricken, she grabbed her bag and Jake's note, locked the door and raced to her car. She was going to have to put her foot down if she was to be at the coach terminal by the time Aunty Flo arrived. There was no time to buy the makeup to hide her black eye.

"Oh, mercy me," said the old lady, who was sitting on a bench at the bus station, surrounded by a mountain of baggage. "You been in a car accident or something? I wondered why you were late."

Molly hugged her warmly. "It's all right. I'm fine."

"Looks as if Frank's socked you one in the eye! He did, didn't he?"

"I don't want to talk about it."

"No, I don't suppose you do, but you'd better get a veil to wear at the funeral or people will talk."

"I don't even want to go to the funeral."

"There, there, Molly love, don't go on so. Here, have my handkerchief and dry your tears."

They stopped to buy the makeup. Aunty Flo smoothed it around Molly's eye, her old, gnarled fingers gentle on the tender skin.

"Can't do much about your nose," she said. "But the swelling will go down by tonight. I'll kill that husband of yours. I always said he was a violent man. Your Dad was worried sick about how you'd go on after his day."

"Don't say anything, please. I can't take much more trouble."

Frank was up and dressed by the time they got back. He greeted Aunty Flo quietly and avoided Molly's eyes.

"I'm sorry," he said. "I was sick in the night. I've put the sheets through the washing machine and made up the bed. I expect you went to the spare room?"

Molly looked at him with her mouth agape. The rotten pig didn't even remember what he'd done. Or, if he did, he wasn't going to admit it. There was more cover-up going on around the situation than cosmetics on her face. The pretence of normality was sickening.

The weekend dragged past despite Aunty Flo keeping her niece busy baking for the condolence gathering which traditionally followed a funeral. Frank, as Molly had expected, refused to get caterers in. She was glad to have something to do to keep her mind busy. She was even more relieved that the arrangements stopped Aunty Flo from prying too deeply into their marital relationship. Those bright old eyes missed nothing, not even the fact that Molly was sleeping on the settee in the lounge.

It poured with rain as the cortege arrived at the cemetery. The mourners huddled under umbrellas as they slopped through puddles on the way to the chapel. There was a good turn-out from Frank's office, including Nina Lavell, in purple drapery and false eyelashes that could have served as windscreen-wipers. There was a giggle of secretaries and a gaggle of black-suited mortgage brokers, including the head of the company, Gary Flatterjohn. There was no Mrs Flatterjohn. He went into a huddle with Nina; the intimacy there had been between them still showed. Nina laughed and they both looked at Frank, smiling like Cheshire cats.

There was a bus-load of people from the retirement home where Mrs Anstruther had lived before taking up residence in the granny flat. Peter Piper was present and Dot and Bud had made the effort. Molly, subdued and veiled, concealed her emotions throughout the sombre service. She stood next to Frank as condolences were paid. Only as they drifted out into the forecourt did she become aware of the council ranger standing at the back of the throng.

She lingered behind the funeral party. Jake touched her on the arm. "Are you all right, Molly? I've been worried about you."

She smiled at him, feeling a tiny glow of warmth in her heart. "Oh, Jake, I'm so glad to see you. I've missed you."

"Ring me at work tonight on my mobile. I know you can't get away to meet me." He slipped her a card.

"Who was that?" said Frank.

"He works for the council. I expect he knew your mother from the nursing home," said Molly, wide-eyed and lying. She didn't give a damn any more. She'd seen Frank receiving Nina's condolences. If body language was anything to go by, sorry had a new meaning for the pair of them.

"You and Aunty Flo go back to the house with Dot and Bud," he suggested. "I've people to talk to before I leave."

"Well," said Aunty Flo, "He'll not get a chance to do more than talk, under the circumstances, but I suppose that's his other woman! That passion fruit who's wrapping herself all over him."

Dot and Bud turned to the old lady, astonished.

"Don't you think I've got eyes in my head?" she said. "Lord, what are neighbours coming to if they can't tell what's going on. That Frank is the sort that will always have another woman."

Dot looked at Molly nervously. "I wasn't sure if you knew."

"Oh, piffle," said Aunty Flo. "Of course she knows what he's like. The only mystery is why she puts up with it!"

It was a strange gathering. Frank's colleagues gravitated towards the formal lounge. The old folk sat round the kitchen table, sipping sweet sherry, but made their excuses quickly as they said they needed a nap before high tea. Aunty Flo was left to entertain Dot and Bud while Molly changed.

"It wouldn't do to be late for my first night at work," she said. "You'll be all right on your own, Aunty?"

Bud patted her hand. "Don't worry, Moll. Flo's coming over to have supper and a game of cards with us. We'll look after her."

*

Bert Welcome was delighted to see his new gopher, but concerned about her eye. He said nothing. He guessed that it was more than walking into a door, as Molly said. He explained the operations of the supermarket and introduced her to the nightfill supervisor.

"Molly'll be helping us with stocktake so you show her the ropes this week. You can meet the butcher tomorrow afternoon but the baker's on night-shift. Come and see if we can twist his arm for some muffins to go with a cuppa."

Molly drew in a breath of pleasure at the aroma of fresh yeast and crusty bread. The baker was a small, wizened man with a floury handshake. He had a wicked supply of wisecracks and a suggestive wink.

Mr Welcome told him to go gentle on Molly.

"Mantovani means no harm but he's a cheeky bugger," he said. "Come on, let's brave the office and you can see why the paperwork is driving me crazy."

Molly was transfixed by the enormity of the task ahead of her. Bert Welcome had simply dumped every month's accounts in a box. There were invoices mixed up with receipts, till rolls among sheaves of wages slips. There were ten boxes lined up against a wall and another half-full beside the desk.

"It's not as bad as it looks," Mr Welcome said. "I've done a trial balance every month. I need help fixing the latest mess and then collating all the accounts from last year onto the government forms."

"It looks like a dog's dinner to me," said Molly. "Go on. Push off home. Let me try to create some sort of order out of the chaos."

By midnight she had worked out how the system worked. She'd sorted out the papers and brought transactions onto the books. There was a pile of bills to be paid and a stack of receipts to be filed. Tomorrow, she decided, Bert Welcome was going to pay a visit to a stationers and buy filing cabinets and a mass of other equipment. She'd already started to draw up a shopping list for her new boss.

Mantovani knocked on the door and invited her to join a midnight feast. The nightfill staff were about to knock off work but gathered in the vegetable preparation room for hot drinks with cheese and bacon rolls, hot from the oven. They were a good crew, obviously happy with their work which was, for many, a second source of income, supplementing low-paid day jobs.

"I finish at 2am," the supervisor said. "Then the cleaners come in. Mantovani here finishes his last bake at 6am by which time the day shift supervisor is in to receive the delivery trucks. You go home at the same time as me, Molly. Eight hours is a full days' work. You have to sleep sometimes."

Molly nodded. She returned to the office and rang Jake's mobile. "When do you finish?" she asked.

"Not until six am," he replied. "Go to my place, Molly, and get a few hours sleep. I'll wake you up with a loving kiss when I come home."

The supervisor walked her to her car, making sure there were no dangers in the shadows. Molly found it strange to be out in the middle of the night, driving along deserted roads. She was cold by the time she got to Cottesloe. A warm shower and a hot drink put her in the right frame of mind to sleep. She slid naked between the sheets and listened to the waves on the rocks and the wind sighing among the pine trees on the grass-topped cliffs. She nuzzled the pillow and slept.

Jake, still damp from the shower, slid in next to her in the light of early morning. He pulled her warmth to him and she turned lazily into his embrace. It was a sweet and gentle joining. His fingers were soothing on her soreness, though he frowned to see the damage Frank had done. Although Molly was still aching from her husband's brutal assault, she welcomed Jake. He turned pain to pleasure, so slowly, so sensitively that her moistness grew and within it the fire in her nerve-endings that set her entire mind aglow. He brought her to a relief that made her cry a little from sheer happiness.

"I must go," she said, caressing his cheek. "Thank you, thank you. That was special for me."

"I wish you didn't have to leave," Jake said. "My arms feel empty without you. You belong in my arms."

"I'll be here tomorrow morning. No, my darling. Don't get up. You rest now."

She sat beside him, stroking his hair until he fell asleep. The curls were soft beneath her fingers. On an impulse she took a pair of nail scissors from her handbag and snipped one off. She was wearing her mother's gold locket. She clicked it open, wound Jake's curl into a tight circlet and placed it inside the pendant. It was a memory of a treasured moment in her life.

Molly was stretched out on the settee in the lounge when Aunty Flo got up for the second time. The old lady smiled. She'd been in the kitchen making a cup of tea at 5am and knew Molly had not been in then. Nor, for that matter, had Frank been home. If Molly was playing goose to Frank's gander, that was fine by her. She was broad-minded. She just hoped Molly had found someone worth the effort of jumping over the broomstick.

Chapter 7

"Have you left me, Frank?" asked Molly, watching the red creep into his face. "I mean, you've not slept at home one night since I started the new job." There was a jagged edge of sarcasm in her voice and a secret laugh. She'd not been in either.

Frank mumbled something about being so upset at the memory of his mother that he'd taken to sleeping at the club. "There's too much here to remind me of her," he muttered.

"Oh, is that it? When do you think you'll get over it?"

He slammed a drawer shut. "I suppose that interfering old biddy's been tittle-tattling to you. When is she going?"

"Aunty Flo? Tomorrow morning. But you needn't think it will make any difference to you. I'm going to sleep in the spare room so that I don't wake you when I finish work."

"Considerate of you," he said. "I've been playing stud poker with the boys lately. I'll be quiet when I come in."

"Thank you, dear. By the way, Dot and Bud are going to water the plants while we're away. At the conference. Remember? We're going to Albany?"

"I've not forgotten the conference. I thought you wouldn't want to come, as you've just started a new job."

"Oh, I told Mr Welcome I had a prior engagement for that period. He's happy about it."

Frank's brow was dark. "I cancelled your booking."

"Well, uncancel it, dear. I'll drive down if there's no room for me on the coach." Molly, guessing Frank was on the horns of a dilemma, hoped he was thrown by the cliché. She had plans for the conference. It would not affect her affair with Jake, who was off to the Eastern States for a week's weapons training at the same time.

"You could go and stay with Aunty Flo instead," Frank

suggested. "You like Dancer's Creek."

"But we've had such a lovely visit from her already. We've talked and talked. You've no idea what we've talked about. Like how to invest my mother's money in a way I'm comfortable with. Now, now, Frank. Watch your blood pressure!"

"I don't know what's got into you, Molly! You've turned into a nagging bitch! It must be that time of life with you."

"Maybe," she snapped. "But it's my life, and I'm the one living it. I've had enough of being pushed around by you. I've had enough of you blaming for everything that goes wrong, treating me like a slave, like a fool. You're a cheat, Frank. Do you know what hurts me most? Why didn't you tell me you'd had a vasectomy? You cheated me out of having children, Frank. That makes me angry!"

"I haven't had a bloody vasectomy!" he yelled.

"You told the girls at the office you had!"

"You've been listening to that bunch of airheads? Molly! How could you!"

"Then why tell them lies?"

"I tell them I've been cut because I'm infertile, Molly. I had the tests done, years ago. You think I'm going round telling my workmates my balls are shot?"

"What? And all these years you've made me think it was my fault?"

"Well, it was at first," he muttered. "I got you in the club easy enough when I was young. You're the one who can't carry babies."

Molly sat down on the bed, her shoulders slumped. "So why did you get yourself tested? And when?"

"When your mother died and you were as miserable as a wet dishrag. If you must know, missus busybody, you were such a boring lay that I went with a whore and got an infection. And, if it's any consolation, I learned my lesson. I've never been with a prostitute since. Now are you happy?"

"Of course I'm not happy. Aren't you even going to say

sorry?"

"Sure I'm sorry. I'm sorry you're a boring lay."

"We can't go on like this, Frank."

"Get off my back, Molly. This isn't the time for one of your moaning minnie turns. Go to work. Get a life."

He stormed out of the bedroom, nearly bowling over Aunty Flo, who was in the hallway. "Been listening at keyholes, you old bag? Much good may it have done you."

No amount of cuddling and 'there, there, there, my love', was going to comfort Molly.

She entangled herself from her aunt's embrace and went to the kitchen.

"You heard?"

"Most of it. You can't put up with much more of this, Molly."

"I can't put up with any of it, but I'm not leaving until I get Mum's money. I promised Dad I'd stick with Frank until I did. Aunty Flo, it's not that I'm money-grabbing, but I've got to live. I've got rights. It's not Frank's inheritance, it's mine. It's Grayson money. I'm not going to walk out on twenty-five years of marriage empty handed. I've worked since day one. I've no children, I can earn a living. Frank would go into a divorce court with a smart-alec lawyer and I'd end up with peanuts."

"There's always a home with me, in Dancer's Creek."

"I know and I thank you. But not just yet. There's someone in the city that I care about, you see."

"I thought there might be. Are you going to tell me about him?"

Molly grinned and shook her head. "No. I'm not. It's very new. It's very precious and it may come to nothing."

Aunty Flo sighed. "I had a man like that, once," she said. "I lost him in the Korean war. I never said a word. Even Uncle Fred never found out."

Molly kissed the withered cheek and gave her aunt a hug. "Then you know why I want to keep it to myself, love. Stolen love is like a dandelion clock. One puff and it might all drift away on the wind."

*

After Aunty Flo's departure Molly and Frank walked delicately around one another, like cats preparing for a fight. Mr Welcome was accommodating about Molly's working hours. Having seen what she had achieved in a week, he was pleased for her to come in whenever she chose, enabling her to match her shifts to Jake's.

Theirs was not a time of unbridled lust, although there was a more than a smattering of it. It was a time when Molly enjoyed many experiences that a forced, early marriage had denied her. Jake took her fishing off the North Mole, since she'd used it as a pretence when they first met. They took a cruise to the wineries in the Swan Valley and got mildly drunk. They went to the zoo in the pouring rain and fed peanuts to monkeys. They walked sections of the Bibbulmun Track in the Darling Ranges, a wild upland trail from Perth to the south coast, and nearly froze. Molly had never been to Rottnest Island, so they took the half-hour ferry trip and spent the day cycling around its coast.

On the first warm day of September Jake unearthed Jen's wetsuit and dared Molly to try surfing. She fell about among the waves, swallowing half the ocean and laughing with the shock of the cold water. He helped her to her feet and guided her out again until she had managed at least a run-in on her knees. "We'll do this again," he promised. "We'll make you a California girl yet."

"Damned Yankee," said Molly, giggling, "But your doodle's dandy!"

Some fine afternoons they simply lazed on the beach, finding a sheltered corner, working on a tan ready for summer. Molly knew that, if ever he left her, one of her most lingering memories would be the smell of coconut oil as she rubbed tanning lotion onto his skin. She would never forget the feel of firm, muscled flesh beneath her fingers. But the best times were when the winds blew wild off the sea and when rain kept them indoors and, for warmth, in bed. Loving, lingering, lasting.

"I had another letter from Jen yesterday," Jake said as they sat drinking coffee. "She still wants to come back to the west coast. Te Pongarani's dumped her in Sydney while he works the rigs. She doesn't like New South Wales."

"What will you do?" Molly asked, forcing out the words past a great lump in her throat.

"Send her money for her fare, I suppose. She only wants a loan. She's got family in the Wheatbelt. She's not staying here, if that's what's making you frown."

"Are you sure you don't want her back?"

"What? Instead of you? Oh, Molly, when will you start valuing yourself? You're the woman in my life. Jen is just a silly kid."

"But you loved her and Morris."

"Sure. It wasn't hard. She was fun. She needed me. I like being needed. And I felt responsible. I thought Morris was a great kid. I didn't know she'd been two-timing me, letting me keep her warm for that big Kiwi ape. I'm not a fool, Molly."

"But I am," she whispered. "There'll be another Jen for you one day and I'll walk out of your life and die inside."

"The hell you will. Root me or shoot me...or shall we go down the pub for a beer?"

"You can't get a man with a gun, so you know what I'd prefer. Are you packed for the morning flight?"

"Sure am. You're so right, Molly. When I come to think of it, I'll be so stuffed when I get back from this course, I may have trouble in even opening a beer can."

"Well, make this one good enough to tide us both over for the week."

It was, but Molly had one final request. Jake laughed as he helped her into her fur coat and pulled a beach-coat over his own nakedness. There were few people on the beach midweek and, while it was cold, it was sheltered in their favourite suntrap. Molly lay down on the sand and opened the mink to reveal herself in all her glory. Jake unfastened his belt and pressed flesh. It was a totally public joining but only the thrust of hips could have revealed their activity, had anyone been watching other than a curious seagull.

Molly laughed and shook sand and dry seaweed from her hair.

"You amaze me," said Jake, gasping for breath. "To think Frank says you're dull!"

"I amaze myself. But oh, what a memory this will be." She ran her fingers through his crisp hair and looked deep into those fascinating amber eyes, imprinting his features in her mind. So dear he had become to her, so very precious. It was not a zephyr of cold air that made her come out in goosebumps, but a chill that started in her mind.

*

Molly had made few preparations for her own trip. Frank had packed his bag and told her to be ready for pick-up at 8am.

"You can have my seat on the coach," he said. "I've business with a developer. I'll drive down in the afternoon. And for God's sake, pack some decent clothes. You look like a wild woman, with your hair all in a frazzle? How did it get in such a mess?"

"I've been swimming. It's the salt."

"You're mad. It's only September. Go to the hairdressers and get smart."

It was a groomed but pretty ordinary woman who stood at the gate with Dot, waiting for the rest of the party to roll up in the coach. Frank was long gone.

"You look as if you're going to church," said Dot. "What happened to the good casual clothes you've been wearing lately?"

"I'm in frump mode," Molly said. "I've been told to look respectable. Smart but dull, like his mother."

"You look more like a granny. Where's the blonde?"

"Had a rinse-in tint. Frank doesn't deserve blonde. Blond is for Jake. Mouse is for Frank."

"You ought to have gone bright red and shocked the socks off your old man."

"Dot, I've learned a lot from Jake and it's not all been about bedroom capers. He's taught me about military tactics, about camouflage and strategic planning, about subterfuge and undercover operations. I'm not going to Albany for the pleasure of the trip. I'm going to ambush Frank. I'm going to plant a time-bomb under Flatterjohn and Associates."

"Strewth! You be careful, Molly. I don't want to read about you falling off any cliffs. Why don't you just go and have a good time?"

"Dot, this will be a good time. I went to see Peter Piper and his lawyer last week. If this comes off, I'm filing for separation. Frank's got another woman."

"I guessed. Good on you, Molly, it's about bloody time. When a man starts seriously knocking you about, it's then you get out. That black eye was one blow too many. Here's your mob. Have fun!"

*

Molly's presence cast a shadow on the brokers' party, which was already into the champagne breakfast it had advertised would be consumed en route. The giggle of young things were at the back, the suits were doing the charming with their toffee-nosed wives. Mrs Flatterjohn, a sour-faced battleaxe of a woman who looked down her nose at Molly as if she was a bad smell, smirked at her condescendingly.

"I bet you're glad Frank's got that Nina off your Gary's back," Molly said to herself.

Happily there were several down-to-earth couples from firms that dealt with Flatterjohn and Associates but were not part of the company. There was plenty to talk about, innocuous subjects that did not tax Molly's brain. In fact, after a glass or two, she found herself nodding off until they stopped for lunch at a winery.

"Frank driving down?" said Gary Flatterjohn, leering knowingly at her.

"He's got to see a developer. The Citrus Court project, I think he said."

"Funny. I thought you'd want to be involved in that. You're happy for him and Nina to organise it?" He was probing her. She could hear the mockery in his voice.

"Why shouldn't I be?" Molly replied, puzzled.

"Oh, nothing. No reason."

There was a whiff of suspicion in her mind. It lingered like the scent of someone sneakily passing wind. So Frank was driving down with Nina, was he? He obviously no longer cared what his wife thought of him; he was getting brazen.

The hotel was plush, close to the sea front with marvellous views of the harbour from most rooms. Molly's looked inland, across the roofs of the holiday homes below the granite mountain which dominated the harbour. To her relief, there were twin beds. She changed for dinner. It was a buffet, laid out in a glassed-in annexe. Frank had not arrived.

She joined a table where an insurance company manager and her husband were seated. They discovered they were all from the Dancer's Creek area and had many mutual acquaintances. Yes, they knew Aunty Flo. They even recalled her father and mother, having been to many bush dances at the Grayson spread in their youth. Sad to see the little country town in decline, they said. Not much tourist trade despite the agricultural museum, Tom Dancer's Mill, the pottery and Bushranger's Rock, scene of a disreputable hold-up in the mid-1880s.

Molly, her head buzzing from too much red wine, went to bed early. She heard Frank come in but couldn't even be bothered to look at her watch. She rolled over and pulled the covers above her head.

By the time she woke up, Frank had already gone to the first seminar and the bus had taken the women shopping. She had a light breakfast on the terrace and decided to walk along the foreshore. Once she'd started, she didn't want to stop. All alone amid the curlews and the sandpipers, she kicked through shells and sand-encrusted weed, banked high by winter storms. There was an arts and crafts gallery on one promontory. She looked at paintings, pottery, textiles, home-made produce such as jams, pickles and marmalade, honey golden in the jar and chutneys dark with figs. She had a hamburger with salad for lunch and dozed in the shade of a huge casuarina on the edge of the shingle. The sun was setting by the time she got back to the hotel.

"God, you're a mess," said Frank, meeting her in the foyer. "There's a cocktail party in the annexe in ten minutes. Do something drastic to your appearance."

Molly showered and washed her hair, knotting it in a chignon at the nape of her neck and tying a chiffon scarf around the tightly bound bun. Her silk trousers and a glitter top completed her preparations but a dab of powder and a slick of lipstick was all she could be bothered with. She was not going to try to compete with Nina, who was clad in a slinky confection of wine-red velvet. Nina was thrusting her bosom close to men who were trying to balance cocktails while being distracted by her cleavage.

It was the sort of affair that she loathed. She made dutiful chit-chat with brokers who only wanted to talk about the Dow Jones Index and the NASDAQ, about futures and commodity prices, about tax-effective investments and venture capital.

"You could at least try to show an interest," said Frank, escorting her in to dinner with a group of his closest colleagues, a valuer and a settlement agent, a merchant banker and their stuffy wives. Molly picked at her food, said little, and was bored stiff. She sat through the speeches but then pleaded a headache and went to bed. There was a disco somewhere in the complex but the noise did not keep her awake for long.

She went on the coach to Mount Barker and the wineries the next day and enjoyed a tour through the Stirling Ranges, where wildflowers were in glorious array. Another day there was a trip to the tall timber country. Molly took one look at the tree-top walk and shook her head. She hated heights. She was damned if she was going to traverse a wobbling suspension track high above the forest canopy. She wandered down a side path and sat beside a small stream, watching the tannin-dark water bubbling over a little waterfall. When she got back to the tree-walk, her coach had gone.

"Maybe they'll come back for me," she said to a sympathetic Conservation and Land Management officer.

"And maybe they won't," he said. "You're a long way from Albany, lady. Let me see what I can do."

Half an hour later she was on board a bus-load of old age pensioners, having the time of her life. She swapped recipes with the women, was told risque jokes by the men, and joined in the community singing with gusto.

"Bugger the wineries," said an old codger. "We're on a pub-crawl."

Molly was tipsy by the time they dropped her off at her hotel. Frank hustled her up in the lift to their room. "You are disgusting," he growled. "You're legless. Go to bed and sleep it off. All the trouble you've caused, you should be ashamed."

Molly replied with a gentle snore. Frank threw a doona over her and went off in a huff. She felt sick in the morning. She dry-retched for an hour then showered and went back to bed. Her head was pounding.

"I've told Gary Flatterjohn you've got flu," Frank said, coming in to change for dinner. "If you want to eat, order from room service. We're all going into town to a gourmet restaurant."

Maybe it really was the flu, thought Molly, who had been feeling under the weather for days. Her head was still aching so she couldn't even read a book. There was a television in the room. She ordered soup for dinner and dry toast, which she ate while watching a terrifying spy thriller. She dressed and went for a gentle walk on the beach, arriving back in time to see the coach disgorging Flatterjohn and Associates onto the terrace. Nina was draped over Frank. Molly watched calmly as the other woman giggled and handed Frank her room keys. They staggered off towards the cabins to one side of the hotel.

"Rather you than me," Molly muttered and went to bed. Three days to go. God, why ever had she come on this trip? She was hating every minute. But she had a mission and tomorrow she was going to activate it.

She woke up with a bad case of nerves. The thought of what she was about to do made her stomach churn. She dressed carefully and took up the briefcase of papers prepared by Peter Piper's lawyer. She marched across the dining room and fronted Gary Flatterjohn.

"I want to see you in private," she said, firmly. "No, not later. Now. There's no one in the reading room."

Startled, he followed her into the foyer and to the book-lined room beyond. "What is all this?"

"Sit down. Your company has invested $140,000 of the money my mother left to me in a project I neither approved nor agree with. I have signed no papers granting your company permission to do so. You have not entered me on the register of mortagees. My preliminary inquiries lead me to believe the project to be over-valued, the development to be over-priced, and the projected investment returns grossly over-inflated. I want my investment out of this project, not next week, not next month, not next year. I do not want to hold a mortgage on anything you handle. I want a banker's cheque from your company within three working days."

Gary Flatterjohn's jaw dropped. "Frank invested that money on your behalf," he protested.

"Frank did so against my express wishes. I have been

demanding that money be returned to me and placed in my own account for six months, Mr Flatterjohn. If it's such a good prospect you will have no trouble selling my share of the mortgage to some eager investor. But I want out, now and fast."

"And what if I refuse?"

Molly opened the briefcase and waved a sheaf of legal-looking papers in front of him. "Then I shall have no hesitation in placing the facts I have established before the Fraud Squad."

"Does Frank know what you are doing? Does Frank know you are trying to blackmail me? Why, you little tart, you could ruin me! You could ruin my company."

"No. You could ruin your own company, if you've been organising crooked finance deals. That's not my fault. I think your company ethics stink, Mr Flatterjohn, but I just want out of your messy schemes."

"Frank will kill you!"

"No, he won't. Not if he thinks he can wheedle the money out of me again. So I'll see you on Monday at 11am, Mr Flatterjohn, in your Perth office. And, in case you think you can pull a smart one on me, I'll be bringing two security men with me."

Molly picked up her papers and walked briskly out of the room. She closed the door behind her and leaned against the wall, feeling the tension draining from her, feeling bile in her throat. She saw a the sign for a ladies room and dashed inside to throw up in the toilet.

By the time she got back to her room and packed her suitcase, the Associates were embroiled in a noisome row. She could hear Gary Flatterjohn out on the terrace, yelling at Frank, and Frank shouting back. Molly took the keys to Frank's car from his bedside table and left via the fire escape. She would drive home in the BMW. Bugger him. He and Nina could come back on the bus with the rest of the bloody brokers.

Chapter 8

There was a strange car in the drive of the granny flat. It was a flash little runabout, a city car, with a pink decal and a metallic green finish. Molly parked the BMW on the lawn and threw her bag into the boot of her old Barina. She gathered a bundle of cleaning gear from the laundry and carried it out. Then she opened the house and left Frank's car keys on the kitchen table.

Dot, eyes wide, was waiting for her at the post-box. "I couldn't believe it when you arrived in Frank's car. He never lets you drive it."

"I didn't exactly ask him. He can walk back for all I care."

"He'll kill you."

"Could be. I'm not staying here for three days in case he flies home to make me change my demands on his boss. I told Flatterjohn to cough up my mother's money or I'd go to the police. I can't get it out of Frank. Maybe his boss can."

"You never did!"

"Dot, it made me sick to do it, but if I don't have a banker's draft for $200,000 in my hot little paws on Monday morning, I'm going to spew information all over the crime authority."

"Do you want to stay with us?"

"No way. I'm not drawing you and Bud into this row. By the way, whose car?"

"Your tenant's. Moved in the morning you went away. You went at 8am, the furniture van came at 9.30am. And guess who was helping with the move?"

"Who?"

"Your Frank. Has Nina Lavell got red hair? Molly, I reckon he's foisted the Other Woman on you."

"He couldn't. He wouldn't dare. Or would he? Yes, he damn well would. I'll throttle him."

"Where will you go until he gets back?"

"Give you one guess!"

Molly had three clear days before she had to return to work. It was long enough to give Jake's place a through spring-cleaning. She was so angry about Frank that she almost scrubbed right through the vinyl floor tiles, went at the dirty oven like a dog gnawing a bone, and took at least a millimetre off the enamel on the bath. She washed and ironed curtains, sheets, cushion covers and polished the windows until they sparkled. She had every cupboard scrubbed out and new liners in all the drawers. She slept dreamlessly in his bed, she ate ravenously and, when there was nothing strenuous to do, she mended and baked.

Anything of Jen's or Morris's, she put in boxes in the hall, intending to take them to the Salvation Army. She ran out of time on Monday morning but left, knowing that when Jake got back, whenever that might be, his pad was now a home.

It was a race to get to Flatterjohn's by 11am. She had first to meet and brief the two 'security guards', who were really off-duty policemen. They were Jake's ex-Army friends. When he'd heard her plans he asked Larry and Dingo to accompany her to the crucial meeting. There was little said. It would have been hard to talk, for the air was so full of frost that it took her breath away. Frank stood and glowered, like an iceberg with designs on the Titanic.

"Frank has been paid commission on this investment," Gary Flatterjohn said. "You should repay that to my company."

"Stuff! You can take the commission from selling my piece of the action to someone else."

"What are you going to do with all that money?" Frank growled.

Molly turned a saccharine smile on him. "Why, I think I'll just put it under the bed!" She took the bank draft and stalked out of the room. The administrative staff stared at her in silence, hostile. She was like an unwelcome alien.

Her teeth were chattering with nerves so Larry drove her car to the bank. He was a lanky young man with red hair and a scattering of freckles. Molly thought he'd have looked well in the country, leaning on a steer, chewing a straw. Larry waited until the bank transfer was effected and M Grayson was considerably richer, then took her home and waited until Dingo picked him up.

"Will you be all right? Your husband looked murderous."

"Thanks, Larry, but I've got to wear the problem. He'll be careful because he doesn't know what I did with the money. And I'm not telling him."

"Jake said to look after you really well, Molly," Dingo said. Jake's other friend was obviously of Chinese descent. He had sleek black hair and a pointed chin. Larry said he was dubbed Dingo because his skin was yellow and his nature was that of a wild dog.

"That Flatterjohn's a sleazebucket. Just you call us if there's any trouble. No, no. We don't want payment. Jake's a good bloke and he thinks the world of you."

"I'm pretty crazy about him, as well."

Dot beckoned from her front door. "How many more good-looking guys are you going to bring home? Coffee?"

"I'd rather have a brandy."

"You back for good or just for now?"

"I'll play it by ear, Dot. I'm not moving in with Jake, if that's what you mean. He's going to East Timor any day. Maybe when he gets back, if he still wants me. Dot, he hasn't asked me to live with him. He's never suggested this is anything more than a passionate affair."

"Would you like it to be more?"

"Do chickens lay eggs? Of course I would, but hell, I'm not the Other Woman, I'm the Older Woman. Anyway, I've got to get free of Frank first. I'm not staying here while he flaunts Nina in front of me."

"I thought it was only the money that was stopping you getting a separation? You've got that now. I suppose you did get it?"

"Yes, but how far will it go? A decent house and that's it. I can get a job but what happens when I'm too old to work? The house is in my name, but can you see Frank walking out? No, he'll make it so horrible for me that I'll really leave, and then he'll keep all the money my father put into this property."

"You've been living with Frank too long, Molly. What makes you think money is important? There are things like freedom, and lifestyle and, what's really important, friends and lovers."

"Oh heck, Dot. You're right." She stood up and yelled. "I don't need your bloody money, Frank! Go stuff it up your khyber!" Then she sat down all of a heap. "The truth is, Dot, I feel so cross with Frank, that I simply want to stop him having it. His bank account is his baby and I want to take his dummy away and rub it in doggy-doos."

"Molly!"

"So? So I'm not a nice person after all. Do you know what I've been most of my life? I've been a shadow, stretched out in the light of Frank's sun. Now it's high noon, Dot, and the shadow's got shorter. What's left is me, Molly Grayson, learning to be my own person."

*

It took courage to stay in and wait for Frank and Nina to arrive from the Flatterjohn office. Frank escorted the Other Woman to the front door of the granny flat. Molly watched their embrace, then let the lace curtain in the front room fall back into place. She went to the kitchen and put on the coffee percolator.

The thing that barged in through the back door was more like a spitball than a human. Frank wasted no time. He grabbed her by the hair and threw her against the wall, slapping her face left and right.

"You've screwed me up big time, you bitch," he snarled. "Gary's furious at having to pay you out. He's given me three days to make good his losses. I'll have to sell at the bottom end of the market."

"Tough," said Molly, glaring through her tears.

"I said he should sue you, for demanding money with menaces."

"You can't sue me for telling the truth. I'd go straight to the newspapers, Frank. And if I told what I knew, your little schemes would come unstuck. Peter Piper says there have already been questions asked in parliament about scams like yours!"

"I could murder you!"

"I expect you could. But you'd better not. I've seen a lawyer about getting a separation order. You'd be in the frame if anything happened to me. You just think about how you're going to meet a divorce settlement."

"You wouldn't dare."

"I want my father's investment as well. And you can tell that tart to get out of my house. My father left that granny flat to me, not to you."

"If you want it, you live in it. Nina can move in here, with me. You can have your separation."

"No way. She goes."

"Stuff you, Molly. She stays!"

"Then I'll go. I might not come back."

"Yeah! Why don't you piss off!"

*

Molly threw a few things in a travel bag and ran to her car. She needed a refuge. She needed Jake. Even if he wasn't back, she could sleep there until Frank calmed down. There was an Army kitbag and holdall outside the door of the apartment. A slouch hat was balanced on the luggage. Loud pop music came from inside. She smiled in relief. He was home.

She put her key in the lock and opened the door. The first thing she saw was a young woman, seated in an armchair, blouse unbuttoned, breast-feeding a large baby.

"Hi. Who are you? I'm Jen," said the girl...she was really little more than a girl.

"I'm Molly." It was hard to get the words out. Molly's mouth was dry and there was a tightness in her throat.

"You're the one who tidied the place up? Thanks. Jake's in the shower. Hey, Jake! Your cleaning lady's here."

Jake came out of the bathroom, mother naked, towelling his hair.

"What did you say, Jen?" He lowered the towel and looked towards the door. "Molly? Oh, shit!" He clasped the towel to his privates and cried, "No, Molly. Don't go. You don't understand."

Molly understood one thing. He hadn't run the flag up the mast for her. She turned on her heels and ran out, clattering down the stairs, blinded by tears, heading not for her car but for the beach. She ran over the road and across the grassy slopes above the sand, slipping and sliding on the dunes, stumbling over rocks, splashing through pools, heading for a place where she could howl like a wolf.

It was an intense, gut-shattering outpouring of grief. It left her limp. What could she have said? Her face had felt as if it was made of plaster, set hard. Her tongue had been super-glued to the roof of her mouth. She had barely been able to take a breath from the shock of seeing Jen and Morris, back in the place they obviously thought of as their home. Not her refuge. Their home.

Molly, who had discovered lust, who had discovered fun, now found bleak. She ran a reality check, an obnoxious term, but one fitting her mood. One by one the bubbles of fantasy burst. Love and tenderness and joy ran down the mirror of her life, leaving unsightly streaks. That happy, fulfilled woman who had looked at herself after loving Jake, was now a distorted image.

"I thought I'd find you here," her lover panted, ten minutes later, running along the path with Morris in his arms. He set the baby down on the sand and flopped beside Molly.

"Hey, I'm sorry. I didn't know Jen and the kid were going to be at the flat. I'd only just flown in myself. I didn't know they'd made themselves at home. All I wanted was a shower after a day on a military transport."

"It doesn't matter." Her voice was wooden. "They belonged. I could see that at once. They belong with you. It was right that they should be there. I was the one who was out of place."

"Not true, Molly. You're the person I was hoping to see."

"It's hard for me to believe that."

"Listen, Molly. Being with you made me see a lot of things straight. Jen's got some funny ways. I could never take her home to meet my family."

"But you could take me to meet your Mom?"

"You'd get on great!"

"Same age, huh!"

"Same age as my sister! Stop putting yourself down!"

Molly sniffed. "That child shouldn't eat cuttlefish," she said.

Jake retrieved Morris from a pile of debris he was exploring and sat him on his lap. Morris snuggled against Jake's shoulder. Big brown eyes looked at Molly shyly. The baby blew a bubble at her, then smiled.

Molly looked away. "I do not belong, Jake. I don't care if you're that child's birth father or not. He needs you. Children need a father. Jen's in trouble, who does she turn to? You. Jen needs you."

Jake was silent for a long while. "But it's you that I need, Molly. I love you."

She turned and looked him in the eyes, blue on amber. "Loving is not enough, Jake. There's duty and responsibility. There's doing what is right. I know about that, Jake. I've been mad these last few months, doing what was wrong. I loved it all, but it was wrong."

Jake groped for words. "It wasn't wrong, Molly. Never think that. You were like a rosebud, your petals closed. You flowered with me and it was something wonderful."

"Tough. My petals have just dropped off and there's only a bunch of dead leaves and thorns left. You look after Jen and Morris, Jake. Forget me."

"It's academic, Molly. I'm only home on a forty-eight hour pass. The East Timorese voted for independence and the massacres have already started. The pro-Indonesia factions have started killing, burning and looting. I'm on combat readiness as from tomorrow."

"Then it's goodbye, Jake. I wish you good luck." How could she speak so coldly? How could she sound so detached when she wanted to throw herself into his arms and confess her passionate love for him? She wondered at herself. "Come home safely, Jake. How long is your tour of duty?. Will you be back by Christmas? Will Jen stay in the flat? It looks as if she's expecting to settle in."

He shrugged, hurt. "Maybe. It would be easier than packing up and moving stuff into storage. There's four months left on the lease."

"That's that, then. I'll think of you. Stay safe." Molly shook the sand off her skirt and got up. She held out her hand to Jake. He grasped it firmly and looked up at her.

"Molly?" He hesitated. "This isn't what I want. Molly, if you need me; if you change your mind about us, you will let me know, won't you?"

"Probably not," she said firmly, and turned her back on him. But at the top of the cliff she looked down into the sheltered cove, where Jake was now sprawling, with Morris clambering over his back.

It was the place where the mink coat had been outed. She shut the Pandora's Box of memory and retraced her steps to the car, moving like a zombie through the deadlands of the heart.

*

The next weeks were difficult. She avoided Frank as much as possible. When they met it was another head to head battle, a session of mental and physical abuse. Frank tore up the separation papers and ignored the new status of their relationship. Molly tried to leave for the supermarket before he got home and went to the spare room in the early hours of the morning, steadfastly refusing to look into the master bedroom to see if the bed had been slept in.

Before retiring Molly set a table for his breakfast. Bacon and eggs were out. She refused to get up to cook. There was muesli and a basket of fruit. Sometimes the tray was untouched. Often she'd find a bank of bottles of vitamins alongside the debris. There were jars with strange labels in Chinese script. Frank was on a health kick. He'd bought track pants and power-walking shoes. He'd subscribed to fitness magazines and she found a receipt from a gymnasium, where he had a personal trainer.

"I have to take my hat off to Nina," she told Dot. "At least she's got him under control. I think he's losing weight."

"And you're putting it on. That baker...Mantovani, is it?...has wrecked your girlish looks. Too many sticky buns in the night, Molly. Go on a diet."

"Odd, when I don't feel like eating at all. I'm not hungry. It's just such a comfort, chomping on a slice of carrot cake, or sinking my teeth into a doughnut."

"You heard from Jake?"

"Yes."

"What did he say?"

"I don't know. I marked it return to sender."

"Molly!"

"It would only make it harder than it is, Dot. Don't you think I want to know where is and what's happening to him? I watch the early news every night before I go to work, hoping he'll be on camera. I read the newspapers cover to cover. Frank is very surprised that I'm interested in East Timor. He's packing himself because it's losing him business. He thinks I'm interested because I want a share of his money. Little does he know!"

"Have you spoken to Jen?"

"God, no. What would I say to her?"

Dot shrugged. She didn't have a clue. She was, as she confessed to Bud, right out of her depth.

Bud looked at his wife gravely. "Leave her be, Dot. As long as that Nina doesn't flaunt herself in front of Molly, she can put up with the situation. So far Nina seems to come and go by the front entrance and doesn't use the garden. They avoid one another. Molly does the same with Jen. She avoids thinking about her or thinking about Jake. Don't you force her to confront the issues."

"But she's not well, Bud. Have you ever seen Molly look so hangdog?"

"Are you surprised? She should start making marmalade again. At least it gave her an interest."

"Frank would be furious."

"Much she'd care. There'd just be another almighty row. Dot, I can't take much more of their slanging matches. I've had a good offer for the house. I'd like to sell up and go on that trip we've been promising ourselves, the round Australia run."

"What, buy a caravan and go gypsying?"

"Give me one good reason why not."

"Your new job?"

"It sucks. Delivering parcels is not the same as working in the despatch office at the pickle works. As the saying goes, you don't know what you've got until it's gone. I liked working for Peter Piper. We all did. My new boss is a pompous git."

Dot's eyes sparkled. "Well, yes, then. It's not the same living here, with the atmosphere next door. I don't want to run out on Molly but..."

Bud shook her knee. "It's me you need to be concerned about, my little possum. Maybe I need another woman in my life!"

"You wouldn't dare!"

"Grubbit," said Bud. "Let's go make tadpoles."

Chapter 9

"Where are my clean shirts?" Frank yelled. "Why haven't you ironed them?"

"Get your fancy woman to do them," said Molly. "I'm making lemon curd."

"You're not starting that nonsense again, are you?"

"Yes. Mr Welcome says he'll sell what I make from the deli counter."

"The gas bill will go through the roof again.

"So what? I pay it these days. You're supposed to move out properly. You've lost interest in the house. You don't support me. You don't give me housekeeping."

"You don't hand over your wages."

"I'm not paying for your Chinese muck. You can afford to buy your own ginseng and ginko and rhino horn, or whatever it is you're guzzling. Nina can cough up for your alternative medicine."

"She knows what she's doing. She studied to be a naturopath. She's a smart woman. Interesting. Well-read. Good-looking."

"So why's she working with you?"

"She took a degree in commerce. She understands finance. The other stuff is just a hobby."

"Well, making marmalade is my hobby. Rack off!"

"I warned you. I'll smash any jars of the stuff that I find. I'll...I'll pee in the buckets if I find any more chopped-up fruit."

Molly laughed in his face. "Just your level, Frank. Toilet talk!"

"If Nina's to do my washing, she'll need the laundry."

"If Nina wants to wash your clothes she can go down the laundromat and put coins in the slot. She can sit there, watching your underpants make love to themselves!"

Frank snorted and stamped. Molly picked up another lemon

and started grating off the zest. "Look, Frank, there's a whole orchard of fruit out there. Why waste it when I can make money from it? That's what you've been telling me for the last twenty-five years. Don't waste opportunities. Turn resources into cash."

"Resources? What the hell do you know about resources, Molly? What do you know about making money?"

"Well, I know a lemon when I see it," she said calmly. "After all, I married one."

*

The good thing about Molly's routine was that, in the afternoons, she had the house to herself. Spring had arrived and the grass in the orchard was full of sweetly scented freesias. The new blossom on the citrus trees spread another heady perfume. She wore long boots to gather lemons for Frank had forgotten to have the firebreaks put in. Molly did not like the thought of snakes, though admitted she hadn't seen one for years. She took only the ripest fruit for, unlike other citrus trees, lemons bore flowers, baby fruit and great golden heavyweights at the same time.

The curd was proving popular. The rich, buttery, sweet and sour paste, rather like the texture of thick cream, made magic tartlets and a tangy topping for toast.

Bud put in an order for a dozen jars. "We'll take it with us when we go," he said.

"Go?" said Molly. "Go where?"

Her neighbour looked stricken. "Hasn't Dot told you? I told her not to, but I never thought she could ever keep her mouth shut."

"Explain, please."

"We've sold the house." The whiteness of Molly's face showed him his wife had been uncharacteristically discreet. "We got a good price. Enough to take us on tour for six months and still buy a new home when we get back. We've ordered a

Winnebago, a home on wheels. We'll pick it up after settlement, in four week's time."

"Only four weeks? You're leaving next month? Oh, Bud, what will I do without you and Dot?"

"Why don't you get Frank to sell your place? There's twice as much land behind you as there is on our block. Yours is a double block, access right through to the road along the creek. You'd find a buyer, easy. The house behind us is sold too, and the one on our other side. Frank must know there's a development scheme for the area."

"He can't sell it," said Molly. "I have the deeds."

Bud shook his head. "Now there's a case of being stubborn as all hell, Moll. Why cut off your nose to spite your own face? You want out of your marriage, and who could blame you. You want your share of the property. Let him sell and give you half. Then you'll be free of him, once and for all!"

"You really think I should do that?"

"Seems sensible to me."

"I'll think about it."

*

She put Bud's suggestion to Frank, who looked at her with a curled lip and gave a flat no.

"Why not?" Molly said. "You always intended to develop the land one day."

"Butt out, dummy."

"Right. So I'm a dummy. Explain. Give me one good reason not to sell while local land is being snapped up."

Frank snorted. "Property dealing in one simple lesson? Big ask, Molly."

"Try."

"All right. All urban land is zoned by the town planners. They give land a residential code. That tells you how many lots you can get out of a hectare. That's about two and a half acres for pre-metric dumbos like you."

"No need to be rude."

"This area is R25. That means a developer can build twenty-five homes on the hectare."

"Bud's place is a quarter acre. How many blocks is that?"

"Two, maybe three. It's negotiable. Might get four if it's old people's housing. Knock down their house, put up a quadruplex, sell each for a quarter mill. Nice profit."

"But Dot says they got $250,000 for all their land and the house. According to you, it's worth much more than that!"

"Hard cheddar, Molly. They could have gone on the open market and got more. But what you have to understand is, the first homes sold in a buy-up are worth less than those that are sold at the end. The last one, that stands in the way of developing what's called a super-block, that's the one that's worth most."

"Is that what you're aiming for?"

His face went blank. She could tell he thought he'd said too much. The clam closed its shell. "Ah, so what. You wouldn't understand."

Molly did understand. To someone used to doing company accounts and handling stocktakes, the mathematics was simple. There was more to it, she knew. She consulted Peter Piper a week later.

He explained about density bonuses and plot ratios and a whole raft of ways in which a super-block could be manipulated. Some blocks might be no more than 300 square feet, given council approval, and council approval could be obtained by lobbying the right people.

"Sometimes the developer has to provide community facilities. Sometimes it's a sweetener to key people," he said. "It's cowboy country, Molly. This ain't called the wild west for nothing."

"Boss, have you heard of a project called the Citrus Court development?"

"Your Frank involved?"

"I think so. I'm concerned about our land."

"Good thing, that caveat, wasn't it?"

"He's said nothing."

"He won't know until it comes to settlement. Be careful, Molly. If he's hanging on until the death knock and finds out you've checkmated him, he could get rough. Why, girl, you could blow any scheme he might have right out of the water. Leave it with me. I'll suss it out. By the way, who did Bud sell to? You could look into that."

She nodded. The boss looked at her sadly. These were bad years for a woman to have to change her way of life, just when her body was shifting gear. He'd been unrealistic to expect Frank to support her through the period. He was pleased Molly had found a job well within her capabilities. He was even pleased she'd had a discreet fling with Jake Morgan, if she had indeed done so. He was not pleased to note the strain on her face.

"I've had a letter from Darwin," he said. "Jake tells me his letters to you have been returned unopened. Is that your doing or Frank's?"

"Mine." She looked panic-stricken. "Frank doesn't know about Jake."

"Keep it that way, Molly. But you've got to be fair on the lad. If he bothers to write, you should at least hear what he has to say."

"That chapter of my life is closed." Her knuckles were white with tension. The boss gave an exasperated huff.

"All I can say it was a damn short chapter, Molly. I hope it was a good read!"

"It was an excellent read." Her cheek dimpled suddenly. "I was sorry it ended. If you write back, tell him I'm all right. Wish him luck and a safe homecoming."

"That's all?"

"Yes. Jake will do his duty. He's a decent man."

*

Molly got no safe homecoming. Frank met her at the door, his face like thunder. "Who is Jake Morgan?" he snarled. "And why was your mink coat at his place?"

There was no explanation Molly could find on the spur of the moment. "What?"

"A blonde bimbo drove up with a kid an hour ago and gave me this big bag. She said to give your fur coat; she found it at Jake's. Said they didn't want to take it to Darwin. I've not opened it yet. I presume it is your mink?"

"I left it there after a party." Molly swallowed hard. That probably meant Jen was joining Jake in Army quarters. One part of her was pleased he was doing the right thing. The other felt bereft.

Frank opened the bag and pulled out the garment. A shower of sand and dry seaweed fell from the hairs of the mink. "It's ruined," he roared. "What sort of a funking party was it, for God's sake?"

Molly met him with defiance. "You said it, Frank!"

"You two-faced whore. You've been giving me the rough edge of your tongue about Nina and all the time you've had an affair yourself. Who is it? Some geriatric old has-been?"

"No. I got myself a toy-boy! A wonderful, handsome hunk. He's dark, he's virile, he's passionate. A young stud!"

"You lying hussy. I don't believe you. No. You haven't been having an affair. You're not the kind. You don't even like sex." He shook her by the shoulders. "Come on. The truth. Who did you lend your coat to? That bird?"

Molly thought like fury. "I dropped it on the beach walking home after a party. This Jake must have seen my offer of a reward in the lost and found column of the local paper." Molly was amazed at her ability to lie.

"Right! Right! That's more like it. Why didn't you tell me it was missing?"

"I was afraid you'd be angry."

"I could have claimed it from the insurance, you dumb cow."

"Give it to me, Frank. I'll see if it can be cleaned."

He handed it across with obvious reluctance, then went out, muttering "Toy boy, indeed!"

Molly brushed out the worst of the mess and threw the coat onto her bed. That night she pulled it beneath the sheets and held it, remembering.

*

The next weeks were busy. Molly spent them helping Dot and Bud to pack and sort their possessions. Bud had arranged a lock-up storage unit for the furniture and their favourite things, while Dot had set aside the bare essentials for life on the road.

"Do you want to put the marmalade in store, or will you sell it through the supermarket, Molly?"

Molly chuckled. "No. I've other plans for it. Most of it's going to Dancer's Creek. I've also spoken to the Army liaison officer and he's agreed to take a gross. It's going on the next shipment of stores to East Timor. It's a sort of Happy Christmas to Jake and the other soldiers in his unit."

"Bit early for that, isn't it?"

"It will take weeks to get there. Where do you two expect to be in December?"

"Tasmania, hopefully. Get away from the heat. And you?"

"I'll be at Aunty Flo's, I expect. She's all the family I have."

*

It took ten days for Peter Piper to get a lead on Citrus Court and on Bridgers Finance, which had been the front for the purchase of Bud's place. He dug deeper.

"You always had a good nose for a rat, Molly. Bridgers Finance is a subsidiary of Flatterjohn and Associates. And guess who the directors are of Citrus Court Nominees? None other than Gary Flatterjohn, one Hariman Hamid of Jakarta, Councillor David McDavies from your local authority and our old friend..."

"Frank Anstruther," said Molly.

"No. The fourth director is Nina Lavell!"

"God, has she got Frank by the short and curlies, or what!"

"Better for him not to be on the board if he's the owner of the property which is the lynch-pin to this project."

"How much land does it cover, now? Is this why Frank's been pleading poverty? Has he sunk everything in buying up real estate? Is this why he won't come to the table to discuss a divorce settlement? Because he hasn't got any money to buy me off?"

"You could be right. He'll be in no hurry. You have to be separated for a year before you can get a decree."

"I have to put up with him virtually living next door for that long?"

"Better than him sleeping under your own roof, Molly. That would make things tricky."

"But he..." Molly bit her tongue. The least said about the night after his mother's death the better. Rape sure wasn't in the separation code of conduct.

"Why don't you go and live with your Aunty Flo?"

"Because I don't trust the big oaf. I want to keep an eye on him."

"You could be wise. I'll carry on tweaking this one. Thank you for giving me an interest in my retirement."

"Bored, are you? I wondered how long it would take."

*

Nina and Frank's cars were both outside the house when she got home. To her surprise they were in her kitchen, drinking Veuve Clicqout. Frank, puffed up like a cane toad, pulled out a chair for her and poured another glass of bubbly.

"We wanted you to be the first to know," he said. "Nina and I are going to have a baby."

The fizz went up Molly's nose as she gasped. "But you can't.

You're sterile."

"I never said I was sterile. I said I was infertile. My crotch is too hot!"

"Pull the other one."

"They were. I had sticky sperm. They were abnormal. Nina's been manipulating me so I'm looser."

"I'll bet she has!"

"And I wear cotton pants now, not nylon. You always bought me nylon."

"Actually, it's the Chinese herbs," Nina said, smugly. "They've done wonders. Got Franky's testosterone boiling away like nobody's business!"

"She says I'm like a young stud." Frank blew out his chest. "Nina says I'm the best but then, she's the best." He chortled. Chor chor chor. Molly had often wondered how a chortle went. Now she knew.

"Congratulations. When's it due?" Molly wondered if she was going mad. One half of her wanted to giggle at the absurdity of it, the other suppressed a cry in her heart which said, "It's just not fair!"

"In the New Year. I want to marry her. Have your divorce."

"We've decided to make you an offer, Molly," said Nina. "I know how much you wanted to give Frank a family. Why don't you go and live in the granny flat and act as the baby's nanny so that I can go back to work after it's born. Frank and I will take over this side of the house and modernise it. It's too big for one."

Molly's jaw dropped. "Over my dead body," she gasped.

Frank frowned. "I said the bitch wouldn't like it," he said to Nina. "The other alternative is for me to pay you one hundred and fifty thousand dollars now, in settlement. That's the fifty thousand your father put into the granny flat and the same price Dot and Bud got for their property. Half each. Fair deal?"

"No," said Molly. "Half of two hundred and fifty thousand is one hundred and twenty five thou, and my father's fifty on top.

That's a hundred and seventy five thousand, but the deal still sucks."

"Why, you little chiseller!"

"You taught me the maths yourself, Frank. Ours is a full acre. That's worth double Bud and Dot's. And it gives two road access to the super-block."

Nina's eyebrows shot up at the mention of the word. "I thought you said your wife was dumb?"

"Not so dumb that I don't know what you're up to, Miss Lavell, director of Citrus Court Nominees! I bet you've got a buyer lined up once you've assembled the land package. I bet you can't move an inch until you get the deeds to this land!"

"You meddlesome bitch!" Frank shouted, dashing his champagne in her face. "How much do you want to get off my back!"

Molly, white-faced, felt numb. She didn't really want any of his money but she was damned if he was going to cheat her. "Half a million." She plucked a figure out of the air. She'd give the extra to the dogs' home, if her conscience pricked too much.

"When hell ices over!"

"Have it your own way. But just consider this, Frank. You raped me the night after your mother died. What happens if I get pregnant as well as Nina?"

He glared at her, veins high on his neck, temples pounding. "You can't get pregnant, you silly bitch. You're past it."

Nina stood up and slapped his face. "You told me you hadn't slept with her since last Christmas. Now I find out you've been with her in the past three months? You eff-wit, Frank. That puts your divorce back. The baby'll be born illegitimate!"

"What's wrong with that," snapped Molly. "The father's a bastard! No, don't bother to make a decision tonight, Frank. I've had the pair of you. When Dot and Bud leave I'm going to stay with Aunty Flo. You can hatch your little plots...and your little heir! But I warn you, Frank, don't try any smart tricks with the land. I've taken legal steps to stop you selling it without my approval."

Frank grabbed the champagne bottle and flung the door open.

"Wait," said Nina. "Three hundred thousand. Half now, the rest when I get the deeds."

"Done," Molly held out her hand to shake on a 'gentleman's' agreement.

Nina opened a briefcase and handed Molly a thick envelope. "Count it," she suggested.

It contained one hundred and fifty hundred dollars bills.

"It's all there."

"Then, if you hurry, you'll get to the bank before it closes."

Molly glanced at her watch. Yes, there was time. Then she could go straight to work. She ran for the door, leaving Frank shouting at Nina.

"You didn't have to do that!" Frank's face was bright red.

"You want her causing more trouble? Poking and prying?"

"She's too thick to work it out."

"Seems she's found out a lot more than you expected. What makes you think she's stupid? You were going to give her that much money anyway!"

"Yes, but we don't need the deeds!"

"The deal with Hamid won't go through without them."

"Yes it will. The deeds aren't worth the paper they're written on."

Molly, who'd paused outside the window to look in her bag for car keys, wrinkled her brow in puzzlement. What was wrong with the deeds?

"What's wrong with the deeds?" Nina screamed. "What have you done now?"

"She'll find out. And when she finds out, you'll find out!"

"You're a fool, Frank Anstruther. Don't you know a wasps' nest when you see one?"

"Bloody women! You're all the same."

"No, we're not," yelled Nina. "You may have slapped Molly around, but you're not starting that game with me! Hit me again and I'll cripple you, just where it hurts most. Your balls will go so high you'll think they're tits!"

*

Molly tried not to cry as Bud and Dot prepared to drive off in their shiny new home on wheels. They'd been such good friends for many years. Dot had been more than a friend. She'd been the only person to whom Molly could confide her negative feelings about Frank and her positive, passionate longing for Jake.

Dot had been shocked to the core to learn of Nina's pregnancy. "Oh, Molly, how could he do this to you?"

"He didn't do it to me. He did it to her. Chinese herbs, indeed. I hope he turns into a Viagra case. I hope he gets brewers' droop. I hope his fancy bits shrivel."

"Judging from the row they had last night after you went to work, it's a wonder he's got any left. You should have heard her carrying on! Worse than his old lady ever did."

"Oh, she's the one who's going to be the master of the house, you can tell. I wonder how he'll like that?"

"Maybe she'll make him stay home and mind the baby. Though, from what she was saying, he's more likely to end up in prison."

"Dear heavens, Dot, what has he done?"

"Don't give it a thought, Moll. You've got a good chunk of money out of him. You won't have to worry about where the next loaf is coming from. Was Mr Welcome decent about you leaving?"

"He was fine. I'd done the business accounts for him, set up a simple system that anyone could operate. He'll get by. He even gave me a decent reference. Not that it will be any use in Dancer's Creek. There's not much work there."

"Then why not come back and find a new place in the city?

You don't have to live in this area."

"Aunty Flo needs me, Dot. She's not as fit as you'd think. She's got mild angina, like my father had. She just won't let it stop her doing what she wants to do."

"Did you write to Jake?"

"Just a card."

"You are a fool, Molly. Why didn't you fight to keep him if you want him so much?"

"Why didn't he fight to keep me?"

"Fat chance you gave him. You didn't even open his letters. Maybe there was a rational reason why Jen was there."

"He was in the nude in front of her. What was I to think? He was aroused."

"Maybe he was glad to see you. Maybe it was a salute to the Marmalady."

"Maybe I interrupted something."

"Molly, he'd been living with Jen for two years. He'd think nothing of going around starkers. Did he go round starkers in front of you?"

Molly nodded. "It was great. I liked looking at him."

"And did you do the same?"

"I got used to it. It was cold, but nice. I used to turn the heater on first thing in the morning. Jake said I looked better without goosebumps." Molly shivered and her body came out in them in memory.

Dot looked at her friend's arms and grinned. "Look at you. You're doing it now. You've tried to block him from your mind, but your body gives you away."

"Oh, Dot. Things were against us. We had so little time together. Maybe it would have grown to a closer relationship, maybe it would have faded away. But there was that bad scene. I made him do his duty by Jen and the baby, and then he was gone. And she's gone to Darwin, waiting for him."

"You don't know that."

"I do so. I went round to the flat to thank her for returning

- 110 -

the coat. The guy in the next apartment told me Frank had it right. She had gone off to Darwin. To join her man, she said."

"Write to Jake, Molly. Write again. Promise."

Molly shook her head. "I couldn't do that, Dot. It's dangerous in East Timor. He needs his wits about him. The last thing I want is to distract him from staying alive."

"You think a gross of marmalade won't distract him?"

"Only one hundred and forty-three jars, Dot. There's one of lemon curd, don't forget. That's for him. That's his favourite. He can give the rest away, to his men or to the locals. I don't mind."

"But fancy taking the rest of the jars to Dancer's Creek. No wonder you had to trade in the Barina for a station wagon. The back of the car must be down on its springs. Why didn't you sell it to Bert Welcome?"

"Mm. You see, I've got a little plan, Dot. I won't tell you about it, but you call in at Aunty Flo's on your way back from the Eastern States. In six month's time I'll be ready to give you a surprise."

*

Frank wasn't there to see Dot and Bud depart. He'd also been absent when the removalists took Molly's favourite furniture to Dancer's Creek. Nina didn't want her old-fashioned pieces, he said. She had better taste. What Molly didn't take with her would go to the Salvation Army. Bud had come out to the truck with several boxes.

"A parting gift, Molly. I'm giving you back your cookery-book collection."

"My old friends. Oh, Bud, I felt quite lost without them!"

He hugged her. "We'll miss you."

"You two are going to leave a huge gap in my life."

She stifled tears as they left. An hour later she stood at the back door and looked down the garden, past the fence to the orchard and out across the creek to the hills beyond. It was strangely quiet. Then a truck drew up in Bud's drive and a demolition crew started unloading gear. A second truck could be seen approaching the block behind Bud's house.

She could see a low-loaders pulling up on the road next to the creek. A small bulldozer was unloaded at the bottom end of the Anstruther land. To her surprise it did not go up the drive to the adjacent land, but came rolling and bumping across the kerb to the citrus orchard. She watched in total dismay as two men, armed with chainsaws, advanced on the valencia, navel and lemon trees and cut them off near the roots. The dozer pushed the greenery to one side, sending a shower of gold and orange fruit bouncing into the long grass. By the time she gathered her wits, the dozer had cut a long brown swathe into the earth and was near the orchard fence.

"Stop it, stop it!" Molly yelled, waving her arms. "You've got the wrong block."

The dozer driver looked at the frantic figure and turned off his engine. He took his ear-muffs off and got out of the cab.

"What the hell's up with you, missus?" he said.

"You've got the wrong block. You're supposed to be next door."

The man pulled a work-sheet from his pocket and looked at it. "This the Anstruther property?"

"Yes."

"Then it's where I'm supposed to be."

"Frank Anstruther told you to do this? Or was it Nina Lavell?"

The man checked again. "Neither, missus. It's signed by the new owner. A Mr Hamid."

"Oh no," Molly protested. "It can't be. I still have the deeds to the property. Citrus Court Nominees don't own the land yet."

"This don't say nothing about Citrus Court, lady. This is a work-sheet from Wintergully Estates."

"What?"

"You go and check with the council, missus. I've seen the subdivisional plans. This whole area's being cleared."

"There's some mistake!"

"Not by me, missus. Now you get your car out of the drive and get out of my way. I'm coming through this fence and taking out that old laundry building. If you want the dunny, you'd better use it quickly or you'll be riding on my dozer blade!"

Molly's head swam. She felt sick with anger. There was a dark haze descending and the world spun. The dozer driver caught her as she fell. The man laid her down on the lawn and fetched a container of water.

"Come on, missus. You can't faint here." He splashed cold water on her face and raised her head to force her to drink. "Come on, pull yourself together and get out of it. You're making a bloody nuisance of yourself."

He helped her to her car. "I need my bag and my cases," Molly said. "They're by the back door.

"I'll get them. You sit tight and have a pull of this" He handed her a hip-flask of brandy. Molly coughed and spluttered on the raw spirits as he opened the rear of the station wagon and stowed her luggage.

"Safe journey, missus."

She gathered her courage and drove off without a backward glance. The local authority offices were only a short distance away. She parked by the council chambers and found her way to the planning department.

"Yes, we know all about Wintergully Estates. You want to see the plans?" The planning officer unrolled a many-coloured sheet, showing internal roads, small lot subdivision and an area he said would be a district shopping centre."

"That's going to be a community hall and library," he said, pointing. It was on Dot and Bud's block. The Anstruther house was marked by pink shading.

"What's happening there?" Molly asked.

"Oh, that's the one block that Mr Hamid hasn't bought yet. Citrus Grove Nominees, who assembled the land package, haven't been able to get title to it yet. Some old biddy's hanging on to it and refuses to sell. Never mind, they don't need title. They can wait until she dies."

"How come?" said the 'old biddy'.

"The owner's husband has signed a ten year lease on the house. Wintergully are going to use it as a sales office and display centre. They're gutting the main house and setting it up to show floor plans of house designs and artists' impressions of how the estate will look. It's a grand scheme. There'll be a car park in front of the house and public toilets where an old laundry used to stand. Tell me, are you interested in buying? Here's the card of someone to talk to."

Molly stared down at the photograph of Gary Flatterjohn. "I don't suppose you can invest in Wintergully Estates?" she said.

"I'm sure you can. Mr Flatterjohn's always looking for people to join his development schemes. He's a mortgage broker."

Molly bit her tongue. She felt like saying, "He's a damn crook!" But what did that make Frank? Oink, oink, oink!

"Can I have your name, madam? The developers like to know who's taking an interest."

"Do you get a commission on referrals?" She smiled as the man's face reddened. She took his pen and wrote in the book he handed her.

"I've put myself down as Mrs Biddy," said Molly. "Mrs Old-Biddy, 123 Main Street, Dancer's Creek. Make sure Mr Flatterjohn sees it, won't you."

Chapter 10

Filthy, stinking hot, air so thick with humidity that breathing was like inhaling chunks of it, the soldiers thought. Perspiration ran down the inner thighs, causing heat rash. There was a fetid, rank smell from the armpits and shirts were stained dark with sweat.

There'd been no chance to wash clothes and personal ablutions had been restricted. There wasn't much water to spare in East Timor. The town they called The Pits, because its real name was a tongue-twister, was little more than a burnt-out shell. The pro-Indonesian militia had driven the villagers out into the night at gun-point, those they had spared. After the looting came the drinking; after the drinking came the wrecking; after the wrecking came the flames. As every water pipe had been smashed, every tap broken off, every toilet and basin shattered, there was nothing with which to douse the fires, even if anyone had dared to do so.

The watchers had seen their homes reduced to charred skeletons. They had wept and, gathering a few salvaged items into bundles, had slipped into the shadows like dark ghosts to make their way into the comparative safety of the countryside.

A little food, a sip of water, a place to rest weary heads, that's all they wanted. The children cried themselves to sleep from hunger, from the pain of blistered feet, from the shock of separation from their familiar surroundings and from fear at the atrocities they had witnessed. Their elders sat like stones, shocked, disorientated, worried about their missing loved ones, grieving for those they had seen die, anguished about the fate of those who had been taken captive.

By day they watched the smoke rise on the plains below, knowing another village had fallen to the men who resisted the very idea of independence. They moved upwards, onwards, deeper into the mountain wilderness, gathering wild fruit and grains as they went, knowing that on their heels came others in search of freedom from the fanatics, the men who would govern by force of arms.

How many days? How many nights? They lost count. They counted only those who died from their injuries, who died from exhaustion, who died from malnutrition.

The sight of ships on the horizon meant little to them. Ships constantly passed through the Timor Sea between Australia and their homeland. They had little hope the ships signified relief; if anything, it was thought that the Indonesian government had sent more troops to back the militia.

The Australian soldiers landed on a hostile shore. They took possession of the nearby villages after sweeping through the ruins, driving out the militia, arresting those who would not lay down their arms. It was always confrontational, sometimes bloody. It was what they had been trained to do, in Townsville and in Darwin, in Army camps throughout Australia. If peace could not be negotiated, it would be enforced.

There were no home comforts. They lived on iron rations. They slept on the ground. They cursed the uniforms that had never been designed for tropical warfare. They sweated and they stank. They were too tired to grumble. The sergeant advised them to sleep starkers under the mosquito nets. It gave the skin a chance to dry out overnight. A rub down with sand in the morning was better than nothing, but the misery of getting back into their stiff and stinking fatigues was depressing. The sergeant allowed no grumbling, setting an example, combing flat the dark hair that sprang into tight curls during the heat of the day. The NCO was a half a head shorter than many of the young men but the look in the brown and amber eyes dared any to challenge a command.

Another dawn. Another patrol. They climbed into the back of a truck for an early morning patrol of a militia outpost, closer to the border with West Timor. Thick vegetation hung across the road. Spiteful vines tore at their faces as they passed, bugs showered onto their shoulders, a thin green snake that fell from a branch was quickly stomped on by the sergeant's size nine boots. The driver was blinded by the rising sun and did not see the ambush in their path.

The sergeant was alert to the possibility. Orders were crisply given. The soldiers rattled the bushes with rapid fire, oblivious to the hail of bullets that greeted them. They took minor damage, flesh wounds that were serious but not fatal. There was the sound of someone whimpering in the bush when silence fell. The serge told them to search for the wounded but, when the attackers had retreated, they had taken their fallen with them.

"God knows what they think we'd do to them," said the sergeant.

"God knows what they'd do to us, if they caught us," a soldier muttered.

"You've seen what they do to their own."

"Mongrels. Sadistic bastards."

It wasn't a thought on which they wanted to dwell. They'd been on burial detail the week before. They'd found corpses of the villagers, piled in a mass at an execution ground. The carcases had been hacked with machetes; some were limbless. All were putrid. All had to be documented for a future war crimes investigation. A small dozer had excavated a grave but someone had to move the bodies. Petrol-soaked rags dulled the smell but nothing could dull the mind. The soldiers threw up from time to time. The job had to be done.

There came a breaking point. It was the body of a small child that reduced the sergeant almost to tears. Arms cradled the little boy, who'd been about a year old. His hands had been severed and he had bled to death. His face had been ravaged by vermin but his hair was still glossy, a mop of dark curls.

"I've one at home, no older than this kid," a soldier said.

The tiny body was laid gently in the grave and the sergeant

covered the child's face with a handkerchief before shovelling earth over the tiny limbs.

The soldiers were moved the next night to a camp on the beach where they were able to take a swim to wash the foulness from their skin. They paid no heed to thoughts of crocodiles or stonefish or the well-fed sharks that had cleaned up the corpses drifting out to sea. Even if the salt made their skin itchy and the sandflies resisted the frequent applications of aerosol insecticides, it was half-way clean. There was a hot meal but no one felt like eating.

They were sent the next day to help unload relief supplies at the airport, transferring them to lorries that would be driven up into the foothills to feed the starving, or into choppers that would drop supplies higher in the mountains.

"Shift your butts; put some muscle into it," yelled the sergeant, staggering under a sack of rice, setting a blistering pace. "The faster we shift this cargo the faster we'll be back at the mess."

Backs ached, hands were rubbed raw from the sacking, sunburn had caught most on the nape of their necks. They stood and watched the transport plane take off for Darwin and civilisation.

There was curry and rice for the evening meal. Rice pudding followed.

"There's a joker in the kitchen," said the sergeant, watching the men push the grains around their plates. "Get it down and you can have your mail."

There was a bag of letters, parcels and hero-grams from Australian school-kids. Most men had been sent cotton shirts and underwear, socks and shorts, for the soldiers' complaints about their gear had made the press big time. Mothers listened, even if the supply department was in need of ear-trumpets.

The men drifted off to quiet corners to read the news from home. The sergeant found a deserted patch of beach and a rock to lean against. There was a letter from Jen. It was short and unwelcome. The sergeant's head dropped. The one page was crumpled into a ball and a broken voice said, "Damn it all to hell."

"You okay, Jake?" said a fellow NCO, who had strolled along the shoreline to sit beside the rock.

"My bird's run out on me again. Taken the kid. She's gone off to Darwin with that Kiwi lout."

"Stuff that. Plenty of others. Go on, open the other card."

To Jake's surprise it was from Molly. It was nothing special. It simply said, "Hope you get the lemon curd in time for Christmas. Yours, Marmalady."

Jake grinned. He felt a whole lot better. It wasn't much, but it was a chink in Molly's armour. He had no opportunity to write more than a brief note. He was unexpectedly sent on leave, on the next flight out to base camp. He'd spend a few days in Darwin, to make sure Jen knew where she stood, to make it plain that Te Pongarani should look after his own child. Then if he could get a flight, he'd go on to Los Angeles. It had been ages since he'd seen his parents. It would give him the chance to talk to his Mom about Molly. He needed her advice. He'd be able to spend a few weeks with his sister and her parcel of kids. He'd be back on duty in the New Year

The lemon curd would have to wait.

Chapter 11

Molly was shaking by the time she got through the city traffic and out to open country on the far side of the Darling Range. She knew she was in no fit state to be on the road, not with the faintness of the morning and the seething anger in her mind. She'd driven to Peter Piper's home after leaving the council offices, but the housekeeper said sir and madam had gone to Singapore.

Molly considered stopping at a hotel for the night but knew this would worry Aunty Flo. She took a turning off the main highway in the state forest and drove through towering karri trees to a tourist spot beside a dam. She parked in the shade and looked out across the man-made lake, letting her anxiety-level drop. The hum of insects was a soporific sound. She put the seat back and dozed off.

It was late afternoon when she awoke but she was refreshed and alert. Luckily the sun was at her back, not glimmering on the windscreen. However, it threw long shadows of trees across the road and she had to concentrate until she came to the rolling open pastures and fields of wheat. It would be dark before she got to Dancer's Creek. That worried her for there was always the chance of hitting a kangaroo at night. The marsupials had no road sense.

She was thirsty and hungry by now, so stopped at a cafe in one of the small towns that served the farming community. Coffee and a toasted sandwich revived her energy. She rang Aunty Flo to warn of her late arrival.

"I'll not wait up," the old lady said. "I need my beauty sleep. I'll leave the door open for you. Have a hot drink and go to bed."

The only thing stirring in Dancer's Creek after midnight was an old black dog. Most of the houses were in darkness but

Aunty Flo had left the porch light on. Molly stretched the stiffness from her spine and flexed hands that were sore from gripping the steering wheel. She looked at her luggage with disfavour. It could wait until morning. The sponge bag with her toothbrush and soap would do for tonight. She locked the car and went quietly along the garden path. She turned off the outside light and bolted the front door.

The floorboards creaked as she walked down the dimly-lit central passage to her usual bedroom. The bedside light was on and the covers were turned down. A small red light indicated that an electric blanket was doing a good job. There was a tray with a thermos of hot cocoa. A tin of biscuits stood on the dressing table. Molly smiled. Aunty Flo obviously didn't want her niece clattering around in the kitchen in the middle of the night. After this treat she tip-toed to the bathroom and did what all good bed-goers do.

Then she took off her travelling clothes and rolled, in her birthday suit, into the warmth of a safe haven.

*

"Time you were up, Lazybones," said Aunty Flo, putting a cup of tea next to Molly's bed. "Lunch will be on the table in twenty minutes. It's only ham and salad because it's building up for a warm day. It'll hold but if you don't get up now you won't sleep tonight."

Molly sat up, clutching the blanket to her throat. "Can I borrow your dressing gown? I want a shower but I didn't bring my cases in last night. I've nothing to wear."

"Tush, child. Your cases are outside your door. I got Fergus to bring them in earlier. He can help you unload the rest of your things later. It will give him a break from digging the garden."

Molly smiled. Aunty Flo's gardener was an old Scot with an irascible temper and an accent so thick it was like chunky Dundee marmalade. He did for her aunt two days a week and worked for the doctor and the bank manager on alternate days.

On Sunday mornings he weeded the cemetery and on Sunday afternoons he got blind drunk.

"It's thinkin' o' the wife and the wee bairns," he'd say. "There, under the cold, cold marble slab."

Molly had thought this a noble sentiment when younger, until Aunty Flo informed her Fergus had never married and was a legend in the liar stakes.

It was luxurious to have a hot shower without the rattle of pipes. It was even better to rinse her hair in water from the rain-tank, which her aunt carried to her in a bucket that had been warmed on the hob. Soon, powdered and fresh, Molly reached for a casual top and a pleated skirt that needed no ironing. One hundred strokes of her rapidly drying hair set her scalp tingling. She was ready to face the world of Dancer's Creek.

She loved Aunty Flo's old house. The ceilings were high and made of overlapping pressed-tin plate, deeply embossed with stylised flowers and painted white a hundred times. There was sprigged wallpaper on the upper half of the walls and timber panelling to dado height. Where later Federation homes had picture rails, Aunty Flo's had narrow plate shelves, for displaying ornaments. Her fine china was on show in the sitting room.

The dining room housed the piggery. Aunty Flo had the largest collection of decorative pigs Molly had seen. There were big fat pink ones in shiny glazes, little porcelain piglets with a self-satisfied sow, and small ivory pigs joined nose to curly tail. There was a surly-looking boar in polished teak and a number of Chinese carvings. Greenstone oinks from New Zealand sat next to alabaster sows in milky white. There were piggy banks painted with flowers and a cute naval pig with a sailor's hat.

"I call him Captain Bligh, from Mutiny on the Bounty. He was a pig," her aunt said. She directed Molly's her attention to recent finds, an Edwardian porker in cast metal and a stuffed toy in the dress and pose of an unamused Queen Victoria, but with an unmistakable snout and ears. A large Miss Piggy sat on a chair at the head of the table. The walls were hung with drawings and paintings of the animals, many of them cartoons or framed copies of Christmas cards with a porcine theme.

"I've been offered a picture of former Prime Minister Paul Keating," she said. "He owned a piggery. But I don't know whether I should make a political statement."

Molly laughed. "If you hang him, I can think of a dozen other members of parliament who should join him."

"Well, you're the expert on porkers. You married one. Are you here for a holiday, or have you finally decided to give him the boot?"

"I think he's given it to me," said Molly, taking her place at the kitchen table. "We've been living apart for months. He finally moved into the granny flat with his lady friend. He's put her in the pudding club."

"More fool she. Help yourself. Go on. Have plenty of ham. I buy a leg every month and cut it into four. I take a hunk out of the freezer every week. It's very fresh and tasty. The tomatoes are home-grown, out of the greenhouse. I made the bread myself. Have cucumber and lettuce. Go on. Eat up, there's a good girl. Then tell me all about it."

It was hard to do justice to the story, taking a mouthful of food in the breaks when Aunty Flo passed comment with a series of "Well, I never," and "Oh, the wickedness of the man." The old lady was so engrossed that she put a spoonful of mustard in her tea instead of on her plate. Molly laughed and jumped up to wash out the cup and refill it.

Fergus came in and helped himself to a mug of tea. He cut a thick slice of meat and put it between two slices off the loaf.

"No airs and graces, have you, man?" said Aunty Flo. "Why can't you sit down to eat your food like civilised people?"

The old man gulped the last of his sandwich and growled. "I ain't civilised, Mrs Frinton. I dinna want to be civilised. You bide along with your table cloths and fancy fiddle-faddles and I'll unload the preserves." He rolled his tongue around the letter R in a furious fashion. "In the garage, would you think, Mrs Anstruther?"

Molly smiled. "Fergus, I never want to hear that name again. Molly will do. I'm Molly Grayson in Dancer's Creek."

"Verra good, then. I knew your father and your puir wee mother well. And I knew you when you was a bitty bairn."

"That's as may be," said Aunty Flo, "But the garage is full of her furniture. Put the rest of the stuff in the empty shop next door, there's a good man."

"Do you own the shop, Aunty Flo."

"Of course I do. It was the bakery. Your Uncle Fred was the baker before he passed on. You remember our bakery."

"Last time I was in it, some young man was running it."

"We've rented it out from time to time, Molly, but the young bakers never stay. They say they can't compete with the sliced bread from the supermarket."

"I wasn't sure. I thought Uncle Fred might have leased it himself. I didn't know it went with the house."

"Got plans for it, have you?"

Molly rubbed her forehead. "I've got the germ of an idea. It needs thinking about. I'll go and help Fergus."

"That you won't. You're not to go lifting heavy boxes in your condition."

"Hey no, you've misunderstood. It's Nina who's in the family way, not me!" Molly gave a soft chuckle.

Aunty Flo looked taken aback. "Well, Molly Grayson, I wasn't the midwife in Dancer's Creek for forty years and more without knowing what a pregnant woman looks like! You've got the look. You've taken. You're not far along, but believe me, you've got a bun in the oven!"

Molly sat down again, shocked. "I can't be. I'm on the change."

"But not on the Pill, I'll bet. Whose is it? That young man who was keeping you out at night when I was down for Hermione's funeral? I saw him talking to you. I saw the sparkle in your eye. You needn't blush, Miss Madam. Fishing, indeed. He got more than his hook into you, didn't he?"

"But I couldn't, Aunty Flo. My periods had almost stopped."

"Hm! Light show? Once every three months or so? You won't be the first that's been caught that way. It's my belief that the body has one last boost before it shuts the system down, especially if you're having fun. It was fun, wasn't it?"

"God, it was glorious! How do I know for sure?"

"Forget about your doctor's tests and rabbit's pee, Molly. You just shut your eyes and open your mind and tell me what you'd really like for supper."

Molly did so and knew at once. "Kippers!" she said firmly.

"See? When did you ever ask for kippers? You hate the damn things. And where, I ask you, are we supposed to find kippers in Dancer's Creek?"

"In the supermarket. I'll walk up the street and get some."

"Lord, Molly. What's come over you? You're sparkling like a set of Christmas lights!"

"That's what I feel like. I feel wonderful. Oh, I'm so happy."

*

Dancer's Creek was just the place for dancing, thought Molly, moving lightly along the pavements. If she was aglow, so was the town. Suddenly her sense of colour seemed intensified. The brickwork of the colonial buildings seemed a deeper red, the leaves of trees a brighter green. Jacaranda blossoms had covered the road with mauve petals.

Main Street, though more or less level through the town, sloped sharply down to the river after one passed Aunty Flo's. On her side of the road the pavement ended in a flight of steps down to the creek, which pooled out upstream of the narrow bridge to the far side of the valley. The bridge could take only a single lane of traffic. Courtesy and patience were required. Across the road the pavement joined a footbridge on the downstream side of the parapet.

Side streets ran at right-angles to the main road, above the valley. They were avenues of wattle at this time of year, the golden flowers shimmering with vitality.

Aunty Flo's home had a wide verandah fronting Main Street. Next to the house was the disused bakery, which shared a common wall with her aunt's kitchen. There was a door to it from the scullery. Molly passed the empty saddlery and the deserted fire station, which had once housed the Volunteer Bush Fire Brigade's engine. It was crumbling into history.

She passed the original post office with its arched entrance of sandstone blocks, the Federal Hotel with wide balconies on the upper storey onto which bedrooms opened, giving shade to the street below and endless opportunity for midnight hanky-panky to the travellers in the days of Cobb and Co. The bank had a modern facade built, despite considerable public protest, over the original bricks. These had been retained as a sop to the heritage lobby, the bank arguing that the olde worlde look could be restored if anyone were daft enough to prefer it. Molly was one who did.

Her smile was infectious. People knew her. She often stayed with Aunty Flo. She was a daughter of the town, come home again to live. They'd thought her a shy and quiet girl. They'd been shocked when she'd been conned by that smart-arse bank clerk who'd taken advantage of her innocence. They'd watched her grow into a shy and quiet woman and knew the hardships she'd faced. They'd shaken their heads in sadness that little Molly Grayson had been dealt a worthless hand of cards. But this was a Molly Grayson they did not know. This was a bubbling, merry, mature woman with an inner glow you could warm your hands on. She smiled at the check-out staff at the supermarket at the far end of town and they, feeling the day was suddenly brighter, smiled back.

Aunty Flo was surprised that there were frozen kippers in town. She'd had to go and have a lie down after Molly went to the shops for, while she was delighted in one way by the development, she could see huge hurdles ahead, problems that Molly had not yet considered.

"You were a fool to have said anything," she told herself. "Molly lost three or four when she was young. She miscarries like other people sneeze. Better to have said nothing and let nature take its course. Better not to have raised her hopes. But what will Frank say? And how will she support herself and a child, if it goes full term. Oh, I can help out a bit, that way, but there's no work here and the family allowance won't go far. Would Frank pay maintenance if he thinks it's his child? Did Molly get a good settlement from him, or has he had his usual dose of the stingies?"

It was all too much for an old chook, she decided, and went to sleep.

*

Molly spent the rest of the afternoon in the garden, weeding the vegetable beds for Fergus. Not only did the garden stretch a full quarter acre behind the house, but continued down the slope to the river in a series of terraces where fruit trees grew.

When the evening chill arrived she went in and finished her unpacking. Aunty Flo drove her out of the kitchen, saying the smell of the cooking fish might ruin her appetite. It didn't. The salty, pungent aroma of smoked herring and browning butter set her mouth watering. She came eagerly to her evening meal and picked out the fine bones with concentration. Aunty Flo ate a scrambled egg. She couldn't even abide the smell of the kippers.

"You'd better go to the doctor's and get yourself checked over," she told Molly. "He'll want to keep an eye on you. Older mothers are inclined to be difficult. He may want you to have a test to make sure the baby isn't handicapped. If it is, you could get rid of it."

"I'd never do that. This is my last chance. You know how I've longed for a child. You know what I put up with from Frank, hoping for one. Oh, don't pull that long face, Aunty Flo. I know you think I'll lose this one, the same as the others. But this doesn't feel the same. This feels right. I feel good. I know, I really know, that this pregnancy is going to have a happy ending."

"But what will you live on?"

"I got Mum's money out of Frank. I got half the money from the house. I've got savings and a good redundancy package from the factory. Frank owes me another hundred and fifty thousand when I hand over the deeds. Aunty Flo, I'm really quite rich. And I'm lucky. Oh, I can't tell you how lucky I am. You and I will never have to worry about money again."

Molly Grayson's happiness came to an end in the middle of the night. There was a sharp pain in her gut and a roiling, spoiling feel in her stomach.

"I'm losing the baby!" she wailed. She staggered to the bathroom and threw up in the toilet bowl. She was there most of the night, off and on. There was plenty going on, but she passed no blood. Aunty Flo heard her and fed her antacids. She gave her a hot water bottle and a dose of peppermint and kaolin to clog up the works.

Towards dawn things settled down and Molly slept, exhausted, wondering how, when and what to tell Jake. Wondering if she should, in fact, tell Jake anything. The dilemma sat as uneasily on her conscience as the kippers had done on her stomach.

Chapter 12

The euphoria wore off as quickly as it had risen to the giddying heights. Molly's fizz went flat. That frightening turn following the kipper fiasco brought back all the memories of her early miscarriages. She had never been past four months before. No sooner had she felt the first flutterings of life in her womb than it had rudely expelled each foetus.

Once more she felt the tightness in her breasts, the tingly, itching feeling of sensitive nipples. She had to use safety pins to fasten waistbands for the buttons no longer reached the holes. Her B-cup bras were too tight. She had to buy the next size up and soon bulged over the edges of those. She had to get up in the night to spend a penny and still the little swelling in her belly stayed in place.

The doctor was ready to confirm her status and handed her leaflets full of good advice.

"I must be sure," Molly said. "My first conception felt like this and it wasn't a baby at all, just a 'katy did'...a sort of mole."

The doctor laughed. He was a young man but knew her medical history. The former doctor had kept medical records from whoa to go on all the people of Dancer's Creek. Those relating to a young Mrs Anstruther and the critical years were still in store. He sent to Perth for later details, and wrote to specialists who had seen her through the traumas of the past.

"We've come a long way in twenty years, Molly," he said. "We'll check by ultrasound that it is a baby, not what you call a 'katy did.' I'm sure it's a real foetus, by the way. We can help you carry this baby to full term. But there is one thing I insist you do. You must have an amniocentesis. The gynaecologist will draw off a sample of the fluid around your baby. They will look at it to make sure there are no genetic defects in the child. They can find out if it's a girl or a boy and make sure it is healthy."

"I won't go back to Perth to have it done."

"No need. There's a good district hospital thirty kilometres away. They could fit you in next week."

"Can they tell who the father is?"

"Lord. I don't know. It would take weeks to grow foetal cells. We don't usually test for DNA until the baby's born. Is it important for you to know?"

"Yes. I'm separated from my husband. We're divorcing."

"I see. It's critical?"

"Vital. You see, unless I know, I can't decide what to do for the best."

"I'll ask if it can be done early. I'll need some hair or nail parings or something like that from the one you suspect is the father. Your husband?"

"No." Molly unfastened her locket and tipped the curl of Jake's hair onto the doctor's desk. "Will that be enough?"

He teased a few strands from the circle of hair and put them in an envelope. "This will do. You keep the rest. I feel it's precious to you."

"It's all I have of him," said Molly, sadly.

The doctor's smile widened. "If he's the father you'll have a lot more of him than what's in that locket!"

Molly's chin came up in the brave little gesture that was part of her nature. "So I will. And that will have to be enough."

There was nothing she could or would do until the tests were done. She refused to contact Frank or Nina. They could wait for their damn deeds. After the trickery they had played on her, she owed them nothing. If it turned their deal sour, she did not care. She knew now that Frank had never intended to share the proceeds of their home equally. She saw how Nina, by pretending to capitulate on a lower price than the outrageous figure Molly had suggested, had put her in the position of half now, half later, while in fact only fronting with the miserly sum Frank had originally offered. What he would offer by way of maintenance, should the baby prove to be his, would be niggardly, she knew. Even if she got Peter Piper's hot shot lawyer on her case, she knew they would have a battle on their hands.

If the baby proved to be Jake's, she could not, in all conscience, expect Frank to pay for its upbringing. If it was Jake's, the burden would fall entirely on her shoulders. She had thought and thought about it. At first, in her joy, she had rejoiced. She'd wanted to write and tell Jake about the baby, to let him know he was, at last, to be a true father. She wanted to shout, "Aren't I clever? Come to me, be with me, stay with me. The baby will be your reward for loving me. I won't double-cross you like Jen did with Te Pongarani. I won't tell you a baby is yours and then wait until you love it before I tell you that I lied."

And then she realised that she was on the brink of doing just that. If the baby was Frank's, she would love it for its own sake, but hate the father while she did so. The child would, she knew, be better off without a father than come under the influence of the oink factor.

But when she remembered Morris, the child with the brown and amber eyes, the child that Jake loved as if he were his own, she recalled her words, the duty and the responsibility she had forced on him. "Morris needs a father. Go. Look after the child and Jen. Learn to love them both." And hadn't Jenny responded and gone to Darwin to be nearer the Army base, to look after Jake when he came back on leave from East Timor?

She fingered the envelope that had been forwarded by the Post Office from Dili. He had replied to her card about the marmalade. Lemon curd, indeed. What must he have thought of her? Such a trivial message after all those weeks of returning his mail unopened. Would he tell her she was a hard-hearted bitch? Would he tell her he loved her? Worst of all, would he tell her he needed her?

Molly, sitting beside the mill-race above the waterwheel at Dancer's Creek, watched the tumbling current and found no answer there. She sighed and tore the letter into shreds. The paper fragments floated out from the shore and went whirling down and over the paddles of the wheel, on to the sea of dreams and futility.

Then, in panic, she realised she had made a mistake. She should have kept the letter until she knew the test results. Too late. Too late. She burst into tears. And, as she did so, felt the stirring inside.

The waiting was a torture. The procedure had been unpleasant. The trip to the hospital, with Fergus at the wheel, a nightmare. If Aunty Flo hadn't driven from the back seat all the way there, Fergus would not have gone to the pub while he waited. If he hadn't gone to the pub, Aunty Flo would not have insisted on driving home herself, with Fergus snoring in the back of the car. If Molly had realised what a lousy driver Aunty Flo was, she'd have taken the bus. So much for the doctor warning her she might feel strange because of the local anaesthetic and recommending she be driven. Why, it had been enough to make her go into labour. As it was she'd had three sets of kittens on the way home.

*

Anything to pass the time, Molly thought. Her quest for local history not only stopped her worrying but had a long-term purpose.

She knew that Dancer's Creek took its name from Tom Dancer who, in the early days of settlement of the South West, had set up a flour mill on the banks of the river. His eagerness to process the local grain led to a certain lack of foresight. In winter the creek was prone to flood, in summer drought to allow no more than a trickle of water to wet the sandy sediment that lay among the granite boulders. He built a dam upstream, in the valley below Bushranger's Rock, to regulate the flow. It was now used for irrigation of arable land.

Tom Dancer next built a granary high on the banks

overlooking the gully, from whence he could pour the grain down a series of chutes to the grinding stones, when the river happened to be at the right level to turn the waterwheel. It had been a novel way of dealing with the problem and, being unique to Western Australia, heritage lovers had sought and obtained government grants to restore the mill to its original condition. They had even started milling again, selling the flour to the few tourists who realised what a fascinating glimpse of bygone days it represented.

Molly, exploring Aunty Flo's bakery, realised quickly that it pre-dated the weatherboard house by more than seventy years. The walls were thickly built of stone and rubble, loosely cemented with mortar. The original bakery was in the front half of the premises, used as the shop and a cafe-dining room. The old ovens were in place and many of the original machines had been slung high in the rafters or nailed to the walls to give an historic ambience. Behind the ancient lay the modern, a place of gleaming steel and rotating ovens, banks of hotplates where savoury fillings for pies could be cooked. There were wide shelves, on which dough could be stood to rise, or knocked down by kneading, flanked by deep troughs for washing utensils. All lay under a pall of dust and cobwebs.

Molly spent hours in the library, built in 1918 as a practical memorial to the fallen of the Great War. Previously the memorial had been a trough to commemorate those who'd died in the Boer War. This stood outside the hotel, where it had served a practical purpose in the days when the farmers came to market in horse and buggy.

She was shown the archives, wherein she found faded sepia photographs of the old bakery. The librarian unearthed fragile letters written by Fred Frinton's forebears to Tom Dancer, placing orders for wholemeal flour and bran.

"They're restoring some old cottages at the mill now. It will be quite a tourist attraction in time," the librarian predicted. She was pleased to find another heritage enthusiast. Few saw potential in a community where young folk went to the city to get jobs and the retired farmers and business leaders stayed only until they wore out and were put under.

Fergus swore that, when some of the oldies got buried, they looked little different to the way they'd been for twenty years or so.

"Och, noo, they're dead from the neck up until sixty and dead from the neck down at seventy. But not Mrs Frinton. Your Aunty Flo will be still botherin' folks when she's gone to meet her maker. I'd bet my last bottle of Glenfiddich that, after St Peter's had six days of her, he'll send her back to haunt us!"

Molly laughed and said she hoped it would be many years before either Aunty Flo or Fergus faced the Pearly Gates.

"What are you up to Molly Grayson?" said her aunt. "Whenever you go all quiet, I know you're up to something. I know you're trying to keep your mind off the baby, but it won't do to worry me as well as yourself."

"Listen, would you let me rent the bakery from you?"

"Rent it? Why you can have it. It'll be yours one day, after all. You're my only surviving relative. What would you do with it? You're no baker."

"No. But I'm a dab hand at marmalade and jam. I've been walking round town for weeks, using my eyes. The gardens are huge and old. Every one has a dozen fruit trees, mainly oranges and lemons. I bet there's a glut of fruit in season."

"There always is. Can't give it away."

"Aunty Flo, if I could persuade Peter Piper to sell me some of the plant from the old pickle factory, I could go into business. I could start a co-operative with the Townswomen's Guild. We could get the men growing produce in the gardens for us to make into chutneys and pickles. The women could learn to make marmalade to my special recipes. We could bake the flour ground at Tom Dancer's Mill. We could serve tea and fresh bread and marmalade."

"Hey, hey. Slow down. What's all this 'we'? I'm gone

seventy."

"Fergus said you're more trouble as you get older. He's offered to put half his garden under pickling onions."

The old lady blew out her cheeks but looked as if she's received a compliment. "You couldn't do all that in the bakery."

"No. But the old saddlery next door is vacant and so is the original fire station. We could rent them and spread out as the business grew."

"And who, may I ask, is going to buy your produce?"

"If we made it interesting enough, we'd get the tourist coaches stopping. They're a good way down the road to that at Tom Dancer's Mill. We could work hand in hand. And when we're in full swing, I'll ask Peter Piper to take an interest. I'm sure many of his old customers would order a gourmet line of country-made produce."

"Molly! Where's the money to come from? It would cost thousands to set up this scheme."

"I've got thousands."

"You're about to have a child to bring up. How much do you think that's going to take out of your savings?"

Molly grinned. "The interest will bring me about $16,000 a year."

"Yes, but you mustn't use your capital."

"You sound like Frank. I think it's a risk worth taking, but if it worries you, I won't. But Aunty Flo, there's something you don't know. I had a win on the lottery in August."

"Gracious. How much?"

"I don't know exactly. Bud said there was a first division pool of two million but there were about twenty winners. That's at least a hundred thousand I could use without affecting my savings. I posted the ticket to you to put in the bank, remember?"

"So that's what it was. I did wonder."

"It's bound to be enough to get us started."

"It's bound to be nothing of the sort. Some weeks there are

fifty winners or more. Why don't you start small, in the bakery? Then, if you go ahead with the full scheme, you should begin the way you mean to continue. If you're going to form a co-operative, you get those that are going to take part in it to take shares in raising the money you need. There may be no work here; they may cry poverty, but they've all got a bit tucked away for a rainy day."

Molly looked at her with eyes shining. "Do you think we could do it, Aunty Flo?"

"Well, I can't see any other way of getting rid of all that damned marmalade you've got stacked in the shop. It will give you an interest in life, if the baby doesn't keep you run off your feet."

"Thanks. I'll start writing a business plan."

"When are you going to make time to write to that nice young man? Hasn't he a right to know you're pregnant."

"He's in the Army, Aunty Flo. He's in East Timor. He's got enough to think about without me bothering him."

"Bothering him? Bothering him? If it's his child, bother him all you want."

"He lives with another woman, Aunty Flo. He's like a father to her son." The whole sad story came welling up. Molly, reluctant at first, was relieved to get it all off her chest.

Aunty Flo watched Molly intently as she spoke of the man she loved. There was no doubt what Molly would like out of life. The old lady felt a great compassion for her niece. Molly was so used to being imposed upon in her personal life that it was hard for her to fight for what she wanted. The man seemed a good person. They sat in silence for some time after Molly had finished.

"You do understand, don't you, Aunty Flo."

"Yes. But Molly, have you ever considered that Jake might prefer to bring up his own child instead of someone else's?"

"Jake? No. I hadn't."

"Well, you should. I've listened to all your reasoning, all your beliefs, all your good intentions and good common sense. There's something missing. There's been a whole load of Molly and damn all Jake. He chose to make love to you. You can't deny him the right to choose whether he also wants to love you and love his child."

Slow tears rolled down Molly's cheeks. "That's not fair. I'm trying to protect him, not to be a burden on him."

"You were his lover, not his mother. Give him the right to make a man's decision."

"Must I?"

"Yes. Now go to bed. There's no point in going over and over this until you get your results."

"And if it's Frank's?"

"Molly, if it's Frank's he'll still have to know. If it isn't, you must still tell him."

"You're hard, Aunty Flo."

"I'm a pragmatist, Molly. I face facts. And one of those facts is that it's two hours past my bedtime. Goodnight!"

There was no way Molly could get to sleep with her aunt's words ringing in her ears. Face facts; face facts. It was refusing to face facts that had kept her tied to Frank. It was refusing to face facts that had made her tear up Jake's letter. It was the refusal to face facts that had left that damn lottery ticket lying in the bank, unclaimed. While it was there she had neither to face the consequences of being a very rich woman or a comparatively poor one. It allowed her the luxury of dreaming.

Aunty Flo had put it in perspective. Molly needed money to go into business; she needed money to bring up a child. It was time she found out exactly where she stood.

The newsagent, a newcomer to town, took the ticket and ran it through the machine that checked each week's numbers. He opened the till and assembled a twenty dollar bill, a ten dollar note, a fiver, a dollar coin and forty cents.

"Congratulations," he said. "You've got a winner!"

Molly was thunderstruck. "But that's a line of correct

numbers. That should be a first division prize! Please check."

He reached for a printed list and thumbed back to the sheet for late July. Then he laughed. "Sorry, lady. You've got the winning numbers for draw 295 all right. The trouble is, that ticket is for draw 296. Easy mistake. $36.40. Take it or leave it."

He handed her the money and the franked ticket. Molly, getting over her initial disappointment, started to laugh.

"Don't spend it all at once," the newsagent said.

"I'm not going to spend it at all," his customer replied. "I'm going to frame it!"

Chapter 13

"There," said Molly, adjusting the picture frame above her bed, "Doesn't that look good?"

"I must say, you've made a tidy job of it, but I'm surprised you're not howling all down the street."

"Hey, Aunty Flo; you're the one who said face facts. Every time I look at that, I'll remember not to trust in fantasies. I'll face the real world."

"Then I hope you're ready for it. The doctor rang. You're to go down and see him. Some of your test results are back."

Chin up, Molly told herself. Straighten your back. The baby kicked. "It can't be worse than not knowing," she said. "I've carried for nearly five months; that's more than I ever did before. I'm more than half way home, Aunty Flo."

"Counting chickens again, Molly?"

"You told me to look reality in the face. You didn't tell me to stop hoping for the best."

The old lady smiled. "I never count that sort of chicken until seven months. But you look well. It would be lovely to have a little one around the house, I must admit. Maybe I should start knitting."

The doctor waved Molly to a seat. "You're all right," he said. "The baby's fine."

"Pardon?"

"But we can't do a DNA match from the hair sample we took. The foetal cells didn't grow."

"Is that serious?" Her heart sank.

"No. It's very common. But we can tell a lot from the amniotic fluid. No genetic defects."

The champagne feeling was back. Molly started to bubble with happiness. "Is it a boy or a girl?"

The doctor tapped his teeth with his pen. "Ah. I hoped you

wouldn't ask me that. We're not sure. There's been a bit of an argument over the results. I'm sending you to a specialist in Perth."

"Why? What's wrong?"

"Oh, I don't know that there's anything wrong. It's just that you seem to be carrying twins."

Dumbstruck. That was Molly. The doctor explained that the district hospital equipment did not give brilliant images.

"Look, Molly, you lost so many babies when you were younger that we have to ask whether you have cervical incompetence. That means that, when the foetus gets to a certain size, your cervix opens and the baby sort of falls out. Oh, that's a bad way of putting it, but there's a simple procedure that can make sure it doesn't happen. The gynaecologist can put in some special stitches to draw the opening of your womb tightly closed like the string on a bag. You get the idea? Then they snip it in time for delivery. It's essential if you're indeed having twins and want to go near full term."

"I don't want to go back to the city."

"Any woman having a first child at your age should be under specialist care. In fact, it's likely that they'll insist on you having the birth in King Edward Memorial Hospital, probably by Caesarean section."

"Aunty Flo will be disappointed. She wanted to deliver it herself."

"Them," said the doctor firmly. "But, much as I respect your aunt's reputation as a midwife, if you think that I'd let her meddle in one of my cases..."

"Say no more," said Molly. "I'll be good."

*

There was no question of Molly driving to Perth, nor any chance that she'd risk herself or her precious cargo to Fergus or Aunty Flo. Molly went by bus. She booked into the County Women's Association hostel in West Perth for the night, glad of quiet comfort and sympathetic company. The other guests knew the problems facing people in rural areas. She talked to them about her ideas for the shop and the future co-operative. They understood. There were rural branches that had run community services of that nature, such as a coffee shop in a mining town. They offered advice on everything from finance to health regulations. They promised to send her marmalade recipes. A vice-president, who was staying in-house, gave her a copy of the Country Women's Cook Book. Molly promised to send a supply of marmalade for the dining room.

Her appointment was first thing in the morning. She took a taxi because she had been told to drink several litres of water and not to pass them before the ultrasound. Molly felt like a balloon of liquid and was fairly desperate for relief by the time she was on the examination table. Midway she was given the chance to let rip. On her return the radiographer applied more jelly to her stomach and moved the sensor across the bulge. He swung the screen towards Molly and pointed.

"There you are, you can see the two foetuses quite clearly."

Molly could not see anything in the fuzz of images until he showed her the heads, the spines, the tiny limbs. As she watched a tiny leg stretched out and she felt the movement against the wall of her uterus. Her smile was infectious.

"Pigeon pair, all right. No problems. No spina bifida or anything. You'll do."

Molly had to wait an hour before she was prepped and taken down to theatre for the purse-string suture to be inserted. She was kept in overnight and told she would see the specialist in the morning.

The doctor greeted her with a smile. "You wanted to know the paternity of your babies, I understand? I'm sorry we couldn't do a DNA test for you, but I can tell you one thing for certain. It's almost impossible for it to be your husband."

"Molly was wide-eyed. "How do you know?"

"From your blood tests. You are rhesus negative but your

blood is full of rhesus positive antibodies. That means you were sensitised in the past. Your blood has been mixed with that of someone who was rhesus positive."

Molly recalled in a flash the night when she had nearly died, the night she'd expelled the first presumed pregnancy. "I had a what I think the doctor called a 'katy did' mole," she said.

"A hydatidiform mole?"

"Yes, that would be it. It was an emergency. The doctor gave me a transfusion of my husband's blood."

"And he's rhesus positive?"

"Yes. After we gave blood for the Red Cross he used to joke about him being a positive person and me being negative. He was a big D, big D, whatever that means."

"You realise that's probably why you couldn't carry any conception more than a few months?"

"Then why are you so sure I can this time?"

"Because the babies are rhesus negative as well. Unless your husband was heterozygous, that's a man with big D and small d, that's one rhesus negative factor, it's odds on that he didn't father them. Is that a problem?"

Molly smiled through tears. "No. Thank you. Thank you so very much."

*

Larry was waiting for her in the car park. She'd rung Jake's friend to see if the police officer was off-duty. While she was in the city she had decided to meet Frank but not without protection. She had the deeds to the Wintergully property in her handbag. Since the lottery had proved a wash-out, she planned to try to prise the promised $150,000 from her ex-to-be and Nina. If they were difficult, she'd tackle Gary Flatterjohn again, but only with a cast-iron witness.

Larry's eyebrows shot up when he saw her coming out of the hospital. "And I thought you were visiting someone," he said, putting her overnight bag in the car. "I didn't realise you were having a baby. Jake's?"

Molly went red. "I hope so but to be sure I need to know his blood group. Do you know it?"

"No, but I've got an old mate who could check the Army Reserve records. You want me to do that?"

"Don't tell Jake, please. I want it to be a surprise."

"It'll be that all right. But I'm pleased and he'll be thrilled. Time he found a decent woman. That Jen was a bad lot. Dingo and I couldn't convince him that she was trouble on the trot."

"Was she?"

"Speed freaks usually are. You don't think Jake would give her money to feed her habit, do you? Then where did it come from? We knew, you see. The vice-squad picked her up a couple of times. When he was on nights she used to get a baby-sitter in and go on the game."

Molly felt as if her heart had been pierced by a corkscrew. She'd not guessed.

Jake, loyal, obviously had no idea. She'd rejected him and sent him back to Jen, loaded him with the responsibility for a drug addict. Dear Lord, she'd been a short-sighted fool. But what of little Morris? Wasn't the child's need of Jake even greater than before?

Larry, puzzled by her silence, said, "You're in charge, Molly. Where to?"

"We'll try Wintergully Road first. He may be in the site office or at home. Nina should be in, even if he's not. She'll surely not be at work in her condition."

The dozers had been busy in the past month. Where there had been two streets of houses there was now a wilderness of newly-turned ground. There were surveyors' pegs everywhere and pipes were being laid for sewerage. There was a clear view to the wetlands along the river and the sparkling waters could be seen through the bulrushes. The Anstruther house stood out like the last tooth in an old man's head. Across the front eaves was a sign, 'Wintergully Sales and Home Display Centre.' The front door was open.

There was an unfamiliar car in the drive of the granny flat. The front gardens and the access to the rear of her old home were buried under newly-laid bitumen. The surface was still sticky and the smell of coal-tar pungent. Molly went up the path to her father's old quarters and knocked. Nina and Frank did not appear to be at home. The curtains were tightly drawn. She looked at the letter box. There were newspapers bulging from the slot.

"I'll go round the back, shall I?" said Larry. "I can get down the side without getting tar on my shoes."

Molly was flummoxed. If Frank and Nina were out, whose was the car?

A man walked out of the sales office and down a path from the door to the drive of the granny flat. It was Gary Flatterjohn. He did not look pleased to see her.

"Hah! The interfering old biddy herself. What are you doing here?"

"I've come to see Frank and Nina. He promised me another $150,000 when I gave him the deeds of this house."

"You've got them? Show me."

Molly took a large envelope out of her bag. "Where is Frank? Your office said he was working at Wintergully."

Flatterjohn scowled. "You'll get no money out of that cheating bastard. He's done a bunk."

Molly shook her head. "I don't believe you. Why would he do a bunk?"

"Because Hariman Hamid paid $8 million into Citrus Court Nominees for title to the Wintergully Estate. That's supposed to go into the trust funds for those who had mortgages over the land during the acquisition stage. Nina and your Frank were both signatories on the Citrus Court account. They cleared it out and skipped the country."

Molly went white. She felt giddy. She sat down on the front seat of Larry's car and took a few deep breaths. "Frank couldn't.

Frank wouldn't. He's a lot of things, Mr Flatterjohn, but he's not a thief!"

"He's a money-hungry con-man, Mrs Anstruther. Who do you think set up these schemes? Santa Claus?"

"Well, it wasn't Frank. He's a bully and a miser and a two-timing skirt-chaser but, knowing him for twenty-five years, I can tell you one thing...he hasn't got the brains to pull off that sort of a double-cross."

"Oh, of course he hasn't got the brains. He does what Nina tells him!"

"I bet you cooked this one up with her!"

Gary Flatterjohn's eyes narrowed. "Think you're smart, do you? You say that in front of witnesses and I'll sue you."

"For what? Money I haven't got?"

"I'll give you the money for those deeds. $45,000 now and the rest in three days time."

"Why?"

"Because it will get Hariman Hamid off my case! He'll go ape-shit when he finds out what's happened."

"You haven't got that sort of money on you."

The mortgage broker opened the briefcase he was carrying and gave her four thick rolls of notes. Then he peeled off half another block of money. Molly took it. There were fifty loose hundred dollar bills. There were more rolls of banknotes in the fat, bulging briefcase, shaped like a doctor's bag.

"The deeds, Mrs Anstruther." He held out his hand.

She studied his face carefully. What was wrong here? There was a shiver of distrust in her mind. He was carrying enough cash to pay her out in full. Why was he doing so? Why didn't he just pay her the full amount on the spot? Why was he telling her lies about Frank?

"Same deal as before," she said, rising to confront him. "You get the deeds in three days time. When I get the bankers' draft. And, Mr Flatterjohn, the price has just gone up. I don't like you. $200,000."

"You bitch! You'll give me those deeds now!"

"Make me!"

He put his hand into the briefcase and pulled out a gun. A gun? Molly's mind shrank from the unexpected turn of events. What on earth was Flatterjohn doing with a gun?

"Give me those deeds," he roared.

Larry, coming round the corner of the house, crept up soundlessly behind the man. He had a neat cosh in his hand. It landed on Flatterjohn's head with a thump. The broker collapsed on the bitumen.

"Oh, tush," said Larry. "He's got a touch of the sun. I suggest we get out of here, fast."

Molly breathed deeply, trying to overcome her fright, glad to be on the road again. "You didn't learn that in the police force, Larry," she said.

"No. Highly unprofessional. But damned effective."

"Was that a real gun?"

"Looked like it to me, but does it matter? What was he doing waving around in public? That's illegal."

"Larry, he gave me $45,000. His bag was stuffed full of money."

"Hm. He's no bank robber. If I had to make a guess, I'd say he was planning to do a runner. Is he in trouble with the law?"

Molly explained the situation. "He says Frank's the crook but I don't believe him."

"I should think Flatterjohn's going into hiding before that Hamid guy arrives from Indonesia. It will take a while before the mortgagees alert the Fraud Squad and we arrest him but the consequences of messing around with Hamid might be worse, especially if Mr Budiman's got buddies on the wrong side of society."

"Will you tell your colleagues what's been going on?"

Larry frowned. "Hell, Molly, I don't know. If we start digging right now, Flatterjohn would immediately suspect you and that could lead to him threatening you further. Best if it comes from a third party. I can't very well admit my involvement in case he does me for assault."

"He didn't see you."

"No, but he knows you were there and, if you had to give evidence, even as a hostile witness, he could find out."

"I'll ask Peter Piper to talk to the police on my behalf. He knows the Commissioner."

Larry saw her to the door of the pickle king's home where she was to spend the rest of the week. He was invited in for a beer and, together, they recounted the afternoon's events. The boss was seriously concerned. He would, he said, take action but discreetly. He walked down to the car with Larry while Rita took her guest upstairs.

"Are you a good friend of Jake Morgan's, Mr Piper?"

"I'd say so. Why?"

"Molly hasn't told him she's pregnant. Says she wants it to be a surprise. She's a deep one, that. I don't understand her."

"I don't suppose she understands herself, Larry. She hasn't even told me and I'm like a father to her. I'm still in shock myself."

"If she tells you, would you tell Jake?"

"No. I know things are difficult. They're two damn fools, afraid to say what they really feel, but they'll get there. I'll keep an eye on the situation. I like Jake. He'd be good for Molly. Now, as to our other little problem, I'll get a friend of mine to ask more questions in parliament. And I'll have a chat to an investigative journalist I know. Let the media do the chasing."

"Good, but be quick. If Flatterjohn's going to skip out, he'll do it soon."

"He worries me, Larry. This is Australia. Men don't go round carrying guns."

"Not unless they mean to use them, Mr Piper. Not unless they mean to use them."

*

It was a hot night. Rita ordered her husband to set out garden chairs on the terrace overlooking the Swan River. As the sun went down the great pool of the river between South Perth and the city centre turned gold, then red, then violet. The tall towers of office blocks on the far shore took over the spectacle, casting reflected lights onto the placid water. The boss cooked steaks on the barbecue while Molly and his wife made simple salads to accompany crisp chunks of French bread. Rita was naturally most concerned with the details of the pregnancy but too tactful to push for the paternity.

Over dinner they talked of the dramatic events of the day and Molly outlined her plans for the future. The boss thought the shop might do very well. He thought the co-operative might do even better. He promised Molly all the plant she wanted from the pickle factory, the slicers and the sterilising units, the bottle cappers and the rotary feeders, the labelling machines and the pressure vats.

"It'll only go for scrap otherwise. I like the plan; in fact, you and I, dear, might take a drive down south to Dancer's Creek to see how we could help Molly set this up."

His wife smiled indulgently. "Well, fancy that. Molly, he's been bored witless since he retired. He's not made to rust out, he's made to wear out. The next thing you know is, he'll be buying a place in Dancer's Creek and running your project."

The boss shook his head. "No. I can be more use in the city, marketing and buying, doing promotions and so on. But we could always get a holiday home down there, couldn't we?"

"Whoa, whoa, how big do you think this could get?"

"Who knows? You could get bulk peel from the orange juicers at Harvey; they discard the skins; then all you want is another source of commercial pectin and some fresh fruit to bulk it out. I mean, it's your good thick chunky recipe that's most popular, isn't it?"

Molly nodded. "But there are all sort of new recipes I want to try, ones with melon bases and apple pulp. We could get those ingredients in bulk."

"If I found an onion supplier in your area, would you make a small run of pickles? I can't stand the stuff in the shops."

"He'll have the saddlery, the fire station and even the town hall converted if you let him have his head," said Rita. "But I think you should also link in to the pottery in town. You could get them to make a line of decorative marmalade jars. And how about Bushranger's Rock pickles? There's a great recipe in one of my grandmother's books for a spiced melon and fig pickle. I always wanted to try that."

Enthusiasm kept them going for hours. Rita seemed as keen as her husband. "We could invest some money in this, don't you think?" she said.

"Hold on," said Molly. "I haven't even talked to the people in Dancer's Creek yet."

"Before you do that, let me see what I could line up for you in government grants," said the boss. "Yes, this is a goer all right."

He poured wine for his wife and himself and looked speculatively at the bottle. "How's the soil down there for viticulture?"

Molly laughed. She drank only ice-water. She was avoiding wine for the sake of the baby...no, the babies. She hugged the knowledge to herself but it crept out in a little smile of contentment.

Relaxed, feeling safe and welcome, she eventually shared her delight in carrying not one, but two babies. The boss, as chuffed as if he were to become a grandfather, gave a whoop of congratulations and insisted on champagne all round.

"Just a sip won't hurt," he insisted. "Think of it as medicine."

"It never hurt me," said his wife. "What does the father think of the news?"

"I haven't told him," said Molly.

Peter Piper shook his head. "You know you're not playing fair, Molly. Jake wrote to me, remember. You promised me you'd contact him. Did you?"

"Just a short note."

"What's got into you, Molly. It's not Frank's is it? I can see you'd be troubled if it was, but why aren't you sharing this with Jake?"

Molly, goaded, tried to explain. It wasn't easy. She'd only just come to terms with her own motivation.

"Look, I love Jake. I always liked him, then when it seemed I could get free of Frank, after I thought I'd won that lottery prize, I wanted him. He turned out to be more man than I ever imagined. But he'd said right from the beginning that he loved kids and, even though Morris wasn't his own, he felt like a father to him. Boss, I knew he couldn't have kids with me. I was too old, I thought. I'd never carried one beyond four months. I lost all my babies when I was young. How could I entice him into such a relationship? So I pushed him into staying with Jen. Then, when I found I was having a child, I thought, no, I have a right to fight for him. I can give him a proper choice. But I didn't know for certain that he was the father, not Frank, until this morning. Now I'm almost one hundred per cent convinced and sure I'll go the distance. Mind, while having twins is a bonus, it's also an greater risk of things going wrong. But there's something else I learned today. And it changes everything."

"Good Lord, what on earth can you find to throw in the path now?" The boss sounded exasperated.

"Jen is a drug addict. She won't be able to look after Morris. Jake wouldn't see the child neglected. It's not fair on him or the boy to ask Jake to shoulder the burden of me and the babies as well."

Rita Piper exploded. "Bull-shit, Molly. Grow up, will you! Start acting like the sensible woman I know you to be and not like a teenager!"

The boss looked at her in astonishment. "I'm glad you said it, love. I just want to smack her bottom!"

Molly bowed her head. "I'll write. I'll write. I promise."

*

It took only two days for the news-hound to get on the scent of a scandal. Details of the mortgage scam were on the front page of the daily newspaper.

'BROKERS ABSCOND WITH INVESTOR FUNDS'

The report said the police were investigating the disappearance of Nina Lavell and Frank Anstruther, last seen at Perth Airport. It said that small investors stood to lose their entire life savings. A parliamentary inquiry into the industry was being set up. Questions were asked in the house. Mr Gary Flatterjohn, of the mortgage broking company Flatterjohn and Associates, for whom Lavell and Anstruther worked, had spoken to the journalist; he said he had been horrified by the theft.

"I knew nothing of this until this morning," he said. "I am shocked and disappointed that associates, in whom I had placed my complete trust, could have betrayed my company in such a way."

Mr Hariman Hamid, of Jakarta, denied any knowledge of criminal activity. He was, he said, an honest developer who had made a multi-million dollar investment in Western Australia and had done so in good faith. His legal entitlement to own and develop the Wintergully Estate was not in question. He held the deeds to the land, had paid for them in front of witnesses and, as the owner, would proceed with the project. That people who had invested in Citrus Court Nominees had lost money shocked him profoundly.

"Such a thing would not happen in Jakarta," Mr Hamid said. "I have often heard Australians say our police force is corrupt. If your police do not bring these fugitives to justice, I would not say your law enforcers are corrupt, merely that they are pretty damn useless!"

It was on the news, of course. Aunty Flo rang, full of astonishment at the matter. "Good thing his mother's dead," she said. "Hermione will be turning in her grave so much that she'll probably drill herself out of her coffin. And it's a good thing you're out of Dancer's Creek. Give the gossips time to forget about it."

The Fraud Squad paid Molly a discreet visit. Larry got his colleagues to come to Peter Piper's for an interview, rather than have her face the stress of going to headquarters. As agreed with Larry, the episode at Wintergully Road was related in detail, but Molly did not mention the involvement of Jake's friend.

"Mr Flatterjohn took ill," she said. "I feel ashamed of myself for not calling an ambulance. He could have had a heart attack. But I wasn't feeling well myself."

She handed them the papers she and Peter Piper had obtained with the help of the lawyer. The boss explained what they had found out about Frank's dubious dealings with Molly's money. The inspector muttered about the Proceeds of Crime Act. Molly looked alarmed.

"What are you saying? That the courts could take my assets from me? They're legally mine, not Frank's. I owned the Wintergully property, not him. Are you suggesting I'm somehow involved in this fraud? I'm guilty of nothing except having been married to Frank Anstruther!"

"Mr Flatterjohn seemed to think you'd been demanding money with menaces," the inspector said.

"Only my own money. His company was quite prepared to steal from me as well as from other investors."

"It will be for the courts to decide, madam."

Molly was seething. "That rat! That little, whey-faced rat! Thank God I didn't let Flatterjohn have the deeds to the house, sicking the cops onto me like that," she said later.

The boss suggested she calm dawn. "Have you got those papers safe?" he asked. "I'm still curious as to why he was so keen to have them."

"Don't worry. I got Larry to stop by a post office and sent

them by registered mail to my bank."

There was so little time, so much to do before she caught the bus back to Aunty Flo's. There was Christmas shopping and a twin pram and cots to select. The boss and Rita came with her. They seemed to enjoy making choices as much as she did. Rita spent madly on baby clothes, two of everything.

On return to the Piper residence, they found it had been ransacked. Molly's room had borne the brunt of the intruders' interest. Her overnight bag had been emptied, the contents strewn across the floor. The lining had been split. Drawers were pulled out, the mattress overturned. The large envelope containing the ultrasound pictures of the twins had been torn open and the contents scattered.

"Are you thinking what I'm thinking?" said the boss.

"Yes," said Molly. "Call the police."

*

Peter Piper drove her to the bus station in the morning. As she joined the other passengers he handed her the plans of the old saddlery which they had looked at the night before, discussing the potential for converting it into a pickling plant. He picked up the suitcase Rita had loaned her and turned to put it in the luggage locker.

A man pushed through the crowd and grasped Molly's arm. "Give me those damned papers," hissed Gary Flatterjohn.

Molly, who had always wondered what it would be like to kick Frank in the groin, found out by testing her skill on his boss. Flatterjohn clutched his injured pelvis and let the some of the saddlery plans fall to the pavement.

"Stop, thief," cried Molly, fulfilling another long-standing ambition. "Stop, thief!"

The broker snarled and drew his gun. He waved it around menacingly, looking nervous. The throng drew back, leaving him isolated, exposed, on view to security guards who were running down the concourse. Flatterjohn spat at Molly and ran for his life.

Chapter 14

Filthy, stinking hot, air thick with humidity. The only difference between Darwin and Dili in mid-summer was the under-scent. Both places smelt of mud off the mangroves, the rottenness of dead fish and seaweed. There was always a trace of dog droppings and blood-and-bone manure. Darwin's armpits were full of the heavy aromatic odour of petrol and diesel fuel. In Dili, where little moved on wheels, the nostrils clammed up against the constant invasion of the smell of death.

Dili, wrecked by war, looked as if it had been devastated by a cyclone. Darwin, which had been blown to buggery a quarter of a century earlier, by Cyclone Tracy, had been rebuilt. It was a modern city, lush with tropical vegetation, affluent with wealth from a resource-rich territory, brash with bronzed men from the bush, dark with the strange beauty of the indigenous people, gold and tan with the skins of multicultural Australia.

There was a large Christmas tree in the reception area of the military airport. Jake took a taxi to the address from which Jen had written. He dumped his kitbag in the hallway of the apartment block and knocked sharply on the door. Te Pongarani opened it.

"Strewth, am I glad to see you," the big Maori said. "Come in and have a beer."

Jake rocked back on his heels. The rigger was the last person he had expected to see. Jen was very much in evidence. She was sprawled on her back on a settee, limbs flopping, mouth open, hair a tangled mess. She was snoring.

"Pighole, man. She always makes a place into a pighole. She trash your pad?"

"Dunno," said Jake. "I had to leave her to it. I had to go."

Te Pongarani ripped the tab off a cold tinny and handed it to the soldier. He motioned him to a seat at a table placed in front of a cooling fan.

"You shouldn't have sent Jen that money," he said. "I'd got her fixed in Sydney with a rehab mob. She was off the stuff, living clean, looking after Morris properly. They looked after her, she looked after the boy. I went back on the rigs. You send her money, she scarpers back to Perth and, as soon as I track her down, she bums a lift here with a truckie."

"What's she on?" said Jake. He only had to look at Jen's arms to see the needle marks, many infected.

"Methylamphetamin, most like. Yakka. Bad muck."

"She wasn't a big user when she was with me. Pot, yes. Ecstasy now and then."

"Man, Jen's always been a speed freak. But she didn't mainline before. Moody one day, on a high the next. Remember? That's Jen. Uppers and downers."

Jake sighed. "God, I wish I'd known. I'd have done things differently."

"Wasn't your responsibility, man. She's my wife, legal and binding. It's for me to sort her out. I'll have to quit the rigs. Stay round. Straighten her out."

"Where's Morris?"

"Took him back home to my mother. Left him with the family in Rotorua. Mobs of kids his age. He'll be cool. He'll be safe."

"He's a great kid."

"Jenny says you were good to him. Man, I shouldn't have pissed you off in Perth. I didn't know Jen had led you on. She tell you she'd got family in the Wheatbelt? Used to go stay with them? Lying bitch. Was meeting me."

"I got a bum deal then."

"You surely did. You stopping around Darwin? You planning to see Jen? Don't mess with her, man. She's been working the streets. She ain't safe."

"I won't even think of it, mate. I've got a lady I care about. That's what I came to tell her. I want her out of my life. She's your responsibility."

"That's what I'm telling you. She's going into rehab again next week. Then I get her fit, watch her like a hawk. Kill any bastard that tries to grab a piece of the action or push stuff to her. Then I take her back to the Maori pah. Make sure she lives clean."

"Good luck with it."

"Here, you want to see pictures of Morris?"

Jake flicked through the snapshots. Morris was walking. He was shown with a happy group of toddlers. "Looks fine."

"You drop in, see him any time you're in New Zealand."

"Maybe I'll do that on my way back from Los Angeles."

"No hard feelings?" said Te Pongarani. "You boys are doing good in East Timor."

*

No hard feelings, just a waste of damn time, thought Jake, strapping himself into his airline seat. Had he known about Jen's habits, he'd have gone back to Western Australia for Christmas to claim Molly. He guessed her reluctance to write came from her determination to make him look after Morris; to do his duty. It was a sour cup she'd handed him. He'd sipped it and had decided to spit it out. Te Pongarani had dashed his intentions to the ground.

"I should have listened to Dingo and Larry," he said to himself. "They tried to warn me about Jen but I didn't want to hear. And what did I keep telling Molly? How much I enjoyed playing father? What was she supposed to read into that? That I didn't want her because she was too old? What a loser. I should kick myself!"

*

Christmas came to the San Fernando Valley with a cold chill that left frost on the trees. Jake had forgotten how cold it could get, or maybe his blood had been thinned by tropical service. It was certainly colder than it had been during his winter idyll with Molly. He could not shake from his mind the memories of that quiet embrace on the balcony, he in her coat, his flesh against her skin, and nothing in it except gentle comfort and caring. He smiled more deeply about the adventure in mink on the beach. But what he longed for most were the shared meals and their wide-ranging conversations, Molly's unexpected innocence and her quiet sense of fun. What he cherished was the feel of her spooned against him, the scent of her hair and the softness of her skin.

"I need you, Molly," he wrote. "The longer I am away from you, the more I want you in my arms. I was wrong about Jen. You were wrong about Jen. She wasn't my responsibility. I never again want to be in a relationship that is based only on responsibility. I want to be with someone who is a whole person, who is independent, who gives, not takes. That's all Jen wanted from me, my money, my roof, my willingness to carry her problems on my back. She wanted to take. When I look back on it, she gave me nothing. Molly, the poor kid didn't have anything to give, mixed up as she was. Little Morris was the only thing she offered me, and he wasn't mine to love.

"You know, Molly, it was a surprise to talk to Te Pongarani and to find out what a decent sort of bloke he really is. After all the bad things I thought about him when he first took Jen away, I could cringe. If anyone had a right to anger, it was him, not me."

He wrote of the encounter in Darwin, of the way Te Pongarani was helping Jen to recover, of the pictures of Morris in New Zealand. He wrote about his arrival in the USA, how things had changed, how much his Mom and Pop had welcomed him and had urged him to go into partnership with his father to run the family business. He told her how Adelaide's kids had grown and thethings they had planned for him. He wrote about life in Dili and the compassion he felt for the children who had lost their parents. He told her about the other men in his unit and related amusing incidents.

He did not write of the danger and the hardship. He did not write about self-doubt and fear, he avoided descriptions of the evil and degradation he had seen. His loneliness and longing were suppressed. If he was to reopen the affair with Molly, he had to do so tenderly, delicately, he knew. He kept his letter newsy but non-emotional for the best part.

But he concluded with a passionate plea. "Oh, Molly, my love, please write to me. I love you so much and miss you terribly. You were a part of my life for so short a time and I needed you forever."

*

When the letter was sent, there was plenty of time to muse about her, as he sat in front of a blazing fire in the family home, reading.

Mom had insisted he rest up. She could see the weariness in his eyes. When big sister Adelaide and her husband Tom brought the kids down from Big Sur, Mom was careful to ensure they did not hassle Jake. Pop and Tom took the young stuff on outings while Addy and Mom did the Christmas baking. When Jake recovered his equilibrium, he took his nephews and nieces for excursions, feeling healed by their bubbling enthusiasm and obvious affection for their only uncle.

"You been killing folks?" asked Tom Junior, a freckled lad with the blonde hair of some Nordic ancestry but with the Morgan eyes of brown and amber.

"I'm a peace-keeper, not a war-monger," said Jake, shaking his head.

"What do you do when they shoot at you, then? Catch the bullets in your teeth?" Tom Junior, who had a passion to be a US Navy Seal, thought life in the Australian Defence Force was pretty tame. Jake did not speak of the atrocities he'd dealt with.

"I'm too small for them to hit. They fire at the biggest soldier in the unit. He's got a helmet like a colander!"

"Are there snakes in East Timor? Big, slimy snakes that swallow you when you're asleep?" Jane was wide-eyed.

"Yes," Jake lied. "But I taste so awful that they spit me out."

The younger children were less curious. They simply wanted Uncle Jake to take them for walks, to drive them to the beach so they could watch the Pacific rollers pounding onto the shore and see the otters riding the waves above the kelp forests. The children ran, heedless of fog and wind, along the pebbles, chasing gulls. Exhausted, they'd drag him back to the car and insist he buy hamburgers at a drive-in eatery. On return Adelaide would order the children to take hot showers and would settle them down in the home theatre to watch DVD films.

"You coming back soon, Jake?" she said one afternoon. "Pop is getting on. It's time he retired. You ought to be here, taking over Morgan Enterprises. Mom's real worried. Too much competition. She wants Pop to diversify into new lines but he says he ain't got the energy."

"I can't come home. I'm in the Army. I've got to go back on duty."

"Well, brother mine, give it some thought. And it's time you got yourself hitched."

Mom shushed her. "You leave Jake alone. You know his relationship with Jen went sour and I can't say I'm sorry, though the little boy looked sweet. No, leave him alone until he can sort his life out. He doesn't need your nagging, Adelaide. I'd rather he had no one than the wrong one."

"Oh, Molly's the right one, Mom, but I can't seem to get her to listen to me."

Of course, Mom then wanted to know everything about his love life and, while she was a little taken aback to find Molly was no spring chicken, but as old as Adelaide, she was quite relieved to find no young Australian bimbo was to be foisted on her. He did not tell her Molly was married and in the throes of a messy divorce.

"I don't know why you're pushing your brother," she said to Adelaide. "After all, it took you ages to find a partner. Quite on the shelf you were until Tom took you in hand."

Adelaide pushed out her tongue and grinned. "We mature women are fussy."

Jake grabbed her and tickled her. "Lord, you and Molly would never give me any peace. You'd make a fine pair!"

"Now then. Pack it in. You just make sure you bring your lady home to see us as soon as you can, Jake. She'd be made really welcome."

*

A heat wave settled on Dancer's Creek for Christmas. Fergus joined Molly and Aunty Flo for turkey and ham salad followed by strawberries and ice-cream. It was too hot for a traditional dinner. The old man wore a formal outback attire, walk shorts and long stockings, old-fashioned maybe, but practical. He had on a short-sleeved shirt and a lurid tie with a South Park design. Fergus was a fan of the programme.

"That Kenny," he said. "Och, the puir wee laddie."

Aunty Flo said the entire programme was disgraceful. There was a heated argument about American black humour. Molly hadn't a clue what they were talking about.

She was on edge; had been for days. She'd done the right thing and had written to Jake, not asking for his blessing but leaving any further action up to him. She'd agonised over it. Her delight about the pregnancy was obvious, she hoped he would share it, but made no demands. She sent her dearest love and hoped that would be enough. All that was left was to wait and wonder.

His letter from America arrived on Christmas Eve. It was not what she had expected. That he was in California was explanation enough. Her news had not yet reached him. She enjoyed his descriptions and appreciated his comments on Jen and Morris. But it was the messages of affection that sent colour to her cheeks and put a sparkle in her eyes. There was hope. She urged her heart to stop fluttering and to beat a steady pace until she could bring her emotions under control.

In the preceding weeks her surplus energy had been spent scrubbing the bakery from floor to ceiling, although Fergus had done most of the work on the ladders. The premises had been inspected by the council health officer and passed. She had registered the name 'Marmalady' and the sign was ready to go up above the bakery door in the New Year.

There were four cafe tables, with bentwood chairs. There was a display case for scones and cakes, for the crusty bread loaves and muffins Aunty Flo's friends had promised to bake. A demon jam-maker had been found and several dozen jars of strawberry and raspberry had been delivered. An apiarist had asked if Molly would stock honey from the red-gum forest. He'd brought jars of gold and amber sweetness by the score.

The shelves were stacked with rough-cut, rhubarb and orange, four-fruits, tangelo delight, whisky and cumquat, mandarin and apple, lemon and orange curd, grapefruit sour and Dundee special. The latter, thick and chunky, also led to the production of a clear, orange jelly. Molly had liked the look of it so much that she'd done a batch of lemon jelly and had experimented with apple and rosemary, cucumber and basil. Before the heat grew intense, and faced with a glut of tomatoes from the greenhouse, she'd processed a new idea, lemon and tomato, unusual but divine.

But her mind was concentrated on one jar and one jar only...the pot of lemon curd waiting for Jake in Dili...the jar with a golden heart stick-pin buried in its depths.

*

Christmas in Dili was quiet. The pro-militia groups seemed content to let the people go to church in peace. Many Timorese were devout Catholics. They took no heed of the devastation of their places of worship, kneeling among the ruins to take Mass.

There was little festive food, for emergency rations were still only distributed from United Nations depots, but aid workers had made sure there were biscuits for the children and extra supplies for the parents, treats such as sugar and tea.

The soldiers had parcels from home. Jake's unit looked at the crate of marmalade and sighed. They were tempted to open it in Sergeant Morgan's absence but decided, to a man, that it should wait for his return from leave.

He flew in on New Year's Eve. He laughed when he saw how much Molly had sent. Each soldier was given a jar of marmalade and he set aside most of his own special pot of curd for breakfast, after opening it to taste the tangy cream. He laughed as he found the golden stick-pin and put it under his lapel for luck.

"We'll take the rest to the orphanage in the morning," he said. "I've got a couple of kilos of lollies for the kids in my kitbag."

Volunteers offered to help the delivery. The men loved to spend time with the children, dark-eyed waifs whose parents had been killed in the fighting or who had simply become detached from fleeing family members and been found wandering and in distress. They had been given refuge in a convent where nuns were keeping them safe.

Jake loaded a dozen jars into his backpack and filled the spaces with sweets. His mates took the rest. After breakfast on Boxing Day they got ready for the short walk. As they left the adjutant called out to Jake.

"You've got mail here, Sergeant Morgan. What shall I do with it."

Jake looked at the thick bundle. "Unbuckle my backpack and slip it inside," he suggested. "I'll read it when we get back."

The soldiers carried rifles. There were still snipers around. The peace of the Holy Day had already been broken at dawn by the sound of an explosion in the hills. They had to be alert for guerillas and mines, for booby traps and ambushes.

The path to the convent was through overgrown cane-fields, snake-infested and dangerous. They were within half a kilometre of the orphanage when the leading soldier spotted a child's toy on the ground. He bent to pick up the little plastic car.

Jake yelled, "No. Leave it. It could be a boob..."

The car, attached to a detonator, activated the trap. It went off in the soldier's face. Jake, spinning on his heel, felt the force of the explosives on his back. He fell forward, conscious off shards of glass in his skin and the trickle of sweetness through his shirt. But this was nothing to the excruciating pain below his waist.

"I can't move my legs," he gasped, and passed out.

*

Jake was back in Darwin within hours, after emergency evacuation. They'd picked the worst of the glass from his flesh. It was the metal shards in his back that were of most concern. Some had gone deep and had carried fragments of foreign material into the wounds. Grass, earth, fabric; each bore infections that could kill as effectively as the severing and maiming of high explosive.

Surgeons worked on his body for hours. On the operating table they removed most of the shrapnel, stitched up the gash in his right kidney, packed his wounds with antibiotics and put dressings over areas from which flesh had been torn and which would have to be patched with skin grafts.

There was one fragment that the surgeons did not remove. They looked at the scans and shook their heads. The small piece of metal lay hard against Jake's spine. The spinal cord was not cut, but was squashed tight by the pressure of the foreign body. To excise it meant to risk further damage. There was no room for even hair-breadth inaccuracy. Jake's blood pressure was plummeting so they decided to do no more. They pumped pain-killers into his back and flooded the area with drugs to fight the bugs. It looked clean but they took no chances. They closed the wound and crossed their fingers. With luck, the shard would work its way out. With no luck, it would paralyse Jake for life.

Then they fought to stop the infection overwhelming his immune system. He lay, face down as they scraped the suppuration from his wounds. He hovered on the verge of unconsciousness, doped with drugs and his blood running rich with antibiotics of rare and costly form. They put him on dialysis for long periods, to help his kidney heal and to remove the toxins from his blood. Weeks later, when his condition stabilised, they flew him out to Perth, for specialist care in a rehabilitation hospital.

*

In the cane-field around the orphanage outside Dili, cards and letters lay among the tall grass, until Jake's mates gathered them up and gave them to the adjutant. The officer dropped the blood-stained ones in a bin and wiped the stickiness from the rest. She placed them in a large postage bag and sent them on to Darwin. They were overlooked for some time but later followed Jake to Perth. He was too ill at first to read the mail but, when the dark clouds lifted from his mind, he opened Molly's letter. He could hardly see the words through the tears. There should have been joy but he found only bitterness in her news. What good was he to her, a broken man? A black depression filled his heart and he wished that he were dead.

Chapter 15

Marmalady opened with a great deal of fuss and few sales. This was no more than Molly had expected. Country folk made their own jams and pickles. They represented a pool of expertise which could be turned to good account.

The intended market was the tourist trade. She had persuaded the WA Tourist Commission to attend the function. Peter Piper spread the word among coach companies and laid on an excursion for tourist operators and journalists. On board were buyers from companies who, he thought, might be interested in buying the Marmalady line when it went into full production. As the outing was catered for by one of Perth's top chefs, and sponsored by a prestigious winery, there had been no shortage of takers.

The Heritage Minister performed the opening of the shop and the restoration project at Tom Dancer's Mill. He was shown over the saddlery and the old fire station and promised favourable consideration of applications for grants to bring these and other old buildings back to their original condition. The shire president made an inspired speech about the vision splendid and promised the full co-operation of local government.

The Country Women's Association, to whom Molly had been given a warm introduction by the vice-president, did the catering, while the Townswomen's Guild showed visitors through the shop and the bakery behind it. There was a jazz band and a sausage sizzle run by the junior football club.

Molly, looking very pregnant...the twins made her belly even larger than might have been expected at six months...was given pride of place, sitting under a large shady gazebo, offering samples of various marmalades spread on bread made from Tom Dancer's flour. Fergus, who had hidden talents, had confessed that he would like to try his hand as the baker. Hadn't he worked with Fred Frinton for years? Didn't he ken just how to make a wee bitty loaf? Aunty Flo nodded. Yes, of course he had, of course he did, but she'd thought he'd wanted an outdoor life.

Fergus said, "Och aye, but the back's no what it was and I'd be glad if ye got someone a wee bitty younger to do the garden."

He found the 'younger' man himself. Wee Bryan was a cantankerous giant of a man who admitted to being gone seventy but had forgotten precisely. He said he was a dab hand at onions but refused to have anything to do with tomatoes.

"Them's love apples, Missus Frinton. I can't abide love, no way whatsoever."

Aunty Flo, who knew Wee Bryan well, told Molly the man had been slighted in 1944, when his girl had gone off with an American submariner who she'd met in a bank in Fremantle. Aunty Flo didn't worry about the greenhouse tomatoes. She said she preferred to look after it herself, having no faith in the male sex when it came to cross-pollination.

The best part of Molly's role was the opportunity it gave her to make contacts. She was a good ambassador for her own scheme. In the weeks ahead she had visits from the regional agricultural officer, the president of the chamber of commerce, enthusiasts from the Tom Dancer's Mill project, who were feeling at a bit of a loose end now that work was nearing completion.

The cafe was busy every morning with housewives enjoying a chance to socialise. At lunch time the bank manager and the school principal led the rush of professionals who popped in for Aunty Flo's ham and salad platters. The workers from the garage and the agricultural showrooms down the street scoffed Fergus's cockaleekie pies, filled with a spicy mix of chicken and leeks thickened with a wee bitty oatmeal. Fergus, brimming over with ideas, looked set to develop a gourmet line of his own.

Molly did no physical work; Aunty Flo had found two school leavers, Janet and Sharon, to help in the cafe and to make new stocks of preserves. Molly, who had decided that cutting up fruit was no great stress, talked them through the processes.

The great thing about the cafe side of the business was that Molly was able to drum up enthusiasm for the grand plan. There was widespread interest in turning Dancer's Creek into a centre of excellence for country produce. Peter Piper and his wife spent a week staying at the Federal Hotel, going over the fine detail before the public meeting held in the shire hall. Around the wall were concept plans, artists' impressions of how many of the derelict shops could look and projected uses for them.

The shire president, who had become a keen supporter, chaired the session. Molly gave a brief run-down of the project then introduced Peter Piper and the rural adviser he had brought from a horticultural college in Perth.

The boss painted a picture of a town changed beyond belief. The citrus orchards were there already, but new plantings would be needed to meet demand when Molly's marmalade factory went into production. There'd be need for fields of small onions, melons, tomatoes, to feed the pickle plant he intended to set up. He suggested there be a herbal shop which would require local people to grow basil and rosemary, parsley by the tonne and mint by the bushel. Some would be dried, most of it made into preserves to Molly's recipes.

The horticultural expert suggested that, as a side line, one shop could specialise in country perfumes. The soil was good for lavender, he said. Lavender and gardenias, boronia and roses. As essences, soaps, lotions, cosmetics, the fragrance and colour of Dancer's Creek could be as attractive to tourists as the flower fields of Grasse, in the south of France. The buzz of interest grew as others put up ideas.

The heritage society chairman said that, in the past, there

had been a small woollen mill outside the town, and in the centre, a cobbler's shop, a millinery business and a book store.

"Some of those buildings are long gone, but we could buy similar ones from ghost towns and jinker them into Dancer's Creek," he said. "We could turn this town into a real-life, working model of a colonial settlement."

The publican said he'd sponsor a small brewery making boutique beers, a group of housewives suggested the sewing club start a quilting workshop, the farrier said he was sick of fitting ready-made horseshoes on show ponies and would welcome the chance to open an old-fashioned blacksmith's.

"We could wear colonial costumes," chirped a member of the amateur dramatic society. "We could put on scenes from history, like the bushranger's hold-ups."

High school girls tittered and said they were not going to wear junk clothes. "But we wouldn't mind running a shop full of clothes from the olden days. Very retro," said one.

It was Wee Bryan who brought them back to earth. "But where is the money to come from?" he asked.

"Ah," said Peter Piper. "I knew this one would come up. I've asked the bank manager to explain the workings of a co-operative."

There was intense concentration as the man spoke. "We're suggesting we issue shares in the community. The community would be investing in its own future and taking from future profits a share according to how much each member had put in. For example, some of you own the empty properties we've been discussing. They're worthless to you as they are, yet you still have to pay rates on them and count them as assets. You still have to maintain them and pay insurance in case of fire. Bill Jones, for example, owns the old saddlery. Suppose it was valued as it is and as it might be. We could strike a deal saying it was worth X amount of dollars to the project and Bill would get X number of shares. This would be one level of the development. This would enable us to invite capital investment from people like Mr Piper, who, as you've heard, is willing to put up seed finance. How many of you could invest in your town's future?"

There were quick consultations and a show of hands. Not all, it seemed, had money to spare or the conviction to go along with the plan.

"All right. Now, on another level, there is supply of materials. Mary Perkins, you've got a large citrus orchard. Suppose we said this would produce a crop worth so much a year and this would entitle you to an equivalent number of shares. Or we could do it by calculating the actual crop at year's end. Similarly with those of you who grew onions on contract, or strawberries or supplied honey. You'd take your share of profits. At the end of each year, we'd set terms and conditions for the next twelve months. For those working for the co-operative's retail outlets or in production, there would be a flat rate minimal wage. There'd be no other cash payments between participants. You'd all essentially be working for the good of the community, sharing equally in its wealth. But you'd all be working; you'd all be achieving; your town wouldn't be dying on its feet. It would be coming very much alive."

Peter Piper stressed that the scheme was in its early stages. There were months of planning ahead. But it was not the sort of planning that could be imposed on Dancer's Creek.

"You have to be involved. We want small workshops to look at different aspects of the scheme. We want students to work out how it would affect their lives, we want the business men and women to help organise the financial structure, we want prospective picklers and jam-makers to learn from Molly Grayson and others who share her skills. We want gardeners and farmers to put their heads together to plan for the intensive agriculture that would be needed. There's enough planning needed to involve everyone."

The shire president, a real estate agent, rose to close the session. He urged people to sign the lists circulating to say which committee they would join, or to write down different ideas.

"And, just in case any of you think Peter Piper is an out-of-towner coming in to stuff city ideas down your throats, I want to tell you this. He believes in Dancer's Creek and Molly Grayson's vision so much that, only this morning, he and his wife bought the old homestead at Dancer's Mill. The Pipers are now citizens of this town and as concerned in its future as all of us."

Molly was stunned by the news. She gave Rita Piper a hug and turned, laughing, to the boss. "You didn't tell me you'd been house-hunting."

"I said we should get a country cottage," he replied. "I didn't expect my good lady to chose anything as fancy as the homestead."

Rita smiled indulgently at her husband. "I'd have seen nothing of you, if I hadn't found a good property. I'd have been alone in that great pile of brick and glass in South Perth and you'd have been out bush, shaking up Dancer's Creek and making yourself worn out. Molly Grayson. I'm not sure that I shouldn't smack you for enticing my husband away from me."

Her comment was greeted by a delighted chuckle from Molly. "I'll love having you here. You are quite my most favourite people, other than Aunty Flo."

"No, we're not," the boss said. "What's the news from Jake?"

"I did write to him. Our letters must have crossed. His was from California but he obviously hadn't got the big news. I expect it's waiting for him in East Timor."

"The meeting went well, don't you think?" said Aunty Flo, joining them.

"Well enough, Mrs Frinton, but we've a long way to go. Molly, we're going back to Perth tomorrow but I'll be in touch if there are important developments. We're going to move our son and his family into our house on the river and just keep a suite there for our own use. My good lady here wants to consult an interior designer to make the homestead something to suit her exquisite taste. I expect she will drive me into bankruptcy doing it."

"Peter! How could you say such a thing?"

He gave his wife a squeeze. "I never question your judgment, love. You spend what you like if it'll keep you happy. Now, Molly, my dear, you'd best be getting home. You're not looking the best."

"Just tired. Very tired. My feet are swollen. It must be the heat."

Aunty Flo frowned. "You'll stay in bed tomorrow; I'll look after the shop."

Molly picked up her handbag and said her goodnights. "One last thing, boss. Have there been any developments over Frank? I can't believe he'd do anything like Gary Flatterjohn suggested. Haven't the police traced them yet?"

Peter Piper frowned. "I'll have to ask Larry. I can't get anything through official sources. I'll see what my newshound has come up with. But don't worry about it, Molly."

"I can't help doing so. I'm so afraid I'll lose all my money and I need it for the babies."

*

It was too hot to do anything more than lie around in the shade. Molly asked the girls to start work at 6am, when the cool of the morning made food preparation possible. By 2am the business had closed for the day. Aunty Flo went for an afternoon nap; Molly took her siesta in the shade of the ornamental grapevine on the patio. She lay back on a sun-bed and wished she could get comfortable. The gross swelling of her abdomen made lying down difficult. Getting up to spend a penny was even more of a problem, especially as the need came with maddening frequency.

Molly rubbed her temples. She had no worries about the

shop. Marmalady was organised to her satisfaction and was drawing a steady patronage. Peter Piper was in charge of the grand vision and had it well in hand. There was nothing she could do about Frank and Nina and the missing millions. Thinking of the scam was too wearisome. The scandal had received national attention. Even Dot and Bud had heard about it while travelling through New South Wales.

There was a long letter from Dot, eager for details not in the newspapers. "I'm dying for news from you," Dot wrote. "I know you couldn't contact us when we were on the road, but we're settled here in Byron Bay for the summer. You can reach us at the caravan park."

Molly sighed and fetched pen and paper. She poured iced tea and sat at the kitchen table, under the big ceiling fan. There was so much to say. Dot and Bud had no idea about the babies; that would be a shock whereas the opening of Marmalady would come as no surprise. In fact, it had been Bud who had sown the first seed of her idea.

Of course, Dot and Bud would want to know about Jake. That would be the hard part. It was the one thing about which Molly was getting seriously worried. Surely he must have had her letter by now? Why didn't he write? She, who had greeted the news with such joy, had she misread his feelings for her? His words of affection in the letter she'd received in December were burned in her mind, but so too was his opinion of Jen.

"I never again want to be in a relationship that is based only on responsibility. I want to be with someone who is a whole person, who is independent, who gives, not takes. That's all Jen wanted from me, my money, my roof, my willingness to carry her problems on my back." That's what he'd said. Would he regard Molly and the babies as a burden, a responsibility that required him to take care of money, provide a home and shoulder all the problems? He'd been home to California. Maybe he'd met someone there whom he liked better.

Aunty Flo woke up and went to the kitchen to make coffee.

She found Molly gazing at the wall, a look of unhappiness on her face, her letter to her friends unfinished.

"Oh, damn the man," she muttered. "Don't say he's going to run out on her!"

She was worried about her niece's physical condition as well as the effect the relationship with Jake was having on her psyche. The former midwife did not like the way Molly's ankles were swelling, nor the puffiness in her legs and arms. There were tell-tale bags under her eyes, not from crying, though there might have been a little of that as well, but her neck had also lost its lean and lovely line. Chin up, was Flo's motto, but which of several chins was Molly supposed to raise? She bore all the signs of pre-eclampsia. That, Aunty Flo knew, was not good, especially as there were several weeks to go before Molly passed the critical seven months mark.

She lifted the kettle and poured it over the granules, talking, as she often did, to her favourite pig, who served as a salt jar.

"Don't count your chickens, I always said. Not until twenty-eight weeks at least. It's time I had a word with the doctor, young whippersnapper that he is."

After her next antenatal visit, Aunty Flo found Molly in the kitchen, looking white and drawn. Fergus, who'd driven her to the clinic, was drawing her a glass of water and bidding her to sit down and put her head between her knees.

"The doctor says I have to go to bed and stay there," Molly said. "My blood-pressure's right up, there's protein in my urine. If I show no improvement in the next week, Aunty Flo, he's sending me to King Edward's until the babies are born!"

Chapter 16

A week later Larry phoned. Aunty Flo took the call while her niece slept. "I'm glad I caught you, Mrs Frinton," Larry said. "If it had been Molly I was going to hang up."

"Good heavens. That sounds ominous. What's wrong?"

"Hey, hey. How about the good news first? We've traced Nina Lavell."

"Well done. Where is she?"

"In Hong Kong, would you believe. Guess where?"

"In a maternity hospital, I'd think, if Molly'd understood the precious pair properly."

Larry sounded disappointed. "Yeah. We figured that too, so we've had a watching brief on clinics all round the world. But the odd thing is, Frank's nowhere to be seen. We've not arrested her or even let her know we're on to her. The Hong Kong police have got an undercover officer working as a ward orderly."

"Using her as bait, are you?"

"Yeah. She's all staked out. It's not just a matter of bringing her to justice, it's trying to retrieve the money they stole."

"That's it?"

"No. Tell Molly Jake's blood group is O, and he's rhesus negative. He's the main man, all right."

"I count that as good news too, but why hasn't he written to Molly?"

"Well, that's the bad news. Do you want to sit down?"

Aunty Flo followed his suggestion, after shutting the door so Molly would not wander in on what sounded ominous.

"Give it to me."

"Jake's been wounded. He's been in hospital in Darwin since the New Year. He was blown up by a land-mine. They've done what they could, patched him up. His Mom and Pop flew over from California to be with him when he was on the critical list. They've gone back. His condition is stable so they've flown him to the rehabilitation unit in Perth, near the Army barracks."

"And what exactly is wrong with him?"

"Spinal damage. He'll end up in a wheelchair. He's a paraplegic."

"Oh dear God," said the old lady. "Molly'll break her heart."

"I don't know that you should tell her, Mrs Frinton. I twisted the Sister's arm to let me see him last night. He's not really allowed visitors yet, only family. But he hasn't any over here, so she bent the rules. She said he is in a terrible way, deep depression, not wanting to see anyone, not wanting to live, even. He hasn't come to terms with what's happened to him."

"Did you mention Molly to him?"

"I tried. He turned his head away and wouldn't meet my eyes. He said he didn't want to know. He said he was no use to man nor beast and that there was nothing he could offer Molly except grief. Then he rang the bell for the Sister and asked her to show me out."

"Cruel, Larry. Life's cruel."

"Sure is, Mrs Frinton. What's to be done?"

"Nothing at present. Maybe my niece is better eating her heart out not knowing anything than facing rejection, and for such a horrid reason. Oh, the poor man, how will he face the future?"

"I don't know. Jake's an action man. Being confined to a wheelchair will be a living death to him. It's not even as if he could get fit enough to do wheelchair sports. There's a shard of metal near his spine and they're afraid it could get dislodged and cut the nervous cord entirely. On the other hand, it might work its way out."

"Long term prognosis?"

"Hey, I don't know, but I'll find out. The Sister's a corker. I'm taking Chantelle out to dinner tomorrow."

The bedroom door slammed as a draft caught it. "I must go.

Thanks for calling, Larry."

*

Molly lay in a darkened room most of each day, her mental anguish dulled by the sedatives she was taking. It seemed that every time she used her brain she thought of Jake and felt like crying. Only the undoubted health of the babies brought a smile, though they made a football field of her stomach. She wondered if they would fight as much after they were born. After all, they were the children of a warrior, a man accustomed to action.

The thought of what her personal experience of that action entailed, the sweet moments of intimacy, were no longer a comfort. Better she forgot the pleasures of the flesh, since Jake now seemed wary of renewing their relationship. Better she forget that he had lit her inner fires, taught her to take pleasure in her body, and in his. Such wasted years she'd endured, married to Frank, the insensitive, the user, the uncaring. Better she had not sought an adventure of the flesh but had endured. Could she, in all honesty, have stayed with him, despite Nina, stayed and become a nanny to another woman's child? No, that had been just a ploy, a ridiculous suggestion made only to throw her off balance.

Aunty Flo had told her Nina had been traced. She didn't know if Frank's child was a boy or girl. She wondered where her errant husband had gone and if he was pleased to be a father. If Frank doted on the child as much as his mother had doted on him, there might be hope for the man. But, she thought, Frank was not likely to spend time staring through the bars of a cot; he was more likely to be behind bars in a prison.

The very thought made her headache worse. Her vision was blurred and the flashing lights of an incipient migraine dulled her brain. She heaved herself out of bed to fetch a glass of water to take another tablet. Aunty Flo was at the front door, talking to a stranger.

"You'd better come into the sitting room," she said, showing the man into the front hall. "I'll fetch Molly."

Molly put on a maternity dress and brushed her hair. She peeped through the bedroom window. There was an expensive-looking limousine parked outside Marmalady. A chauffeur sat behind the wheel, reading.

She cupped her abdomen with both hands, as if to make it lighter, and made her way slowly to meet the visitor.

"This is Mr Hariman Hamid," said Aunty Flo, who was pouring tea from her best silver teapot. "He has a proposition for you."

Molly, startled by the name, and with no preconceived good notions about it, looked at the Indonesian businessman. He was small and brown, his dark hair smooth and glossy. He wore a lightweight suit of some lustrous fabric. His nails were cut square and were rather pink. There were heavy gold rings on his fingers and a hint of gold in the shy smile he gave her as he rose to his feet.

"I am more pleased to meet you than you are to see me, I expect." He pushed the John Lennon glasses he wore back up his rather broad nose. "I need your help."

Molly felt bewildered. "My help? In what way can I help you?"

"You still own the Anstruther property. You hold the deeds to the land."

"But you don't need my land. You have a lease over it."

"Indeed I do. Mr Flatterjohn was quick to assure me it would make a good sales office and, I must say, he has made a good job of fitting it out for the purpose. Why, he took such a personal interest that, as he told my agent, Mr Rampal Preddipatan, he even laid the car park himself. But it simply will not do. I must buy that land from you."

"Why?"

"The council want to build a children's playground on the river foreshore. It had been our intention to drive the access

- 178 -

road for the estate from the road along the river through the lower half of your land, and form a tee-junction with the internal roads of the estate. But the State Planning Commission has refused to endorse the council plans. It said there would be too much traffic conflict with recreational users of the foreshore, where there will be a cycle-path and walkways. They say I must come in from the higher block, which means demolishing your old home. We will then build the community hall next to the river road."

"It makes sense," said Molly, "But why didn't Gary Flatterjohn just say so? Why all the drama about trying to get the deeds from me by force? I offered to sell them to him."

"I think Mr Flatterjohn is more interested in acquiring money than parting with it," Mr Hamid said. "He did not seem to want me to have the land either. But I cannot ask his reasons. He, too, has disappeared from his usual haunts. He may be avoiding me or it may be more sinister."

Molly's head was spinning. "Mr Hamid, I still can't believe Frank has cheated you."

"So? I have not met your Frank. I can only go on appearances."

"But you were a director of Citrus Grove Nominees. You must have known my husband."

"Alas, I was only a director in a purely titular capacity. Mr Preddipatan negotiated with him, as the associate who was raising capital to acquire the land through mortagees. I, as the end-buyer, dealt only with Mr Flatterjohn and Miss Lavell. They came to Jakarta to arrange the project. I was rather surprised to find Mr Anstruther had absconded with Miss Lavell. My informants, and I have a good network of what you would call spies, Mrs Anstruther, led me to believe that it was Mr Flatterjohn who was intimately involved with the woman."

"But she's having Frank's baby!"

"She told you so, I suppose. Mrs Anstruther, my information is that, although the police have made no arrest, they know where she is and that she has already had the child. Curiously, by my calculations, nine months from the date of her delivery, she was in Indonesia with her other lover. You think your husband may also have been duped?"

"Perhaps. Nina ran rings round him. Do you think he is hiding somewhere near her? That he is, perhaps, waiting until she gets out of hospital?"

"Would any father stay away from the mother of his child at a time like that?"

The words cut Molly. She almost winced at them. She pushed Jake's image to the back of her mind.

"Frank always said the last block in a deal was the most valuable," she mused.

"I am prepared to be generous." The small man's eyes twinkled at her. "Your neighbours sold for $250,000. Your block is twice the size but more strategically valuable. Shall we say $750,000?"

"I've already been paid a deposit for it," Molly confessed.

"By Miss Lavell? Your husband's money, I expect? In other words, your own money."

"I suppose so, since you put it like that. But Mr Hamid, as Frank's gone, the only asset I have with which to raise my children is that land."

"Ah, so you are going to play hard to get, I can tell. If I pay you $950,000 can I have the deeds today?"

Molly gasped with astonishment. "But, but..."

"Plus $50,000 then. It is my final offer," he said, taking out a cheque book and writing a fabulous sum.

Molly gawped. "But it will take three days to clear..."

"And you've learned not to trust people? No problem. My chauffeur will drive us both to the bank and you will find that, for a sum like this, your bank manager will be quite accommodating. He can witness your handing to me of the deeds and I will send you the settlement documents next week. I will, naturally, pay tax and other costs on the land transfer. I am, as you can guess, eager to get the estate developed. I can take no profit on the investment until I start selling the lots for housing."

The deal was soon done. Molly was dropped off at Aunty Flo's. Mr Hamid was driven away. She let herself into the house and leaned against the wall in the hallway, feeling desperately tired.

Her aunt bustled out crying, "Molly, Molly, did the cheque go through? Isn't it exciting!"

But Molly, richer than she had ever in her life expected to be, burst into tears.

*

The doctor, called urgently to a patient whose headache had become a firework show of whirling Catherine wheels and Chinese crackers, snapped at Aunty Flo.

"I warned you not to get her worked up," he said. "I told you not to let her get excited."

"Couldn't be helped," the indomitable lady snapped back. "What's happened means she'll never have to worry about money again. With a cool million in her account, she can bring those children up in comfort."

"Damn you woman, if I can't get her blood pressure down, there'll be no babies and there may be no Molly as well. You know how dangerous this condition can be."

"She shows no signs of throwing a fit."

"I'm giving her no chance to convulse. She's out of here this evening. There's an airstrip at the homestead at Dancer's Mill. I'm calling for an emergency flight. She's started to pass blood."

*

Molly was frightened. She'd been frightened before, on the night when her dream man had taken her after the dance and she had followed her heart, not her conscience. She'd been frightened when she realised she was pregnant and frightened that, if Jake didn't want her, she would hurt for the rest of her life.

She was more frightened now, when she started bleeding and the pain knifed at her head. She was alone while Aunty Flo rang the doctor who gave her a cursory examination and had rung for the Flying Doctor Service to take her to Perth because what was wrong with her was more than he could handle.

She recalled the men carrying her to the station wagon and driving her to the airstrip in the paddock, and the merciful relief of being lifted into the plane and tended to by ambulance officers. The next hours were a haze.

The hospital nurses put her on a drip and administered a sedative. She remembered the sound of the ambulance and the trolley rattling down the corridors to the antenatal ward and the quick stab that brought oblivion. In the morning she was sore and clumsy, the great mountain of her belly humping up the sheet, the other three beds in the room empty.

She looked bleakly at the gynaecologist.

"It's all right," the specialist said. "We've stopped the bleeding. We think it was from a small burst blood vessel in the cervix but we'll keep an eye on you in case it's a placenta praevia. That's when the placenta looks like being born first, Molly. If that happens we'll do a Caesarean. You're in the best place. We'll monitor your blood pressure and protein daily. We'll try to stop you going into labour for another four weeks. But if it looks as if the twins are not thriving, we'll induce labour earlier."

"I feel so ill," Molly whispered.

"That's not surprising," the gynaecologist replied. "You are."

*

Less than five miles away, Jake swore at the physiotherapist who was massaging his upper back.

"That hurt," he said.

"That's good. You shouldn't have to be worked on in this area. You should be exercising these muscles yourself." The girl tweaked the hairs on his shoulders. "Get that?"

"Bitch," said Jake. "You've a nasty streak in you, Irish." He called her Irish because she was from Belfast and had the accent to prove it. She was short, stocky, with dark curls and the fresh rose-tinted complexion that comes from the Emerald Isle. She was used to treating the victims of bomb attacks, thanks to the sectarian violence that had troubled Northern Ireland for decades. She'd got out. Now she was faced with another case similar to those that had turned her stomach in the past.

"You're going to need your shoulders and your biceps to get around in a wheelchair," she said. "It takes more strength than you'd think. Your back's healing well so it's time you started on the weights."

"And if I do, what'll you be doing?" Jake mumbled, his face half-buried in a pillow.

"I'll be working on your legs and your lower back. You won't feel a thing."

"I know. That's the trouble."

Irish showed him a series of isometric exercises to accustom his upper body to a strenuous regime. She looked at the mass of scar tissue on his back and sighed. He'd been a fine figure of a man, she reckoned. Broad in the shoulder, narrow in the waist, his skin tanned where the surface was unscarred. Now he was a mottled mess of new pink skin, shiny ridged tissue and reddish patches where inflammation had left its mark.

She peeled back the blanket and looked at Jake's buttocks. The huge scar above them marked the track of the metal that still rested against his spinal cord, pressing into it and cutting off sensation to his legs. She avoided the area as she started to knead the flesh above his kidneys, gently stimulating circulation. She kneaded his buns. It was important to keep the blood moving, to stop him getting bed sores.

Irish turned her attention to his feet, manipulating them,

bending his toes, squeezing the instep, rotating the ankles. Then she worked on his calf muscles, his knee joints and his thighs. He had a pad above that for, though he had lost all sensation, all control of movement, the sympathetic nerves still operated his internal organs. It was, she knew, one of the most humiliating aspects of paralysis. It was not her job to see to this sort of care.

A nurse came to his aid and, having cleaned him up, helped Irish get him on a Stryker frame which immobilised his back so that he could be turned over.

"Two lovely ladies and I can't get a twitch out of seeing you," Jake said, sighing. He raised his head on his arms and looked down at an unresponsive organ.

"Twaddle," said Irish. "That will work perfectly well if its stimulated. You'll have to get your woman to do more work, that's all. You have got a woman, haven't you?"

Jake's face twisted. "I had. I can't expect her to want me back, in this condition. It's over."

"Double twaddle, man. If she loved you before, she'll love you now."

Jake shook his head. "I don't even want her to know about me. I'm just going to quietly fade out of her life."

"Then, to be sure, you're a silly bugger. You'll just have to get used to playing with yourself. Got two good hands, haven't you?"

She covered his hips and handed him a pair of dumb-bells. "Thirty minutes in each hour, lift and stretch, lift and stretch," she said. "See you tomorrow."

Jake worked with the weights until his muscles ached. It stopped him thinking about Molly. It stopped him thinking about golden curls brushing his cheeks as she rode above him; it stopped him remembering the feel of her body and the brush of mink against his skin. It blocked his memory of her gentle laughter and her words of love and surprised rapture. It blocked his feeling of being lost and left longing. The pain in his arms, however, reminded him of the pain he must be causing her. He was driven by guilt and frustration back into the dark pit of despair in which he wallowed most of the time.

Chapter 17

Larry and Dingo visited the rehabilitation hospital often. Dingo was easier company because he was not so deeply entangled in Molly's life. He played cards with Jake and talked about football and cricket. Larry, in contrast, tried to make him face issues. Larry, dead-pan, talked about Molly, even when Jake told him to shut up and go away. Jake heard all about Marmalady and the purchase of the Dancer's Mill homestead by Peter and Rita Piper. He heard about the trouble with Frank and Nina and the pressure Gary Flatterjohn had brought to bear on Molly. He was told of the deal with Hariman Hamid.

"Thank God," he whispered. "She'll be okay for money, even if the courts confiscate the cash Frank gave her."

Larry gazed at him sternly. "That don't let you off the hook, my friend. You'll soon have a family to support."

"I'll send her maintenance," said Jake. "I'll get compo from the Army. She can have that, too."

"That's not what she needs, you selfish bastard. She needs you to tell her you love her. Don't you?"

Jake glowered. "Of course I effing love her, but I'm not going anywhere near her, Larry. She's got enough to bear without having to look after a bloody cripple for the rest of her life!"

"You're a wanker, Jake. You don't deserve someone like Molly. I used to look up to you, man. You were strong and reliable and brave, Jake. Hell, you can't hold a candle to that little lady. She's got guts and determination. She's been through hell with that rotten bastard she married and now you're putting her through even worse."

"If you're so keen on Molly, you marry her!"

Larry went red. "Sorry, mate, but I've got my eye on someone else."

The charm of Sister Chantelle Hood was a welcome change

of topic. The conversation moved off sensitive matters to a lighter vein, but Larry's admonition still rankled. Jake was left in a state of utter confusion. Was he doing the right thing? Was it possible that Molly could take him, as he was, half-helpless? Could she bring herself to do the sometimes disgusting physical things that had to be done? She couldn't lift him, small as she was. Not only would she have babies to care for, but another full-grown dependent who was certain to be even more of a burden. A child, after all, grew out of the nappy stage.

Nor could he, proud as he was, ever imagine asking Molly to be the dominant partner in love-making. Oh, it was hopeless, hopeless! She was lost to him forever.

*

Larry had not told him Molly was in hospital herself, so near and yet so far. He had talked the matter over with Peter Piper and his wife. They had agreed that, while Jake was in his current frame of mind and still in recovery, worrying him about the danger Molly faced was pointless. The Pipers knew because, on their most recent visit to Dancer's Creek, Aunty Flo had told them.

"It's only a threat at the moment; she's only got pre-eclampsia. But if it develops into the real thing, it's the most dangerous complication of pregnancy," Aunty Flo said. "And I should know, having nursed many a woman through it, and some not through it. Even in the very best hands some women die from eclampsia. Even with modern medicine, it's a twenty to one risk. And it's even worse for the babies. One in five don't make it. God knows what the odds are on twins."

Aunty Flo was in a quandary. She wanted to be in Perth, near Molly, but on the other hand, she felt duty-bound to keep Molly's business going. Marmalady was doing well. An Eco-tour had included it in its itinerary and there were several other coach companies that dropped in on the spur of the moment if they were running ahead of schedule on the way to Tom

Dancer's Mill. Janet and Sharon were kept busy making rough-cut under her eagle eye and several ladies from the Country Women's Association had come in as volunteers to make speciality marmalades. Fergus had mastered the ovens and had now taken over the task of baking scones, but the production of cakes and sponges were still her province.

"It keeps my mind off things," she told Rita Piper, who had dropped in for coffee to show her the plans of renovations at the homestead. The boss was busy at meetings about co-operative deals and property transfers. The machinery from the pickle factory was due to arrive any day and the fire station was being done out to house the display area. The shire president had turned up trumps, persuading councillors to pass plans for a modern factory unit at the rear of the old building. That had gone up in a trice, pre-fabricated in the city and jinkered to the site. Roads had been built to it from behind, so that the street front preserved its air of olde worlde while technology reigned behind the Federation facade.

Yet they all knew that, while technology also reigned behind the red brick facade of King Edward's, Molly's condition was critical. Molly didn't know. Just as her friends had kept her condition from Jake, she was totally unaware of what had happened to him. She lived in a haze, giving blood to the technicians, passing urine to be measured and tested and drinking the copious amounts of water needed to keep toxins from building up in her kidneys.

She greeted visitors with pleasure but often fell asleep while they were present. Rita washed her clothes and bought cosmetics or other things she fancied. She was happy to hear about developments at Dancer's Creek and sent her love to Aunty Flo and Fergus. News of the grand vision passed over her head. Her headaches were still frequent and her bad eyesight made watching the news a misery. She couldn't handle a newspaper, for the bulge of the twins was too large. She knew nothing of what made the headlines. Why, she could have won the lottery and not known it.

*

Jake could read the papers. He had progressed to being allowed a bed over which loops hung so that he could reach up and pull himself into a sitting position. "Stick a couple of pillows behind me, Dingo," he said. "I'd no idea how heavy my bum was. It feels like I'm dragging a tonne weight. Where's Larry? I haven't seen him for weeks."

"Lucky sod's been attached to the major crime squad. I'm still on traffic, hooning around after bikie-gangs."

"Bit of a hoon yourself, weren't you? Despatch rider when we were in the Army, weren't you?"

"Yeah. Speedy Gonzales. Still, it beats writing tickets for traffic offences."

"Larry still seeing Sister Hood or did that whimper and die?"

"What? Chantelle? No, he's keen as mustard. Jealous?"

"Nope. Red-heads aren't my scene. I prefer blondes."

"You think that Irish would come out with me? She's a little corker."

"Ask her. But I warn you, she's got fingers that can kill!"

"Mate, I wouldn't let her practice massage on my shoulders. I could find something better for her to get stuck into."

Jake winced at the thought. Dingo was welcome to Irish's skills. The only thing sharper than her hands was her tongue.

Irish had lashed him into activity. "Get off your backside, Jake." She'd heaved him up.

"You'll not be allowed in a wheelchair until you can sit properly," she'd said. "You work those shoulders and exercise that spine. Just because your bum is frozen it's no reason to let your upper spine lie idle. Twist and shout, man!"

Dingo pulled out a pack of cards. "Cribbage or canasta?" he asked. "Or do you fancy a hand of whist?"

"You cheat."

"Only at stud poker, Jake. Only at poker."

Jake sighed. "My days of being a stud are long gone, Dingo. How about a hand of rummy?"

*

Frank Anstruther made the headlines the next day. It was a good thing Larry had rung the hospital and warned them. They put Molly into a ward on her own and removed the television. They promised to screen visitors and to allow only police into her room. There were fears that she would be besieged by journalists wanting her reaction to developments. Molly, so groggy that she rarely knew what time of day it was, barely noticed the move. She shed a few tears for Frank and the young Molly's long-dead dreams. She hung in there.

The Piper's got the inside story first. Larry called in for a beer, as he'd got in the habit of doing. He was the filter between the police and Molly.

"It was the damnedest thing," said Larry, opening a can. "Once he'd got the deeds Hariman Hamid could hardly wait to get a demolition licence to pull Molly's old house down. Gary Flatterjohn, who we thought had done a bunk, came out from cover and did everything he could to stop it going ahead. We were keeping him under surveillance again, you understand. He tried to get that crook councillor to block it in the chambers, but he was over-ruled. He and Hamid nearly came to fisticuffs over it. We were called to a disturbance at the hotel where Hamid was staying. We charged Flatterjohn with disturbing the peace and old Hariman took out a restraining order against him."

"Damn fool, that man. Carrying a gun, for God's sake. Where does he think he is, America?"

"Yeah, well he wasn't carrying the gun that day, but he's used it in the past, I reckon. Hamid finally got the bulldozer in to demolish the house and the block was clear, apart from the car park. That was the last thing the dozer went at and it was a good thing the operator was told not to take too deep a cut. Guess what he turned up?"

The Pipers sat, entranced. "Go on," urged the boss.

"Frank Anstruther's body. He'd been shot through the head."

*

Jake heard the news. For once he was glad to see Larry, who came, not bringing a mood of censure, but with Sister Hood on his arm. He was carrying a large magnet.

"Look what I've got for you!"

Jake laughed. "Am I supposed to fish for pins with that, or what?"

"Mate, I reckon that if that's iron you've got in you, this little beauty should be able to pull it out."

"Damn nonsense," Jake snapped. "It would never work."

"Sister here says it won't hurt to try. Come on, my precious flower, let's roll this miserable son of a bitch onto his face."

Jake exploded in laughter. "Precious flower? Precious flower? He doesn't really call you that, does he, Sister?"

She grinned, then pulled six inches of sticking plaster off a roll, cutting it with scissors she wore hanging from her belt. "Oh, your Larry has a fine line in sweet talk," she said, watching the police officer as he wrapped the magnet in cotton wool. "About here, would you say?"

"Hell, that will be awkward to lie on," Jake protested.

"You won't feel a thing," Larry said.

Jake, remembering his paralysis, grimaced. "No, I suppose I won't. But I still think it's a silly idea."

"So do I," Sister said. "But when Larry gets a bee in his bonnet, nothing will shake it. But I can't see it can do you harm."

"Aw heck, roll me back over and tell me the inside gossip about Frank Anstruther."

"We reckon we've got enough on Gary Flatterjohn to charge him with murder," said Larry, "But we haven't been able to do so. When the major crime squad went to his place it was deserted. His office was in a shambles. It looked as if he'd been trying to burn his records. His wife was having hysterics because he'd emptied the safe at home and taken his gear. Mind, she was most upset because he'd emptied her jewel case. We traced him as far as the international airport, but there's no record of him getting on a flight."

"Tricky bastard, isn't he?"

"I'll say. Trouble is, he has a forgettable face. Dead ordinary."

"Frank have any of the missing money on him?"

"What would you think? Not a dollar. And, what's more, there's no record of any major sums passing through his account, bar the $150,000 Nina gave Molly."

"Did he pay back Gary Flatterjohn for the money for her mother's investment?"

"Nope. Maybe that was what the row was about. I presume there was a row, but there's no one living around there any more. No witnesses. We found a gun in his office and we presume it's the one he used to kill Frank."

"He wouldn't leave a firearm for you to run ballistic tests on. Bet you he's got another one. Useful to have if you're on the run. Gun freaks tend to collect them."

"Perhaps. So much for our strict firearm legislation. We've not given up finding him yet. My guess is he'll turn up in Hong Kong with dear Nina. We've still got a watch on her. Got herself a nice little Chinese amah. One of ours. Well, one of the local police force, to be precise."

"Did you know Flatterjohn's got a private pilot's licence? Molly mentioned that he took them up for a joy-ride one day."

"And he's got a sea-going motor cruiser. But we'll get him."

"Larry, I warned you he'd a tricky fellow. He could be anywhere. He could even be in Dancer's Creek. He's got a score to settle with Molly, after all. She screwed him right up by selling the deeds to Hamid."

"Then it's a damn good job she's in King Edward's," Larry blurted out. Realising his gaffe, he went red.

Jake looked at him gravely. "Molly's in hospital? Why?"

"Shite," said Larry. "I'm off!"

"Come back here, you frigging grommet, you low-down dag, you lump of roo poo..."

"What ever is the matter?" said the Sister, flinging open his door. "What's the fuss?"

"Get me a telephone." Jake snapped. "Now!"

*

Peter Piper was in a fine temper when he got to the rehab centre. "How dare you accuse us of keeping news of Molly from you, when you didn't even have the decency to let us know what had happened to you!" he said. "If it hadn't been for Larry, we'd still be no wiser."

"You didn't come to see me, boss. I could have explained."

"Larry said you weren't allowed visitors, except him and Dingo. And just as well, because I'd have torn strips off you then, just as I'm going to do now. No need for you to scowl at me like that, Jake. You've been behaving like a self-centred drongo and I'm surprised at you. Leaving Molly not knowing about your injury, letting her think she was just another good time girl, a woman you'd had a brief affair with and then cast aside. That's what you've done, isn't it?"

"No!" Jake yelled. "That's not it. That's not it at all. I love Molly, boss. I love her too much to want to mess up her life."

"What, you're not messing up her life to leave her to carry your babies on her own? It's not messing up her life to father not one, but two kids, and duck out of your responsibilities? It's not messing up her life to leave her feeling unwanted, used, rejected?"

"I'm no use to her or any woman. Look at me. Go on, look at me! Half a man. That's all I am. Christ, boss, I can't even shit on my own!"

"So that makes it all right to shit on Molly, does it?"

Jake was white, his hands clenched round the loops above

the bed, trying to pull himself up. His pillows slipped and he lost balance, sliding back against the bed-head with a crash. His eyes filled with tears of anger and frustration as he tried to hide his face from the boss.

A large clean handkerchief was pressed into Jake's hand and an arm eased round his shoulders. Peter Piper helped him into a sitting position and replaced the pillows. The old man blew his nose on a tissue and turned away for a moment, staring out of the window. Then he fetched a chair and sat down at Jake's bedside.

"I'm sorry, lad. I was hard on you. But I was that mad. I've been bottling it up for months. And I'm that worried about Molly."

Jake sighed. "To tell the truth, boss, so am I. I had no idea she was ill until Larry let it slip. I've been imagining her in Dancer's Creek, happy, just waiting for the baby to be born. Hell, boss, she didn't even tell me she was having twins."

Peter Piper took his hand and squeezed it. "Yes. I see. I can't say I see eye to eye with you, but I can sympathise. Eh, lad, I don't know what I'd do if I were in your position."

Jake glared. "Don't give me sympathy, Mr Piper. It's the one thing I find I can't handle. It's, well, it's as if people are pumping marshmallow into my system when what I need is a bottle of rum, something to fire me up and keep my spirits going. Do you know what it's like to be trapped in bed for months? Do you know what an anchor legs are when you can't move them? I can't even use a wheelchair yet. They won't even let me try until I can swing myself into one. And they won't let me swing myself until the medicos check how Horace is doing."

"Horace?"

"Yes. That's what I call the little monster in my back. That fancy chunk of pro-Indonesian militia hardware. Horace the Horrible. Now tell me, boss, exactly what is wrong with Molly?"

Jake's brows drew down over the amber eyes as he listened to the situation. The gravity of it became clear to him. "Keep me informed," he said, shaking the boss's hand. "I care more deeply than you can imagine. You see, if she dies, the fault is ultimately mine, isn't it? If I hadn't got her pregnant, she wouldn't be suffering this way."

"She'd never want you to think that, Jake. You see, I don't think there's been anything else in her life that has given her so much joy as carrying your child. Pain, yes. Hurt at your apparent disinterest, but to be the mother of your children...not anyone's, mark you...but yours, why, to her that has been a thing of wondrous fulfilment. It means she's going through hell at present, but she'd dare it anytime for your sake."

"God, you make me feel like a heel. There must be something I could do."

"Try prayer, lad. It often helps."

The nurse chased Peter Piper out of the ward and called in the aides to take her patient down to have his back X-rayed and put under a magnetic resonance scan. The specialist looked with surprise at the magnet which was still stuck to his skin. Sister Hood and Larry had replaced its covering regularly.

"You didn't really think this would have any effect?" she said, ripping off the plaster.

"No, but it keeps my mate happy. He thinks it's going to work miracles."

She chuckled. "Well, we'll see."

When the plates were developed she put up the films on a light board. "No miracles, Jake. If anything, I'm afraid there's even more pressure on your spinal cord, but perhaps not as much danger. See here, this thickening of the tissue around the metal?"

"Yeah, around Horace the Horrible. He's made himself a little nest."

"Hm. The fragment's become encapsulated by scar tissue. That's pressing even more into the nerves that control your movement. On the other hand, Horace can't go walkabout and slice into your cord. Some good, some bad news. But I think it's safe for you to try that wheelchair you're nagging me to let you into."

"Great. Because as soon as I'm mobile, I'm going to run off with you!"

She smiled tolerantly. "Oh, are you, Jake Morgan. Well, be careful, if my fiancé wasn't a big hunk, I might run off with you myself!"

She sighed as he was wheeled away. Heavens, it didn't cost anything to put a little bit of heart in her patients, to flirt a touch, to make them feel they were still whole and manly. Jake Morgan must have been quite a head-turner in his younger days. Now he was a man with a handicap that was as much in his mind as in his body.

Chapter 18

Irish was pretty pleased at Jake's progress. She showed him how to pivot his hips from the waist and use the overhead chains to manoeuvre himself into the chair. When she was confident he could get in and out without falling onto the floor, which he did a few times, she let him try a short trip down the corridor outside his room. It was not as easy as he'd expected. He felt quite exhausted by the exertion and his hands ached from the friction.

"That's enough," said Irish. "Tomorrow I'll show you how to get dressed. Then you can take me down to the cafeteria and buy me a cup of coffee."

"Is Dingo picking you up when you go off duty?"

"To be sure he is. Do you want to see him especially?"

"I surely do."

The requests Jake made left Dingo thunderstruck. "Are you sure about all of this?"

"Quite sure. Aunt Flo's got power of attorney and signed what's needed. She's sworn to secrecy."

"Why didn't you ask Larry to do it?"

"Larry wouldn't. He's an old stick in the mud about some things."

"Lord, mate. What a lark. Right, Jake. I'll get going on it in the morning."

*

Larry looked sheepish when he finally showed his face.

"I should twist your balls off," said Jake. "Fine sort of a mate you are, not telling me about Molly. How is she now? I presume you've been to see her?"

"She's pretty stable, but the docs are getting worried about the babies. They may bring her on, if you know what that means."

"Am I an uncle four times over or what? Of course I know what it means. You seeing her tomorrow?"

"Can't. I'm on duty. Got a lead on Flatterjohn. He's slipped our net again. Got to drive up to Geraldton tonight. Take us half a day to get there. The local crayfishers have found a motor launch washed up on a beach. Could be his."

"Told you he was a fly customer. If it is, I'd bet he'd arranged to be picked up by a bigger ship. You've lost him, mate."

"Pessimist."

"You traced his money chain?"

"As we thought. Cook Islands. Dead end."

"Bloody tax havens. There ought to be a United Nations veto on them. Be as much reason to set a peace-keeping team onto the international drug traffickers and other mickey mouse money launderers as there is looking after the East Timorese."

"Who's arguing?"

Larry, obviously reluctant to expose himself to Jake's ire over Molly, made his excuses. "Taking Chantelle to the movies," he said. "Got to go."

Jake sighed with relief. He did not want to risk Larry interfering in his plans. He was up and dressed by the time Dingo arrived in the morning.

"I'm taking Jake here for a walk around the park," Dingo said to the ward nurse. She nodded absent mindedly for she was busy putting together the tray of daily medications.

It was only a short push to the train station. The electrified railway had carriages designed for wheelchair access. Ten minutes later they got off near King Edward's.

"Get a move on," Jake urged. "The booking's for 11am sharp."

"Shut up," Dingo said, panting at an uphill section. "Speed depends on the pusher, not the pushee."

"You get the paper-work done? Special licence? The stuff from the US Consul?"

"Yup. All present and correct, Sarge."

"You picked up what I ordered from the jewellers?"

"Yup. If it's not right, they'll change it."

"You talk to the matron?"

"Yup. She said fine."

"Talkative aren't you?"

Dingo put the brakes on. "For Christ's Sake, shut up, Jake. You're a pain in the butt!"

"I bet that's the one we're meeting; her, standing at the main door. The one in the long dress. She's brought the flowers. Come on, Dingo. Wouldn't do to keep her waiting."

"You know what you're doing, Jake. You're certain sure?"

"No way, but I can always say you pushed me to it!"

"Huh! You, Jake Morgan, are a durr-brain!"

"There's a nice thing for a Best Man to say to the Groom!"

The celebrant led the way to Molly's ward. Jake manoeuvred the wheelchair to her side and sat there, looking at her. She was asleep. Her face was puffy, her hair lank. She did not look like his Molly. In fact, she looked bloody awful. His heart sank but he plucked up his resolve and shook her arm.

"Jake?" she said, in wonder. "Jake?"

He nodded to the celebrant who opened her book and started the short service. Molly responded as if in a trance. Jake held her hand tightly and spoke his lines firmly. Dingo handed him the ring which was the largest in stock. It slid over the puffy fingers easily.

"I declare you man and wife," said the woman in the white kaftan.

There were papers to sign and signatures to witness. Molly's was a scrawl but it was legal and binding.

"Help me out of this chair, damn it," said Jake. Dingo and the celebrant lifted him under the armpits and stood him upright at Molly's side. He leant forward and kissed her.

"I do love you, Molly," he said. "Whatever happens, remember, I do love you."

"Me too," she whispered. "I love you Jake Morgan." And with that her eyes closed and she drifted off again.

Dingo concluded the business with the celebrant, who bent over and kissed the groom.

"I've asked the nurse to put the flowers next to her bed," she said.

"There's a card to sign?"

"You want a pen?"

Jake wrote carefully on the florists' message sheet. He wrote, 'I love you, Molly Morgan.' And through it he stabbed the golden stick-pin.

"Come on." Dingo put the card in the flowers that had just been brought in. "The nurse says we must go as the doctor's on his rounds. Back to the rehab centre?"

"Not on your Nelly," said Jake. "Down the pub. I think we should drink a toast or two."

That afternoon Molly woke happy from a dream and smiled at Rita Piper. "Oh, that was so lovely. I dreamed that Jake was here. I dreamed that we were being married. It was so wonderful, like a fairy-story."

She glanced up to see the boss reading a card which he'd plucked from a beautiful bouquet of roses and lilies. His mouth was open and he seemed lost for words. He handed it to Rita, whose brows shot up in astonishment. Molly looked down at the message in bewilderment, then down at her ring finger.

"I don't believe this," she said. "I simply don't believe it."

*

"I don't believe you could do such a thing!" Peter Piper roared. "How dare you? How could you? How could you trick Molly like that!"

Jake, who was more than a little inebriated, grinned foolishly. "No trick. Meant it. Make Molly mine. Least I could do. Love her. No good to her, but can give her ring. Make her happy."

"I suppose you thought that if Molly dies you would come into the million she's just banked."

Jake's lip curled. "If I could stand up, I'd knock you down for saying that," he said. "Come here and let me sock you!"

"Jake, Jake, I'm sorry, but why did you do it?"

There were two Peter Piper's at the end of the bed. Jake focussed on one of them. "My babies, not Frank's. Give them my name. Morgan. Decent, honest name. Molly wouldn't want to be reminded of that damn crook, would she? Molly Morgan. That's it. Mrs Molly Morgan."

"But why the hurry. Why not do things properly?"

"Was proper. Was legal. Get Molly my Army pension. Had to hurry, boss. I'm going back to America on Friday."

"The hell you are!"

"Yup. Mom's found a specialist she wants to look at me. Got to do what your Mom says, boss. I'm going home in two days time because that's the only time that the quack can fit me in. Boss, I ain't coming back unless I'm on my own two feet. I can't stay around for the birth. But hey, give Molly her marriage certificate, will you? And tell her I love her. I'll write to her tonight, when I sober up."

*

Larry, when he got back from Geraldton, frustrated by another trail that went nowhere, blew his stack when he found out about Jake and Molly. He pounded on the door of Dingo's flat, disturbing an interesting entanglement with Irish, and thumped his friend on the nose. Dingo reeled back with a yelp.

"You slob! You rotten slob! How could you pull such a stunt?"

"Lay off him," Irish yelled, holding Larry's arm to stop him swinging another punch. "What's he done that's so wrong?"

"Sneaky! Tricking Molly into marrying him!"

"You're nuts, Larry," said the physiotherapist. "Wasn't marrying him what Molly really wanted? Didn't she need to know how much he loved her? What better commitment does a woman need than that?"

"But he tricked her."

"No, he didn't," Dingo said. "She was fully conscious. Groggy, perhaps, but she knew what was going on. Hey, man. The look of happiness on her face when she saw him. You'd not credit how good that made me feel."

"But why? Why the rush job? Why not a proper ceremony with her friends around her?"

"Hell, Larry, you think the doctors would have let him out if they knew what he wanted to do? He's only been allowed out of bed this week."

"And we'll make damned sure he doesn't escape again," said Irish. "If he's to catch that flight to America on Friday there's a whole lot of treatment he's got to have. He's got to have his blood thinned down, for a start. With his lower body immobile he stands a greater risk than most of deep-vein thrombosis. If he gets a clot in his legs it could end up in his lungs and kill him."

"Then why risk the journey?"

Irish sighed. "Look, Larry, it's a slim chance this surgeon, Fingiano, can do something to improve matters. Jake's specialist says Fingers, that's what they call him, is the top man in the field. Cut his teeth on vets from the Gulf War and on accident victims. He plays the spinal cord like others play the piano. He's done wonders with some of the British soldiers injured in Northern Ireland. But he's so busy that he's damn hard to get hold of. Jake's Mom went to school with Fingers' Mom."

"What chance?"

"Sod all, quite frankly, but you've got to try, haven't you? Would you take the risk in Jake's position?"

Larry fell silent for a while. "I suppose you're right. Dingo, mate, I'm sorry. I hate seeing Jake as he is. Could have been either of us, any time, if we'd stayed in the Army."

Dingo shook his hand. "Right. Forget it. You seen Jake

today?"

"No. Peter Piper told me. I've just got back. That rat, Flatterjohn, has made fools of us again. Oh, it's his boat all right, but it wasn't washed ashore. It was driven aground deliberately. Couple of guys living in a beach-shack further up the coast said there'd been an old Land Rover parked up in the dunes for a couple of months, covered over with brushwood."

"Didn't they wonder whose it was?"

"They thought it was something to do with drug smuggling and left it well alone. People in that part of the world turn a blind eye to a lot of goings-on."

"Dangerous not to mind your own business sometimes," said Dingo. "So the shyster didn't leave the country again."

"Maybe we closed off the airport and ports before he could get away. There were road blocks on the Nullarbor highway. He didn't go through them."

"Seems to me he didn't plan to leave the country at this time. He'd have planted that four-wheel drive with every intention of using it. Larry, he didn't need to stick to the highways if he had an all-terrain vehicle."

"But why hide up? Nina has the money. Why hasn't he tried to join her?"

Dingo scratched his nose. "Perhaps Nina's double-crossed him as well."

"Is she the one in Hong Kong who's had the baby?" Irish asked. "You watch that she doesn't slip out of the country. I bet she's waiting until the baby's old enough to travel then she'll be away. Come to think of it, if she's that cunning, what's to stop her abandoning the kid and slipping off on her own?"

"Cook Islands?"

"No need," Irish said. "If Flatterjohn and she moved money off shore she'll have made arrangements to draw it anywhere in the world. In fact, it's probably already been transferred from one tax haven to another. I can think of a few places where it's hard to get an extradition order. Australia's never been able to

- 203 -

get Christopher Skase back to stand trial after he did a bunk with millions. And what about that Aussie crook that did a runner to Ireland, twenty years ago. Trimboli, wasn't it? Drug baron?"

"How come you're so smart?" asked Larry.

Irish grinned. "My dad was a copper."

*

The golden stick-pin made Molly smile. She glanced at it every couple of minutes, remembering the day she'd made the lemon curd for Jake and the impish delight with which she'd put it in the jar. She wondered under what circumstances he'd found it. Had he taken it to California with him and opened it there on Christmas morning, or had it waited until he returned to East Timor. She longed to talk to him about such trivia. There was so much to say, so much to share. She twisted the ring on her finger and remembered the touch of his hand on hers.

She knew that Peter and Rita Piper were furious with her new husband. She knew Frank must be dead. She knew that Larry had thumped Dingo. Irish had visited her and relayed the news. She'd learned exactly why Jake had to go back to the States. She understood. But her heart ached with the thought that it might be months before she saw Jake again. She shrank from the possibility that he might not return. Why would he have married her if he had not intended to be a part of her life. Giving the babies his name was surely not a good enough reason. Or was it? She'd never intended letting them be known as Anstruther; Grayson would have done well. She chuckled to herself. "But Morgan is better," she whispered. "Mrs Molly Morgan. I like it."

She dozed off but woke to the unwelcome feeling that she'd wet the bed. The nurse who answered the bell took one look at the sheets and scurried out of the room.

"Mrs Morgan's going into labour," she said to the Sister. "Her waters have broken."

"I'll call the gynaecologist at once. She's going to be one of the tricky ones. And let the nursery know we'll have a couple of premmies coming in a few hours."

"She's too early, isn't she?"

"Thirty-four weeks. Not bad for twins and with her condition. Let's hope the labour doesn't send her into full eclampsia. We don't want her convulsing in the delivery room."

Dingo, who was on duty driving the paddy-wagon that night, ready to throw drunks in the back, dropped in to see Molly during his tea break. He met Larry and Chantelle Hood in the foyer, waiting for visiting hours to begin. They went up the stairs together. They had to stand back against the wall outside Molly's room as nurses pushed the bed into the corridor and rattled off towards the lift with it.

"Go home," Sister said. "The babies are coming. You can't see Mrs Morgan tonight."

"Does her husband know she's gone into labour?" said Larry.

"We don't know how to contact him," Sister said. "He left no address for us."

Chantelle looked at Larry. "I know what you're going to say and you think I'll try to stop you, but I won't. Dingo, is your paddy wagon big enough to take a wheelchair? I've got the keys to the back door of the rehab ward. Come on, men, let's go and get him!"

*

The pain of the contraction was equalled only by the pain in Molly's head. They put a blood-pressure collar on her arm and frowned in alarm. She winced as icy-cold antiseptic was sponged onto her back and a needle inserted into her spine. The epidural anaesthetic numbed the agony that rippled from her uterus, but could not counter the entire sensation. She was quickly soaped and shaved, and other preparations for delivery were made. Her legs felt like lead weights.

The gynaecologist laid cold hands on her stomach and felt

for the position of the babies. He called for a mobile ultrasound machine. "They're lying well," said the radiologist. "The first one's head is coming down into the pelvis but the second looks like a breech unless you can turn it. No need for a Caesarean, I think. She should deliver naturally. She's a small woman but her pelvis is wide and the babies are under-sized."

"So we let nature take its course?"

"I reckon. But I'll stand by for more scans if you need them."

There was a commotion at the door of the delivery room. Molly, gritting her teeth against another contraction, heard someone say. "You can't come in here," and another voice saying, "I bloody well can!"

The doors swung closed, shutting out the sounds of argument. Five minutes later a figure, clad in green theatre garments, was pushed next to her bedside.

"Hi, doll. You didn't think I'd want to miss this, did you, Molly? Come on, my love. Let's see how clever you really are."

She reached out to grasp Jake's hand and concentrated on looking into his eyes. She knew that, if he could have done so, he would have borne the pain for her. She was tiring but drew strength from his very presence as much as from his words of encouragement.

She panted when she was told to pant, she pushed when she was ordered to do so. She felt the incredible size of a baby's head entering the birth canal. No anaesthetic could completely block out the feeling of impossible pressure and the urge to be free of the burden.

The gynaecologist's fingers slid inside her and snipped the purse-string stitch that held her cervix closed. The baby's head started to emerge.

Jake, catching the midwife's nod, cried, "Push, Molly, push!" and she did. The gynaecologist stood to one side and watched the midwife take over the delivery. Jake was crying as he saw the baby's hair for the first time. It was dark, like his own. How could Molly, little Molly, accommodate the head buffeting against her tightly-stretched vagina, a place that had once felt so tight against his thrust? It was awesome to behold.

"Push, Molly, my darling. You're nearly there."

Molly bit her lip and bore down as the strongest contraction yet sent the first twin into the world. Would she ever forget that sweet and searing relief?

"It's a boy," said the midwife, handing Jake the scissors. "Would you like to cut the cord, Mr Morgan?"

Jake, his fingers trembling within the surgical gloves, pressed steel against flesh. He leaned back, trembling, as the midwife turned to him and laid the baby in his arms.

"It's normally a mother's privilege to hold her baby first, but she's still got some work to do."

Molly looked down at the sight of her son and Jake in utter delight. And then the contractions began again.

The gynaecologist ordered another scan and tried to manipulate the twin into a head down position but it seemed to have a mind of its own.

Jake handed his first-born to the midwife and watched the hands of the doctor on Molly's stomach. He fixed his attention on the activity then shouted, in his best sergeant's voice, "Baby Morgan! About Turn!"

And the baby did. The gynaecologist looked at Jake in surprise. "Well, I'm damned," he said.

The noise startled the first-born into a lusty cry. Jake thought it the best sound he'd ever heard. There was no more trouble after that. Molly, though more weary, now knew what to expect and was not hindered by fear that tensed her muscles against the contractions. Her daughter made a smooth entry into the world and cried immediately she was delivered. This time the baby was put into her arms after Jake had done the work with the scissors.

"Beautiful," he whispered, even though Molly looked far from lovely, unkempt and flushed with exertion, her cheeks still puffy and her eyes deep-set and dark.

"Molly Morgan, you are the most beautiful woman I have ever known and I love you from the bottom of my heart. Never forget that, Mrs Morgan."

He took her hand to his lips and kissed it tenderly. His gazed went to the twins, now tucked up in their incubators. "Are they healthy?" he asked. "They're very small."

"Nonsense," said the midwife. "They're quite big for premmies. Isn't that so, doctor?"

The gynaecologist looked up from delivery of the afterbirth and grinned. "All parts present and correct, Sergeant Morgan. Now soldier, it's about time you did an About Turn yourself and let this clever little lady get some sleep."

Jake kissed her hand again and said, "I have to go, Molly. I'm sorry."

"No," she whispered. "Don't be sorry. Do what you have to do. Go to America but come back soon because we love you, Jake. I don't care if you're any different from how you are now. I'll love you always, just the way you are."

Larry and Chantelle were in the waiting room, their faces aglow with the news. Larry hugged his friend then dialled Dingo on his mobile.

"Come in, you old dog," he said. "And bring that Daddy-wagon with you."

Chapter 19

The morning sun came up on a patient who stubbornly refused to get out of bed. The cleaners polished the floor around Jake and he did not even stir. They pushed the bed to one side of the room so that they could take down the privacy curtains to wash them. Chantelle Hood, who'd come on duty just as tired as Jake, pulled his sheets off and put an ice-pack on his back.

He opened one eye. "Bitch," he said, yawning, and tried to go back to sleep.

"Oh, no, you don't, Daddy-O. You get showered, shaved and ready for Irish. She's promised you a good work over before you get on that plane."

"Let her come. I feel as if Larry and Dingo have jumped on me."

"Sook. It was Molly who did the work, not you!"

"Hey, Chantelle? You serious about Larry, or what?"

"What is this? This Jake Morgan marriage bureau? Instant weddings by appointment?"

"I'd like to know. Larry's a good mate. Dingo too."

"I'll let you in on a secret. Dingo's proposed to Irish."

"Did she say yes?"

"Ask her."

Irish came into the room bearing a bottle of champagne. "Don't you get the wrong idea, Jake Morgan. After your little pub-crawl with Dingo you're not drinking any of this. I'm going to use it to give you a rub down."

"That's cruel. I'll reek on the flight. No one will want to sit near me."

"You can wash it off! No, come on Jake, I don't mean it." She whipped three glasses out of her overall pocket and poured the bubbly. "Congratulations, father of two. Now you can drink a toast to me and Dingo!"

Things were a bit of a rush after that. Chantelle dosed him with the last of his course of heparin, to keep his blood running smoothly, and Irish fitted him with thick elastic stockings.

"They'll be hot," he complained. "Oh, I know. I won't feel a thing!"

Larry's lady love fixed him with a stern eye. "Now for the parting lecture," said Sister Hood. "I know you've had trouble coming to terms with your disability, but there are many worse off than you, Jake. You haven't been down to the quadriplegic ward. There are patients down there like Christopher Reeves, Superman, you know, who've lost the use of all their limbs. There are children who've been born without limbs, or poor little ones who can't control them. There are babies with spina bifida, where the covering of the spinal cord never formed. They, poor mites, will never know the pleasure of walking. You can use your arms to get about; you can dress yourself and feed yourself. You can, with a bit of encouragement, even make love to Molly, when the time comes. Go on, go to America and see what Fingers can do for you, but if it's nothing, you count your blessings."

"I do, Chantelle. I do. I remember that my corporal, who took the main blast from that damn bomb, he didn't make it."

"So none of this damn nonsense about not coming home unless you can walk. If you think you'll be too much trouble to Molly, think again. You can employ a carer to help you do what you can't. She's got the money. You'll get a pension. Come back and help her bring up the twins."

"Well said," Irish added. "You come back and love her. You cared enough to marry her. Now you stand by her. When you put that ring on her finger, it stopped being me, me, me, Jake Morgan. You turned it into us. Us, us, us."

"Nagging bleeding women," said Jake, grinning sheepishly. He blew them kisses and wheeled himself down to the taxi for the handicapped that was waiting outside.

He had a police escort to the terminal. Larry and Dingo followed discreetly through the city centre, then overtook the taxi and cleared the way to the airport with flashing lights and sirens.

"Clowns," said Jake, laughing, as they carried his baggage into the check-in counter.

Larry, who had a taste for air hostesses, scanned the queues for any crew that might be boarding. He suddenly went still and sharp. He dug Jake in the ribs.

"Hey, you recognise that guy in the blue baseball cap and the purple anorak who's checking in at Thai Airlines?"

"You're right, Larry. Go on, Dingo. Go get the bastard."

Gary Flatterjohn, who'd obviously dressed to blend with the crowd of holiday makers who were bound for the beaches of Phuket, did not see the police officers until they were almost onto him. He left his baggage where it was and ran. Ten minutes later, Dingo, out of breath, reappeared by Jake's side.

"We lost him. He got in a car and drove off. Larry's on his tail. I came back to get his luggage. Let's see what he was carrying."

Dingo snapped open the lock of the fat black briefcase and whistled. He showed the contents to Jake.

"Well, he won't get very far without his money bag," he said. "I wonder what he'll do without hard cash?"

"Let me know how it goes, mate. I've got to go. We're boarding."

*

The flight was uneventful. Jake, who'd been assigned a steward with medical training, who helped him with the sordid necessities of life with a handicap, found boredom his main problem. Irish had loaned him a portable massage unit to use on his legs and that kept him busy for fifteen minutes in the hour.

The hardest thing to bear were the looks other travellers

cast him. His life post-war had been mainly in a hospital environment or in the pub of the Perth suburb where the medical centres were clustered. He'd not become used to seeing the world from everyone else's waist level. He'd never before noted the many inconveniences the disabled faced in a non-disabled world. It was impossible, for example, for him to get his luggage off the carousel at Los Angeles. He had to ask for assistance. He couldn't balance his case across the arms of his wheelchair and still propel it. He sat there, lost, until a youngster in board-shorts and a Lakers sweatshirt took pity on him and escorted him through Customs.

He was met by Adelaide and Tom. Adelaide looked as if she'd been crying.

"We've left the kids with Tom's sister," Adelaide said, after kissing her brother soundly. She knelt beside him with her arms around his neck. "I'm glad you're here, little brother. Pop's had a heart attack. Mom's at the hospital. We said we'd go right over."

Tom and his sister lifted Jake into the back of their wagon. Jake used his arms to settle himself while Tom folded the wheelchair and put it in the trunk.

"Did you find a male nurse and get the equipment I'll need?"

"Yes, we're all set up at home for you."

"Then let's go there."

"But we're going to see Pop first."

"No," said Jake, firmly. "Oh no, we're not."

"Well for mercy's sake, what's got into you now?"

Jake grinned. "You'll soon find out!"

Adelaide looked back at her brother and realised what he meant. She quickly opened the window and told Tom to get to the Morgan house as fast as possible.

She had received her first lesson on the indignities of Jake's condition. By the time Jake was fit for company, she'd rung the hospital. Pop was in recovery after a by-pass operation.

"He's doing swell. Mom's coming home. There's nothing to be gained by going to see him. She says tomorrow will be better. He'll be conscious then and able to enjoy talking to you."

"Good man you've found me," Jake said, relieved. "Norm says he'll be happy to help with Pop when he comes home. Trust you to find me a carer who comes with a lap-top computer. Norm says it passes the time. He's taking a degree in Egyptology."

"I hadn't realised the problems," Tom said. "It can't be easy."

"It's not. Maybe now you can see why I want to see Fingiano."

He waited until his mother arrived before passing on other news. Adelaide kept up a flow of chatter about the kids and the things they'd planned for Uncle Jake. At first he looked at her bleakly, realising, as she did not, how many of her excursions were likely to beyond his capacity to enjoy. He yawned and nodded off, wishing there were some way a wheelchair could be cranked into a reclining position.

"For Pete's sake, Addy. Stop talking at the man. He's dead beat," said Tom. "Come and help me get dinner ready."

Norm, a stocky ex-Marine in his fifties, wheeled Jake to his room. He lifted him upright, eased his hips onto the bed and expertly rolled him under the blankets.

"Poor young bugger," he said. "You'd have been better off in a sarcophagus."

Mom, who had iron-grey curls, was distracted when she got home. She was torn between worry about her husband and worry about Jake. She talked up a storm. Before Jake could get a word in she'd laid down the law.

"One thing's clear, son, whether your operation's successful or not, you're not going waltzing off to Australia again. Your Pop needs you by his side to start learning how to run the family business. No, no, I know what you're going to say. You can't run it from a wheelchair, but you can. You can hire a manager to do the groundwork, but the administration, the marketing and promotion, that's all a desk job. That's by phone or e-mail, and there's a good secretary who'll see to letters."

"I've ties in Australia," Jake protested.

"Forget them, son. Your duty's to your Pop, let alone to yourself, for the business will be yours when he retires."

"But Molly expects..."

"Jake, if this Molly means so much to you, you get her to migrate. Start the paperwork. You ring immigration and find out what you have to do."

Jake bit his tongue. He didn't foresee any problems, given that he had already married Molly and that the children had an American citizen as a father, as well as holding Australian nationality. The crux of the matter was that, according to Peter Piper, Marmalady was a rip-roaring success and he doubted that Molly would want to pull up her roots. And, beyond Marmalady lay the grand vision for Dancer's Creek. He knew Molly was committed to creating a tourist village of country excellence. While others had been inspired, Peter Piper said, it was Molly's ideas and sheer common sense that the whole scheme depended upon. More to the point, she had invested most of her capital in the co-operative. While retaining that which she had wrung out of Frank and Gary Flatterjohn, most of the Hariman Hamid buy-out had been sunk into shares in the revival. One million dollars of commitment, that's what she'd made. Those were deep and clinging roots.

And what would he have to offer? A crippled body, hard work in a business that his father could no longer manage, in a town that was as moribund as Dancer's Creek. What sort of life could he offer her in Bernadette? Oh, it might have been a thriving place, a staging post at the time the pioneers had first crossed the ranges into the San Fernando Valley, but the interstate highway had by-passed it, the spur line on the railway had been closed. There was better money to be made on the coast so there had been a drift away from the Valley of young people and their inherited money. They were slowly being replaced by retirees seeking a quiet area in which to spend their closing years, but that made a society with one foot in the hereafter. Oddly, Jake knew he could fit in. He'd not be the only one in a wheelchair, although the others were mainly rather geriatric.

"I can't ask that of Molly," he told Mom. "It's not the answer."

"No. The answer is to get you standing on your own two feet and your father back to full health. Say no more, Jake. Forget about Molly. You'll get over it."

So much for her views at Christmas. Bring Molly over, we'll surely make her welcome.

Jake was uneasily aware that his mother had pronounced views about divorcees, even though the fact that Molly had been a new widow might avoid her censure. Mom was also very old-fashioned about pre-marital sex. Molly the girl-friend was one thing, Molly the eager lover was another. Molly the pregnant would, in Mom's eyes, be Molly the trapper.

This was not the right moment to tell his mother he was married and certainly not the occasion to inform her she was a grandmother for the fifth and sixth time. She would be rapt about the twins, of course, but when it came to the way the wedding ceremony had been conducted, her censure would not fall on Molly. In that instance it would be her son who would be held at fault. Jake was uneasily aware that, while his motives had been good, his conduct could well be called reprehensible.

Pop's condition was the main thing on her mind, however, so while she was mulling the by-pass over with Addy and Tom, Jake wheeled himself to his father's den. There was a phone call he simply had to make. He rang Australia and was put through to the Sister of the ward where Molly was now a patient, in the post-natal unit, rather than in the wing for expectant mothers.

The Sister was blunt. "Your babies are holding their own although, remember, they are very premature and their lungs were not quite ready for birth. The boy is also jaundiced. The major problems are with your wife. She convulsed shortly after she arrived on this ward and her blood-pressure remains critical. I'm sorry, Mr Morgan, but she seems to have developed a full-blown case of eclampsia."

It was like a fist in the centre of the Jake's chest. Wham! "Will she be all right?"

"I told you, Mr Morgan, it's critical. But modern drugs should do the trick. We're keeping her under heavy sedation. However, I do need to confirm where I can contact you as next of kin, in case there's a change for the worse. The number you gave us before rang out with no answer."

Jake explained about his father and that everyone had been either at the airport meeting him or at the heart clinic. Sister's tone softened. "Then I'm indeed sorry to bring you such bad news, Mr Morgan. Sometimes sorrows come not singly, but in company."

"I think I've got a whole platoon of them," Jake sighed. There was definitely no way he could talk to his mother. More heartache she could do without. He thought she looked ill herself, tired and very care-worn. She was certainly greyer than when she'd sat by his bedside in the Darwin ward, helping him pull through his own danger zone.

In the days ahead Jake waited anxiously, reassured by frequent calls that Molly was in a stable condition, though only semi-conscious. They were, however, expressing her milk for the babies. When she recovered, she would be able to feed them herself. It was, strangely enough, the one item of information that lifted his spirits. If they were talking about breast-feeding, they must have a positive view of the outcome.

Pop returned from hospital and came under the tender care of Norm, who had been rather bored by the little that Jake required of him. The pyramids got a rest as Norm took to Pop's well-being with a vengeance. However, it was the promise the old man exacted from Jake that put peace back into his sleep. Pop simply wanted an assurance that Jake would take over

Morgan Enterprises. Sooner, not later. He'd been unable to face arguments; Jake had felt unable to put them. He'd nodded and kissed his father's cheek.

Jake's own operation was scheduled for the following week but, when he had his initial consultation with Dr Fingiano, he was taken aback.

"Come in tonight. We'll prep you first thing in the morning," Fingers said. "No point in hanging around, young man. Let's get to it."

Fingers Fingiano looked rather like a Thanksgiving turkey. He was bald but wattled, red in the face, with an air of hauteur yet surprise at what life had in store. By the time he saw Jake in person, he had ordered scans to be taken of the wound from every angle and by many different techniques.

"See here, Aussie, you can see the track that missile made through your bum. Good job it was no higher or it would have mashed your kidney. Good job it was no lower or you'd have had two fart-holes."

Jake started laughing. Fingers gobbled. "Pay attention, soldier! Now this thickening of the tissue, that's where the schmucks cobbled you up. Should have left them in the outback, sewing up wheat bags. Right. Now you know the metal junk's encapsulated? Yes? And they've told you that scar tissue is pressing hard on your spinal cord? Worse now than it was?"

"I can't tell," Jake said. "I can't feel any difference. Feeling's not one of my party tricks below the waist."

He drew a snigger from Fingers. "That's a good one! Party trick. Ho!" He poked Jake in the chest. "Now, you tell me what that thickened tissue means, soldier? Does it not mean we have some room to play with? Does it not mean we can cut through the scar itself and excise the intruder along with his little hidey hole?"

"You can take Horace the Horrible away?"

"This is Horace?" The surgeon pointed to the scan. "Yes, out he comes and so does all this other embroidery where you've had soluble stitches. Out it all comes and then I'll glue you together."

"Cripes. Will that work?"

"Huh! It can't make it any worse, can it? Unless you get an infection, and I'll have the guts out of any germ that dares lurk in my operating theatre, you should start getting some feeling back in your legs within a month. Mind you, soldier, it will hurt like hell when you do."

"To hell with it," Jake said. "Do your damnedest!"

He never knew the tenderness with which Fingers cut through ravaged flesh, nor the anger in the face behind the mask when Horace was prised loose and dropped into a kidney dish with a small metallic ping.

"Souvenir," said Fingers. "He'll want that."

He never knew the intensity with which Fingers peered into the magnifying lens above the scar tissue next to his spinal cord, nor the breath-taking moment when he cut, leaving only a wafer-thin; no, a tissue-thin; no, a mere film between it and the power-house of Jake's spine. He did not hear Fingers whisper, "Now, let's give this a helping hand."

The surgeon suctioned the remains of the film away from the cord, allowing it room to expand back into its natural course. Nor did he feel the strange compound, which Fingers called glue, though it wasn't, sticking the edges of his internal wound together above the cauterised ends of severed blood vessels that had been sealed off.

What Jake knew next was a white light hurting his eyes, and the sensation of being drawn towards it through a great sea of darkness. As his senses returned he realised it was daylight from a window in the intensive care unit. With the light came the feeling that a great tiger had fastened its claws into his back. He groaned with the pain. A nurse bustled across and injected morphine into his thigh.

Jake winced and said, "Ouch!"

As the agony receded he realised that it had the significance he had never thought possible. Feeling had returned. He sent a message to his toes and felt the movement against the sheets. It was no more than a fraction but it was there.

If there was hope, he could bear the pain. If there was hope, the whole future could change. There might be Molly, there might be the pleasures of being a father, there might be a whole new world.

He realised that despair had been sitting on his back, not like a monkey, but like a ravening monster, gorilla-sized. He bucked it off and felt relieved of its burden. And when he slept, the dreams were good again, no longer nightmares that spilled over into each awakening.

Chapter 20

The window next to Molly's bed was open and a gentle May breeze, bearing the faint wood-smoke scent of early autumn, set the curtains flapping. It reminded Molly of waking up in Jake's flat, locked in his arms, with the wind off the sea billowing the drapes. How well she recalled the feel of his body spooned against her back, one arm across her waist, the other under her neck, his breath soft and slow upon her neck.

She realised she was lying on her side. On her side? She hadn't been able to do so for months, with the great bulk of the babies making it difficult, even with a pillow under her uppermost knee. The babies? Her questing hands no longer sought for the memory of Jake's touch but for the lives that had been so active within her. Her breasts were swollen and her nipples oozed with milk. The dream of motherhood was no fantasy; that strange realm she had drifted in for weeks, touching one world but separated from it by a dark veil that lifted from time to time but never enough for her to be fully aware.

As clarity returned they'd taken the tube from her throat and started feeding her with a spouted cup. Whose hands had they been? Sure it was Aunty Flo's face that came so close to hers, coaxing her to eat, Aunty Flo's lavender cologne that had bathed her brow, her sharp voice that had urged Molly back from that other place?

The babies? Smiling, she remembered the feel of tiny mouths upon her breasts, Aunty Flo insisting that the nurses not express Molly's milk with a pump, but 'put the nippers on the teat'. Old arms holding new flesh against the mother's chest, old fingers teasing open tiny gums and inserting sore yet flowing nipples. The images were real enough, not plucked from her imagination.

She looked across the room to where her aunt lay, sleeping on a daybed. Where were they? This wasn't Dancer's Creek. She rolled onto her back and slowly sat up. This was the maternity hospital where the babies had been born. This was where Jake had married her and where he'd spent the long, long hours of the night of pain and fulfilment.

"So you're awake at last!" said a nurse, entering the room with a vase of flowers. "We thought you were coming to the surface. Feeling better?"

Molly had to seek for words. Her throat was still sore, her mind unaccustomed to translating thought to speech. She had to run a muscle by muscle check of her well-being and found, to her delight, that she felt remarkably good. So she said so.

"Then I'll wake Mrs Frinton and we'll fetch the twins."

Aunty Flo came to with a start, then hurried to Molly's side. Theirs was a tearful embrace. "Oh. Thank God you've come round at last," she said. "You've given us all such worries."

"I deserved a rest, after all that hard work." Molly's spirit was getting the hang of it. "Oh, Aunty Flo, let me have the babies."

Such a precious armful they were. The boy had a shock of dark hair, fine and straight, and his father's amber eyes. The girl was smaller, her scalp covered with silver hair so light it was almost invisible. She too had golden eyes and a rosebud mouth, already making sucking motions at the smell of her mother's milk.

"They're both over five pounds," said Aunty Flo proudly. She had no time for new-fangled metric weights. "We can all go home once the specialist checks you out. Always the same, Molly Grayson. Keeping us waiting!"

"You'll wait a little longer, Mrs Frinton," said the nurse. "Mrs Morgan's got to get used to feeding the babies herself and get some strength back into her legs."

"Well, before we do anything else, nurse, there's a promise I have to keep." Aunty Flo opened her handbag and took out a disposable camera. "Pictures for Jake."

The nurse, who helped arrange the pillows to good advantage and even popped a pretty bedjacket on the model, promised to get the photographs developed when she went off duty. Then, as Aunty Flo took the boy from her arms and rocked him, Molly fed her daughter. "Have I enough milk for both?" she asked.

The nurse beamed. "Little milk factory you are, and who'd have thought it, from a size 10. But we're giving them supplementaries as well. They're used to the bottle from the first week and you'll be glad of the break if Mrs Frinton here will do the night feed when you do go home."

"How come you're here?" asked Molly. "Who's minding Marmalady?"

"If that wasn't the darnedest thing. Rita Piper and I talked it over and she agreed to come and take charge while she supervised the work at the homestead. She'd just got Sharon and Janet working like a team and not plaguing the life out of Fergus, when this damn great camper-van pulled up. Dot and Bud, back from their trip around the Eastern States. Between them the Pipers dragooned Dot into managing the shop and Bud into supervising the setting up of the pickle plant. The Langfords are, I hear, now looking for a house to buy in Dancer's Creek. They like it there."

"How wonderful. They are such dear friends. I can't wait to see them. And Jake? How is Jake?"

"I thought he'd be the first one you'd want to know about."

"And I thought he'd be the first one you'd tell me about. What's wrong?"

"I don't know, and that's the truth. I phoned America when you got sick. Peter Piper had the number. Jake's mother answered. I said I was Molly's aunt and she bit my head off. I asked to speak to Jake and she said Molly had no right bothering them when there was such trouble in the family, with her husband at death's door and Jake in intensive care. I said you were pretty ill yourself. She was quite nasty. She said too bad because Jake wasn't coming back. If he got over the operation, which was by no means certain, he had promised to stay in California to help his father run the business."

Molly's colour drained from her face. "Didn't she even ask about the babies?"

Aunty Flo shook her head. "Molly, I don't even think she knew about the babies. I don't think she even knew you were married to Jake. I don't think she meant to be rude but she was certainly ill-informed. She hung up on me. I haven't dared ring since."

The chin came up, the shoulders straightened. "Then we shall just have to get on with life without him, won't we?" Molly's voice was very small but full of determination. But her head whirled with bewilderment. Why on earth had Jake kept his relationship a secret? She would never understand the man.

*

Larry and Chantelle were her first visitors. Larry, who'd been told of developments by Aunty Flo, was ready to strangle Jake, but let no hint of his anger show to Molly. He steered clear of the subject, telling her instead about the hunt for Gary Flatterjohn and the abortive chase from Perth's international airport.

"The crafty weasel ducked into the casino car park and by the time I'd realised he'd peeled off I was stuck in the wrong lane and had to do a bouncer across the median strip to get back on his tail. Ploughed up the council's flower beds. They were pretty choked off about it. We found his car but he'd scarpered. It's like a maze in the underground car-park, doors everywhere, lifts to the hotel and showrooms, tunnels from the gambling area, paths around the river that we couldn't get to. Oh, he was long gone."

"There've been sightings," said Chantelle, "But he's got one of those ordinary faces that look like everybody else, if you know what I mean. You do, of course."

"It's not his looks that put me off him from the start, but the way he looks at you. He's got eyes like slime. They slide over your skin and leave you feeling dirtied."

Larry said, "Puke! But it's not his eyes I'm after; it's his scrawny neck and his sticky mitts. There was $50,000 in the top of that bag and rolls of the stuff in the lining. We didn't get his wallet. God knows how much he had in that, but I'd bet he was ready to grease a few palms if anyone had questioned the amount of currency he was carrying."

"I wonder how long Nina will hang around waiting? And is she waiting for Flatterjohn or Frank? She may know nothing about Frank's death."

"Hm, but I can tell you one thing for sure; Frank's isn't the name on the birth certificate. She put Gary boy in the hot spot."

Molly gasped. "Then what was all that business about, her and the 'Oh, I've made Frank a new man with my Chinese herbs,' and 'Franky-boy's testosterone is raging,'?"

"Sounds like she played your ex for a sucker," said Chantelle, begging Molly to elaborate on the episode.

"It's like a Neil Simon farce. Me playing up with Jake and Nina playing Frank and Flatterjohn off against one another. It would be comical if it wasn't so damned tragic. But then, real life is stranger than fiction."

Larry gave her a brotherly hug before they left. "I'm sorry about Jake," he said. "He was my best mate. I can't understand him."

"Nor can I. Larry, will you and Chantelle be godparents? If the twins aren't going to have a father, I'd like to be sure there are some good people looking out for them."

Chantelle stopped to talk to the Ward Sister on the way out. They'd trained together at Curtin University.

"It's a damned shame that Mrs Morgan's husband has abandoned her," said Chantelle.

The Ward Sister looked puzzled. "But he rings to find out

how she is almost every day. We tell him she's as well as can be expected, but that's all. There's been nothing else to report for ages, has there? And Matron advised us to answer that way because Mr Morgan isn't her only caller. There's another man who keeps ringing to see if she's regained consciousness. It may be Mr Piper, of course, but he just hangs up."

"Strange," said Chantelle. She hurried off to catch up with Larry who'd gone to buy a box of chocolates for Molly from the kiosk.

"Got to go," he said. "I'll be late for duty. Can you get back to the rehab centre on your own?"

Chantelle nodded. The information about Jake would have to keep.

*

Molly, having sent Aunty Flo back to Peter Piper's house, where she was supposed to be staying, was not surprised to see Dingo enter, his face hidden by a huge bouquet of flowers. He was still in uniform, dark blue strides and light blue shirt. But when the flowers were laid on her bed, she realised it was not Dingo. Nor was it a real police officer. It was the last man on earth she wanted to confront.

"Congratulations, Molly Anstruther. I'm pleased you're back in the land of the living. You and I have a little unfinished business," said Gary Flatterjohn. "There's a small matter of $200,000 which you owe me."

Molly blanched. "That was down to Frank," she gasped. "Frank was to pay you! You were to dock his commission."

"I'm not arguing about it. I want that money. There is also the small matter of you double-crossing me and selling those deeds to Hariman Hamid, Mrs Old-Biddy!"

"I haven't got the money," Molly protested. "How can I have that sort of money when I've been here, in hospital for months. Anyway, it's invested."

"Then uninvest it," he hissed. "I warn you, I'm going to get it out of you, if I have to break every bone in your babies' bodies."

"I'd kill you first," said Molly.

Flatterjohn laughed. "Fine talk. Now you ring your little pals in the police force and tell them what I've said. If I can walk into their headquarters and walk out in police uniform and not be noticed, what chance do you think they've got of stopping me?"

"You're mad. Stark, raving mad."

"I prefer to think of myself as a genius. And a very determined one at that. Which way is the nursery? Shall I go and take a look at the kiddy-winkies?"

Molly picked up the heavy glass water-jug from beside her bed and hurled it at him, screaming.

"You missed! You'd never make the Australian cricket team," said Flatterjohn. "Goodnight!"

*

"The man's a loony, completely off his rocker," said Dingo, who'd arrived in the midst of the commotion and alerted the authorities. "But the weirdo got away again. There's a policewoman on duty outside the nursery and the hospital security team is on alert, Molly, but I don't think he'd be back. Larry and I think you'll be safer in Dancer's Creek, where a stranger sticks out like a sore thumb. I'm going to hire one of those people movers; it takes ten passengers so there'll be room for everyone."

"Will the doctor's let me go?"

"Hey, you'll have a nursing sister on board as well as Aunty Flo. Chantelle Hood is coming with us, and Larry. I've even persuaded Irish to ride shotgun and she's got a formidable fist. Anyway, we've heard so much about Dancer's Creek that we want to play tourist. That suit you?"

"Oh, yes, Dingo. Take me home. Please, take me home."

*

Networking is a wonderful thing. Chantelle got through to Dr Fingiano's clinic. Ten minutes later she rang again and this time was able to talk to Jake. She explained precisely what was going on, the current dilemma, and the story of past misunderstandings.

"I knew I should have told Mom but there was never the right moment," Jake said. "She was so worried about Pop and after that, I was so worried about Molly."

"Had time to worry about yourself? How goes it?"

"Too damn slowly. I can feel my feet but they don't go where I want to put them. Fingers says not to worry but swim more until my muscles regain their tone. Tell Molly I'll call her at Dancer's Creek, but not to expect me back for ages."

"Your Mom told Aunty Flo you're not coming back at all. That you're staying to help your father in his business."

"Yeah. Well, I need to talk to Molly about that. You just keep her safe and look after the kids. Has she chosen names for them yet?"

"I guess she was hoping you'd do it together."

"Hey, say I suggest we call the boy Sandy and the girl Shelley. She'll know why. But if she looks blank, just say Mink!"

*

Molly went bright red when Chantelle passed on Jake's idea. "Well, really," she chuckled. "The very thought!" She went even redder. "Well, I never!"

"From the look on your face, that's a lie," said Larry. "I'd say you certainly did, and very thoroughly at that!"

"Jake hasn't been telling tales, has he? I'd like to think a few of our intimate moments remain private!"

"Get on with you. I'm only teasing. Jake's the original clam. That'll be why he had so much trouble talking to his Mom."

Coming home to Dancer's Creek was like sailing into a harbour after a stormy sea voyage, thought Molly. Why, they'd even hung out flags and decorated Marmalady with balloons.

The Pipers were on the porch with Dot and Bud, while Fergus, still in his baker's hat, came running out with flour on his hands. He grabbed Aunty Flo and fairly danced her into the house.

"Och, it's no been the same wi'out you and your havering," he said. "I've missed the edge to your tongue, Flo, and that's the truth!"

The Country Women and the Townswomen's Guild had gone mad with baking. The tables were groaning. The cricket club's urn was set up in the kitchen and the Parents and Citizens had loaned the large teapots used for school fetes.

Molly, relaxing in her bedroom, was thankful it was a double bed, for there was room for Sandy and Shelley either side of her. It seemed that, in the hours of that long afternoon, every man, woman and child peeked in to say hello to her and the twins. Aunty Flo and Chantelle, however, screened them. Anyone with a spot or so much as a sniffle was told to come back when they were well. They made sure no one would breath germs over the first twins Dancer's Creek had known for thirty-five years.

Larry and Dingo warned people to be on the look out for strangers. They could almost feel the townsfolk draw a protective shield around Molly. As the new mother's strength faded and feeding time approached, Rita Piper rounded up Irish and Chantelle and Jake's friends, and led the way to Dancer's Mill homestead, apologising that she didn't have enough double beds to go round. Dot and Bud, having made supper while Aunty Flo bathed the babies, made a quiet retreat to their camper-wagon.

Wee Bryan, sitting on the porch with Fergus, drained the dregs of his beer and wished a rather damp Aunty Flo good night.

"I'll be off now, Mrs Frinton. But you bide a while with Fergus. He's got something to ask you, I reckon."

Aunty Flo flopped down on the bench and asked for a lager. "What's biting you, Fergus," she said. "Come on. Spit it out."

"It's a wee bitty delicate," he mumbled.

"Don't give me your flummery. What's wrong?"

To her surprise the old man knelt in front of her and took her hand.

"I'd be having your wee hand in marriage," he said. "Och, Flo, it's no the same when you're awa'. I'm a lonely old man and sad for your company."

Flo looked at him seriously. Well, he wasn't a bad looking old boy; better in fact than Fred Frinton, who'd had awfully bandy legs and a pigeon chest.

"I won't say yes and I won't say no," she said. "I'll probably say yes, but it would have to be a long engagement. To get us used to the idea, Fergus."

"Aye," he said. "I wasna thinking o' tying the knot until the wee bairns were weaned. I'd no be happy having them wake me up in the middle o' the night."

"You'd want to move in here?"

"Aye. It would be handy for watching to make sure the bread was rising in the night."

Aunty Flo put her head on one side like a cheeky sparrow. "Fergus, if the only thing you can get to rise in the middle of the night is a batch of dough, you can forget it."

Chapter 21

Mom Morgan, sitting beside Jake's bed in the Fingiano Clinic, was nearly in tears. Her son had just finished calling her a lot of extremely disrespectful words.

"I'm ashamed of you, Mom. Molly's my wife and the twins are my kids. How could you have spoken to Aunty Flo the way you did?"

"I'm mortified," she said. "Jake, I'm sorry. It makes me sick to think of it. What must that poor woman have thought. And keeping it from you that she'd called. Oh, whatever must she have gone through, hearing me calling Molly names and telling her to get out of your life?"

Jake sighed. "You were thinking of Pop, Mom. You weren't seeing things clearly. You weren't exactly rational when I first got home and I was too darned tired to care."

"You should have told me."

"How. When? You'd pushed me into making that damn-fool promise to Pop. If I'd argued with him it would have made his condition worse, if I'd argued with you, you'd have clonked me on the head with a frying pan. By then I'd rung Perth and knew Molly was in a critical condition and that the twins were having trouble breathing. Mom. What point would there have been in telling you about it when I knew I could lose them all?"

"They're all right now? The twins look cute."

"Yes. I've talked to Molly. She's not very happy about you wanting her to leave Australia but she says she'll fill in the immigration forms and argue with me about it later."

"Maybe Pop and I could just sell the business and retire to Big Sur. Adelaide and Tom's kids like it there."

"Pop would hate it. He doesn't like fishing."

"He could play golf."

"Big deal. The business is his life. No, we'll work something out when I'm better."

"How long, Jake? How long before you see any results?"

Jake gave her a twisted smile. "Mom, in some ways I'm worse, not better. I can feel my legs. I can stand up. I can even take a few steps between the rails but I have to tell each foot where to go. That's half the problem. My feet are numb. You know how it is when you get pins and needles? It's like that all the time. So I'm not sure if my sole's flat on the floor. Makes it hard to get my balance. But the negative's the pain in my back. Fingers is going to take another look this week, to see if he can pin-point the nerve that's causing the trouble."

"But you can keep yourself clean now? Can I let Norm go? Your Pop's much better and Norm's been asked to take on another case in San Diego."

"Sure. Tell him thanks, Mom."

Fingers was not happy about Jake's progress. Further scans showed that two discs had been displaced by the blast. The damage had been obscured by the swelling caused by Horace. Now they could be clearly seen. Fingers said a rude word.

"I could fuse the vertebrae either side of the damage but that would mean another operation," the surgeon said. "I don't guarantee success. Or we can try a new technique to reduce the displacement under ultrasound and put a synthetic cushion between your poor old bones. I don't guarantee success with that either. Or we can try to isolate the pain nerve and freeze it dead. But if we get that wrong, you could be back in that wheelchair."

"No more operations; at least, not yet," said Jake. "Try your cushions. Your glue worked. Just get me half-way mobile so I can get back to Australia."

Fingers pulled an ear. "Right, soldier. Let's put the springs back into your back-bone."

*

The sheaf of immigration papers gave Molly a headache.

"I don't know why you're bothering with those when you don't mean to go to America," said Aunty Flo. "Burn them."

"I promised I'd fill them in. It will take months to process them and I don't have to follow through even when I get a visa. In any case, love, I'd have to pay a visit to meet Jake's family. His Pop can't travel again. His Mom thinks the stress of coming over to Darwin after Jake's wounding helped bring on the first heart attack."

"Well, she would. Does a good line in guilt trips, that woman." Aunty Flo had taken against Mrs Morgan. "The things she said!"

"She's written; she's very sorry. She sounds very nice and caring. Try to forget the past, Aunty. Look to the future."

"If you think I'm planning a white wedding, forget it. I'm not even sure that marrying Fergus is the right thing to do. Maybe we should live de facto."

"What, and shock the whole of Dancer's Creek? Anyway, Dot and I have been house-hunting. I've put in an offer for that cedar home on Twogood Street."

"The Rankin's place?"

"That's right. Three bedrooms, parquet floor, big picture windows to the garden and a huge patio area where the babies can play. It's got air-conditioning for summer and a log fire for winter. Good kitchen with a dishwasher. Come and see it tomorrow. Mrs Rankin won't mind."

"I should think not. I delivered both her children. When does she move?"

"Next week. She's just about finished packing. They're going to her son's in Melbourne. I can get possession then. I paid upfront."

"You're not still holding all that money in a cash account, are you? You're not still expecting Flatterjohn to ask for it? He must be long gone."

"To tell you the truth, I haven't thought about him for weeks. I've just not got round to talking to the bank manager about term deposits and superannuation."

Aunty Flo shook her head wonderingly. She was pleased Molly had found a place of her own. It was another thing to tie her to Dancer's Creek, to make it hard for Jake to pressure her into migrating. It also solved the delicate problem of how Fergus was to fit into a family with two noisy babies.

*

"Nina's on the move," said Larry, who phoned at least once a week to find out how his godchildren were. "She's dumped the baby on the steps of police headquarters."

"They're certain it's hers?"

"Sure. Plenty of girl babies get abandoned from the Chinese community, but there aren't many Caucasian males. Anyway, he still had his hospital birth tag on his wrist."

"After all this time?"

"Yeah. The amah told Nina it was illegal to remove it until a child was six months old and she believed her."

"What'll become of the boy?"

"The amah's got a thing going with this butch policewoman from Kowloon. They're going to foster it. Bring it up to be a Hong Kong copper."

"When will they arrest her?"

"They're holding off until my Inspector and I get there. We fly out tonight. They say it will be less paper-work if we take her into custody under Australian law and bring her back here to face trial. If they make the arrest we'd have to go through the extradition procedures. Pain in the butt. They know where she is. She's holed up in a boarding house near the port. They think she's arranged to get off by sea."

"Be careful, Larry. You couldn't find the bullet that killed Frank and Flatterjohn swears he didn't shoot him. I wouldn't put it past Nina to be armed. That's one very twisted lady. If she didn't have a gun when she left the country, she may have got one by now."

- 233 -

"I'll be careful. I've too much going for me now to take chances. Chantelle's agreed to make an honest man of me. We're tying the knot at St Andrews in three week's time. You'll come?"

"Wouldn't miss it. But I'll have to get someone to mind the twins."

"No you won't. Fine godfather I'd be if I let Sandy and Shelley miss the fun. No, you come up to town with Peter Piper and Rita. I asked your Aunty Flo but she said she had other things to do."

Molly laughed. "I expect she's planning a dirty weekend with Fergus. I cramp their style a bit and Flo says she's not marrying him until she's sure he's in working order."

"Would Dot and Bud like to come? The more the merrier."

"Send them an invitation. They've not had a chance to get to Perth since they got back from their tour. They'll be glad of an excuse to get their things out of store. They're planning to rent a place here."

"Going to be a swish affair," said Larry. "I've even laid on a police guard of honour."

"Then check that Chantelle hasn't also planned to line the aisle with guys in wheelchairs with crossed crutches over your hopeless heads!"

He laughed. "Give the twins a kiss from Uncle Larry and tell them I'll bring them some Chinese lanterns to hang in the nursery."

*

It sometimes rains in Hong Kong. It rains so hard that the slopes of the mountains in the centre of the islands give way and topple whole apartment blocks. On such nights the entire police force is called for emergency duty, rescuing citizens trapped in the rubble. Rain-slick roads reflect the myriad neon signs and the pixel lights from towers where thousands live. Cars skid on the greasy surface and collide at intersections.

There are ambulances and tow trucks racing to accident scenes.

The team of police expected by Larry and the Major Crimes Squad inspector was reduced to four men. The amah had been dismissed when Nina dumped the child and moved to her present hide-out. There was only one man watching the unit and he was huddling in the driest spot around, even though it gave only a partial view of the building.

Larry, feeling water trickling down the inside of the neck of his rain-coat, was not enchanted by the beauty of Hong Kong. The docks area was on the nose. Luckily the storm had kept marine activity to a minimum. It was a foolhardy captain who would leave anchorage to head out into the path of a typhoon. If Nina had planned to leave on the next tide, she'd have to think again.

"We can't wait for her to make a move. Let's take her in now," said the Australian inspector to his Hong Kong colleague, who was standing near the door with a battering device which crashed through lock and bolt alike. Nina Lavell, taken by surprise by the rush of police into the dingy room, drew a gun. She backed away as they froze. She scooped up a bag and let herself carefully through a back door. This led to a bin area behind a wall, and had therefore not been noticed.

Larry, bringing up the rear of the posse, dropped to the floor and, hidden by the legs of the other officers, backed out of the room into the darkness. Once clear, he ran round the back of the building, heedless of pools of water and piles of refuse. He raced down a back alley after the fleeing woman, who turned and fired at him. The bullet hit him in the shoulder, just above the collar bone. Larry reeled back from the shock and lay helplessly as the lone watcher leapt from his observation spot and brought Nina down with a flying tackle.

She screamed and spat and scratched as they handcuffed her. She yelled abuse as the Australian police read the charges. She fell quiet when the inspector told her that his men had spent weeks examining the debris from the Anstruther home on a demolition dump and had, by luck, found the bullet that had killed her lover, Frank.

"I don't know whether we'll get a match from your gun or from Gary Flatterjohn's, when we catch him," the inspector said. "But if you're not a murderer, Miss Lavell, I'm damn sure you're an accomplice. But for now, we'll settle for attempted murder of a police officer."

Larry, bandaged and sore, clenched his fist within the sling he wore, and thought his inspector a fool. Why let her know that Flatterjohn was on the loose? Why not let her assume him to be in custody and persuade her to spill her guts? There was a mean flash in her eyes and then she started yelling again, complaining of police brutality.

"Sedate her," the station commandant said to the doctor on duty. "Shut the bitch up and you two get her out of the country. The last thing we need is an international incident on a night when there's a civil emergency. Get her to the airport and take her back to Australia. She's your problem from here on in."

It was not the easiest journey back to Perth. The evidence from Nina's room had to be bagged and sent to the departure area. There was a hassle about getting a flight on Qantas and they had to travel on another airline. There was no room in economy so the inspector had to get clearance to book business class. Nina's passport could not be found, so her bags had to be unpacked and searched again. The vital document, and a list of bank transactions, was found in the lining of her cabin bag. Her handbag was full of American dollars. She had obviously not been intending to leave by any official gateway from Hong Kong.

She made a scene when the boarding call was heard and struggled as they dragged her across the passenger bridge. The inspector, who had come prepared for the possibility, gave her another shot of sleep-maker. Larry, whose shoulder hurt like hell, wished he too could have a dose of instant oblivion. As it was, the best he could obtain was a couple of strong pain-killer capsules. It was better than aspirin but not a lot.

"You'll get a medal for that wound," said the inspector, helping him fasten his seat belt.

"I'll get a bollocking," Larry replied. "I'm getting married at the end of the month and my fiancée will be ropeable if I can't cuddle her properly."

As Dingo said later, a sore arm wouldn't stop the wedding plans. "Had you been hit in the nuts, maybe, but Nina only winged you, for God's sake."

"She didn't. The bullet went in one side and out the other."

"Good thing she didn't get your head, then. It wouldn't have done any damage as your brains had gone missing."

Larry, who was healing quite well but was feeling sorry for himself, pulled a long face. "But it's my favourite drinking arm," he whimpered in self-mockery. "How can I lift another beer?"

"The same way as you lifted the last," said Dingo. "It's your shout."

*

The church was packed by the time the Pipers arrived with Molly and the twins. Rita carried one, Molly the other. Dingo, usher for the groom's side, showed them to a pew near the front, just behind Larry's parents. Irish was already there, looking a picture in a fine green woollen dress, edged with heavy lace. Molly's new sky-blue suit showed off her figure, quite restored to its usual slim lines. Her wide-brimmed hat had the high crown fashionable that season. Irish, who'd found a cream straw in the same tone as the traditional lace, admired Molly's outfit.

"Can I nurse Shelley?" she asked.

"You'll give Dingo ideas if he sees you getting clucky."

"As long as they're the right sort of ideas."

Rita Piper popped a pacifier in Sandy's mouth and wiped a dribble from his chin. "I thought Dingo was to be best man, Irish,"

"He'd have done it, but he said he was better at directing traffic. Anyway, Larry'd made other arrangements."

"He's late," Peter Piper muttered, consulting his watch. "He's supposed to be standing at the altar, chewing his nails like every other bridegroom."

"He said he would wait in the vestry until the last minute as he wasn't going to have everyone looking at him if Chantelle decided to ditch him at the last moment."

"Irish! She wouldn't."

"No. I think she's going to beat him to it, in fact."

As the organ music filled the church, every eye turned to the doors where three little bridesmaids, in pale apricot tulle, were solemnly waiting to take their position. Behind them came the bride, in a froth of creamy lace, her auburn locks glossy under a wreath of roses. Her father led her proudly towards the altar where Larry was waiting, having taken his position while attention was on the bride.

And, beside Larry was a wheelchair, from which a figure was unfolding stiffly. The best man stood awkwardly, his balance kept by the arm crutches he was using.

Jake turned his head and smiled, not at Chantelle, but at his precious Molly, down whose face tears were running unchecked. She wanted to run to him at once, to cry out her joy, but she knew she could not spoil this special service. She had to wait. But, when the vows were made and the bride and groom made their way from the church, she was out of her pew and into Jake's arms, faster than he could swing his way across the aisle to meet her. He kissed her as she had never been kissed before. Her hat fell off and she didn't care. Jake hugged her so tightly that she could hardly breathe, yet knew she needed breath to kiss him back.

Dingo, coming up behind them with the wheelchair, laughed gleefully. "Put him down, Molly, before he falls down. He's not crash hot on two pins yet. Sit down, Jake, and let's get you out to have your ugly mug preserved for posterity. Hey, Molly, he may have duff legs, but there's nothing wrong with his arms. Give him the nippers to carry, while I get this show on the road."

"Best kept secret in Perth, wasn't it?" said Larry at the reception. "I don't know how Aunty Flo was able to keep a still tongue in her head."

"It's Mr Piper I thought would give the game away." Irish had taken a shine to the boss. "He was so full of plans and plots. He's got your new house ready for you to move into tomorrow, Molly. That's why Aunty Flo wouldn't come to the wedding. And he and Rita are baby-sitting tonight."

"I thought I was staying with them," Molly said, weakly. She had only just stopped pinching herself.

"Well, if that's what you'd prefer," Jake replied. "But I've booked us into the bridal suite at the Sheraton Hotel."

"Oh," said Molly. And later that night she said "Oh, ooh! Oooh!" as Jake showed her there was more than one way to make love. Then, "Oh, Jake, I love you so much," she whispered, as she looked down upon his dear and longed-for face, and lowered herself tenderly onto his readiness.

Chapter 22

Bud had been acting as consultant to Fergus for weeks. The old man, having had his proposal provisionally accepted, had realised that, despite having occasionally used professional services in his younger days, he did not know much about how married people went on behind the bedroom door.

Wee Bryan confessed that he was a confirmed neuter. He'd never had an interest in man, woman nor even self-gratification. "I leaves that to the birds and the bees," he'd said.

Fergus decided Dot was a happy and womanly person and therefore Bud knew the art of keeping her that way. He'd been taken aback at first then, recognising that Fergus was deadly serious and that this was a cry from the heart, had spent hours talking him through the ways of true love.

There was a great deal of home-brew consumed in the process, down in the garden shed at the end of the onion patch. There was a considerable amount of, "Och, no. She'd niver dae that!" and "Isna that a wee bitty rude, Bud?" and "Nae, I couldna bring myself to take advantage."

Eager anticipation gave way to grave misgiving by the time Larry's wedding came around. When Aunty Flo handed the babies in to Rita and Molly and slammed the car door on the Piper party, Fergus tried to sneak away while his intended was still waving.

"Oh, no you don't, Fergus. You're not going to go to the Federal and get drunk all afternoon. We've the Larkin house to get ready for Molly when she gets back. No. You don't have to bake this afternoon either. Marmalady is closed for the rest of the week. I've sent Sharon and Janet off on holiday."

Fergus sighed with relief. At least the crucial test had been postponed.

They found Bud and Dot hard at work, hanging curtains,

making up beds, unpacking china and glassware, pots and pans, arranging newly-delivered furniture. Dot drove Aunty Flo to the supermarket to fill out a comprehensive grocery order. Milk and butter, cheese and cream, everything from pot-scourers to breakfast cereal had to be bought. All except marmalade, and several jars of lemon curd.

"And Molly knows nothing of the move or what's planned for the wedding?"

"She hasn't got a clue. And you see it stays that way. What time are you and Bud leaving for the city?"

"After the evening news. Bud doesn't like driving into the setting sun so we'll wait until dark. We'll get as far as we can tonight then park the camper-van at a rest stop. It's the beauty of a home on wheels. We'll be away at first light and in plenty of time for the service. Back the day after tomorrow, if all goes well."

Fergus felt his knees buckling after he'd carried in the last of the groceries. Bud put the beer in the bar refrigerator and took two cans out to the patio.

"One for the road," he said.

"I wish weel that I was ganging wi' you," sighed Fergus.

"Nonsense, man. You know what to do, so do it."

"Och, Bud. It's a wee mousie I've got in my trews, not a bluidy caber!"

Aunty Flo took Fergus by the arm, dropped the keys in the meter box, and marched her fiancé back to her house. She left him sitting among the oink collection while she heated a casserole for supper. He stared disconsolately at the display of pigs while she laid the dining room table and lit candles in sconces held up by cute porkers dressed as schoolgirls, complete with gymslips. There were crystal glasses and a carafe of soft red grenache blended with merlot. Fergus looked at it in dismay. He had no head for wine.

"One glass and I'm anyone's," he muttered.

"Two glasses and you're mine," said the amorous pensioner.

- 241 -

He ate lightly, finding the beef stroganoff tasted like sawdust, so nervous was he. He dropped cutlery, he knocked over his wine. He stuttered and said things he knew were nonsense. To his surprise he was offered a large cigar after the meal and, while he sat and savoured it, Aunty Flo whisked away the debris. She could be heard clattering around and running the water in the bathroom.

"In with you," she said. "I'm not going to bed with you until you are clean from top to toe, Fergus. I'll be in to scrub your back."

The bath-water smelt like a flower garden. Fergus looked doubtfully at the froth of bubbles and the steam rising from the tub. He was more accustomed to a cold shower and a hard scrub with a loofah. He stripped and gingerly lowered himself into the water. It was a huge, old-fashioned bath on claw feet. The water came well above his privates, he noted with relief, starting to wash his arms with soap and a thick flannel.

"That's the way," said Flo, coming in with a tot of whisky for him. "This will buck you up."

Her hair was loose on her shoulders, She was wearing a pink chenille bathrobe, tied by a sash at the waist. Fergus looked at her nervously.

"Will ye want the water when I'm finished, Flo?" he asked.

"Not likely," she laughed. "I'm getting in with you."

They were both pink and crinkly by the time they got out. Fergus's hands now knew the feel of her, and his skin the feel of her fingers on his body. Yet he still shivered as she towelled him down and led him through the warm passage to the bedroom. She eased him down onto the sheets, warm from an electric blanket, and covered him over. Then she turned off the light and crept in alongside him, mother-naked.

"Ah, weel, Flo. You will be gentle wi' me, won't you?" said Fergus.

Aunty Flo left her lover to his rest in the morning. He'd done well for an old bloke and, in fact, had surprised her by some of his more innovative suggestions. But there was no doubt, old bones couldn't stand too much of a good thing, and old joints creaked at the most frustrating times.

Flo dressed as the kettle came to the boil. She made her coffee and took it out onto the porch. She sat in the sun and watched a cat chasing a leaf down the road. She did not hear footsteps behind her, nor notice the shadow that fell across the polished floor. The pad of chloroform across her nose and mouth was a complete shock. She gasped for air, breathing deeply of the chemical that robbed her of her senses.

*

It was gone noon before Fergus woke up, groaning as he tried to straighten his limbs. He felt as if he'd been pounded by a gold battery. He recalled his prowess with a blush. To his amazement, he realised he'd actually done rather well. To his amusement, he admitted he'd thoroughly enjoyed himself. "Bud would've been proud o' me," he muttered. " Up wi' ye, man. Up and gi' the wee woman a bitty kiss and a taste o' bristle."

The fire in the kitchen had gone out. The kettle was cold. The front door was wide open and there was no sign of Flo. There was a broken cup on the patio and the dried up remains of spilled coffee.

Wee Bryan arrived for an afternoon of digging. "I seen Mrs Frinton driving off early with that commercial traveller who's been staying at the Federal," he said, when prompted. Wee Bryan was not one to speak unless pushed to it. "She looked to be fast asleep. What did you do last night that made her want to run away from you?"

Fergus looked at his feet. "Och, weel, I think we should go down the Federal and talk about it," he suggested. "To tell the truth, I could do with a beer."

Wee Bryan shook his head. "I told you to leave women alone," he said. "Stick to potatoes. What I say is, women is worse than tomatoes."

*

'Do Not Disturb' notices do not control the telephone. Peter Piper rang to say that he and Rita had fed the twins and would be around to pick up Molly in a hour's time. Dingo would collect Jake and take him to the Army Headquarters where he had discharge papers to sign. Then they would pick up Irish and head for the Piper's homestead for a few days.

"I'll only be an hour or so," said Jake, smoothing Molly's stomach. "We'll be right behind you."

"Don't," she said, trembling at his caress. "You know what'll happen if you do."

"I can wait until tonight, Molly my darling. Then we'll dance the dance of love in Dancer's Creek."

Molly giggled. "The way we went at it last night, I'll feel more like creaking than dancing."

The Piper's were amused by her air of languid fulfilment. She fed the babies on the way, pleased there was enough flow to replace the drain on her breasts overnight. Jake had been hungry for her bounty. "The taste of Molly is the taste of paradise," he'd crooned.

Molly had laughed and told him he sounded like something from the pages of a romantic novel. "Over the top, Jake. Definitely over the top."

"You mean like this?" he'd said, swinging his leg across hers and pushing her gently back against the pillows.

"I thought you had a bad back?"

"Mm, but I didn't know this was the best way to stop me thinking about it."

Peter and Rita got little sense out of her on the journey to the country. She slept much of the time. When they got to Dancer's Creek she offered them tea but they turned her down.

"We've not had chance to air the bed for Dingo and Irish," said Rita. "You go on in with the babies and tell Aunty Flo all about the wedding. We'll see you both tomorrow. You can bring

Jake over to see our new house."

Molly put the twins in their pushchair while the boss carried her luggage onto the porch. He gave her a kiss on the cheek. Molly waved and pushed the sleeping babies into the hall.

"In here, Molly." Aunty Flo sounded quite hoarse.

Molly stepped into the dining room, dragging the babies with her. Aunty Flo was not present. Gary Flatterjohn leered at her from a seat at the end of the long table. He levelled his gun at her and told her to sit down in his place. She did as told, feeling as if she was part of some surrealistic movie.

"I've come for my money," he said, flicking the brake off the pushchair and pulling it closer. He rocked it gently up and down as he continued. "You did do what I told you and drew the money, didn't you?"

Molly nodded, her throat dry.

"And you did put it in a safe deposit box, didn't you?"

"Yes, but I thought you'd forgotten about it. I took it back to the bank for safe-keeping. I couldn't have that much lying around the place."

"Silly girl." Flatterjohn left the twins and took a handful of china pigs from the display unit. He stood them on the shelf behind Molly and took aim. The gun made a dull whuffing sound. It was silenced. The pigs shattered and fell among piles of other fragments. He'd been using them as target practice. The noise woke the twins who whimpered.

"I've got plenty of bullets," Flatterjohn said. "I'm having fun."

"Where's Aunty Flo?" Molly, scared that the twins would scream, popped dummies in their mouths.

"Mine to know, yours to find out. I've got her tucked away nice and quiet. She can't get out. It's quiet as the grave where she is." He tittered and looked down at his hands. "But, oh, the blisters. Still, it doesn't take long to dig a hole."

"You've buried her?"

"Hm. But she was still alive when I put her in. She's got plenty of air. I put boards across the top before I covered it again. She'll not get out, Molly. And I'm not showing you where she is until I've got the money."

"You're mad."

"As a hatter," he said, placing the ivory piglets on his make-shift range. "Shall we go for a stroll up to the bank and get the safe deposit box?"

He pointed the gun at Molly who rose and, like a sleepwalker, went before him. "No, Molly dear. Take the pushchair. Just remember, any smart tricks and there are two lovely little piglets in the pram. I don't like babies."

"Then why did you have one?" Molly lips were stiff.

"With Nina? A moment of careless rapture. Refused an abortion. Paid me back though, didn't she."

"By going to Frank?"

"Stuff Frank. Who cares. By cheating me. By cleaning out our bank account. By running out on me." He was getting agitated.

Molly, feeling as if she was handling explosive that could detonate any moment, took the handle of the pushchair and set off up Main Street, past Marmalady and its Closed sign, past the saddlery, deserted because Dot and Bud were still in the city. The whole town seemed to be frozen in time. There must have been a good mid-day movie on the television, or everyone had gone for an afternoon nap. Never had Molly's feet felt so leaden or the push-chair such a dead-weight. She could feel the silencer pressed into her back. Flatterjohn had draped his jacket across his arm, concealing the weapon.

The teller, though surprised, took Molly's key and fetched the box. She took it with shaking hands and, following whispered instructions, put it in the shopping compartment behind the babies' seats. Returning, she noticed Flatterjohn's Land Rover parked on the far side of the road, near the footbridge. A quick glance down the slope to the pool above the bridge showed her no truants wagging school to catch marron. She could not yell out and expect a gang of teenagers to come charging up the bank to her rescue. She realised she could not have called out in any case, and subjected young people to a gun that she knew Flatterjohn could handle with considerable accuracy. As they drew level with Marmalady the shop door opened and Fergus looked out.

"Where's Flo, Molly? Och, lass, Wee Bryan and I have looked for her all over."

Flatterjohn raised the gun and struck Molly on the temple with it, obviously unwilling that she should speak. She collapsed onto the pavement as he grabbed the box of money and gave the pushchair a mighty thrust towards the road, down the slope to the river steps.

Dingo and Jake, coming into town, assessed the danger in a flash. Dingo braked hard on the bridge and Irish cried out. Jake pushed open the passenger door, on his feet, running, running, throwing his body in front of the fast-moving carriage, steadying it as it threatened to topple. Sandy and Shelley squealed with delight and showed him gummy smiles.

Dingo had picked up speed, driven round Jake and the babies and had parked outside the shop. Flatterjohn, seeing his way of escape blocked, pushed Fergus aside and ran through Marmalady to the bakery beyond. The back door was open. As he made for the exit, Wee Bryan walked in, carrying new supplies of beer.

The old gardener paused. He did not like guns, especially ones that were pointed at him. He pulled a glass stubby from the six-pack and threw it at Flatterjohn with all the power he could muster from a life-time of hard work on the land. It hit the broker's wrist with such force that the sound of the bone snapping could be clearly heard amid the shattering of glass. The gun flew across the room and landed at Fergus's feet.

"Right," said Fergus, picking it up. "Where's Flo? Molly's told me you've got her."

Flatterjohn giggled, a high, hysterical giggle. Seeing Molly coming up behind Fergus with Jake, who was leaning on Dingo heavily, he screamed, "Where's my effing money, bitch?"

"Let me have him," said Jake.

Fergus, clutching the safe deposit box, glared. "It's my woman he's got, mon. Dinna meddle."

"I'm not telling you until I get the money," Flatterjohn screamed, bracing his wrist with his other hand.

Fergus looked at Dingo. "Policeman, aren't you? Why mon, it would be a wee bit tactful if ye'd go and put the kettle on. Molly, why don't you show the lad where the teapot is?"

Jake leaned back against the stainless steel bench and watched the scene with avid interest.

"What are you going to do with him?"

"Och, mon. It seems an awfu' shame to waste that nice baker's oven." He nodded to Wee Bryan who grabbed Flatterjohn from behind and propelled him towards the huge doors. The broker screamed that his hand was killing him. His eyes were rolling with fear and he wriggled like a maggot. Fergus pulled out a couple of shelves and grabbed Flatterjohn's legs. "In wi' ye. And you'll not come out until you're ready to talk."

"What temperature?" Wee Bryan had his hand on the controls.

"We'll bring it up slowly," said Fergus. "We'd no want him to roast until he's told us what we want to know."

Dingo came in five minutes later, with the wheelchair. "I thought you might be glad of a push, Jake."

His friend nodded. "I ache all over. Mind, some of it is from laughing at this pair."

"I don't see a thing, gentlemen. Just let me know when you need me to make a formal arrest," said Dingo. He glanced at Fergus, who was now loading a large pan of marmalade onto a burner. "I won't ask what that's for."

Fergus put his hands on his hips and gazed sorrowfully at the policeman. "Aye, my ancestors had some terrible cruel ways with the Sassenachs," he sighed. "But I've nae got a vat of boiling oil. I doubt he'll stay quiet for long."

Irish and Molly did their best to clean up the dining room, once Dingo had fetched his camera and documented the damage. The boss and Rita turned up to find why Molly wasn't answering the phone and why Irish and Dingo had not arrived.

"Line's been cut," said Dingo. "I've called regional HQ on my mobile. I hope the squad's not too quick. From the sounds of it, the boys haven't finished."

"That's terrible. Rita, take Irish and the babies back to our place and bed them down for the night. I'd say take Molly but I don't think anyone could separate her from Jake at this moment," the boss suggested. "I'll stay. We may have to raise a search party."

It was another twenty minutes before Fergus came into the house, looking grim. "We know roughly where's he's got Flo, but the silly bastard didna leave markers. He said he'd know the spot by day, but he's not got a clue at night. Tae be honest, and that's damn hard for the twisted wee devil that he is, he admits he had nae intention of ever going back for her, curse his black heart."

"Okay, that's enough. I'm asking my colleagues to call in the tracker dogs." Dingo raised Regional and relayed the request. "Got a map? Mark the rough location, Fergus. Jake, pass on the information when the squad gets here. We'll take my car. Mr Piper and Wee Bryan can ride in the back with the prisoner; you act as guide, Fergus. With luck we'll have her out before we need to deploy a full scale search party."

The boss handed Jake his mobile phone. "Act as command post," he said. "I know you'd rather be in the thick of it, but you've done your heroic bit for the day."

"And I'm paying for it," Jake admitted, wincing.

By 9pm the State Emergency Service and the Volunteer Bushfire Brigade had joined the hunt. There was an area of State Forest five miles from Dancer's Creek, around Bushranger's Rock and the dam. Flatterjohn, who had gone from a state of blabbing wildly to near catatonic, was securely locked in the back of a police wagon, handcuffed and guarded.

Early attempts to find the burial site had proved abortive. Flatterjohn claimed all fire breaks looked the same to him. Many had tyre tracks near their beginning. It was a popular spot for courting couples to park up on a Saturday night. It had come down to an in-line search, volunteers prodding the ground in front of them with staves, hoping for the hollow sound of a cavity. The dogs arrived at last. Molly had given the handlers items of Aunty Flo's clothing. Fergus, hollow-eyed, sat exhausted near the van from which the search was being conducted. He was sipping tea made by volunteers from the Salvation Army. Wee Bryan was whittling a length of stick. He had reduced five branches to shreds since the professionals took over the hunt.

It was gone midnight when frantic barking was heard from the far side of the ridge. "They've got her. Fergus, they've got her," yelled Dingo, phone to his ear. "She's cold, she's sore, and she's in the wickedest temper you can imagine."

"Aye," said Fergus. "There's more fire in Flo than in a whole bottle of best malt."

Wee Bryan looked up, beaming. "Have you got one?"

"One what?"

"A whole bottle of best malt."

"Aye."

"Then why don't we take Flo home and drink it?"

"No. You can take the bottle back to your place and drink it, Wee Bryan. My intended and I have got some unfinished business."

"Such as?" said Dingo, curious.

"Well, there's the wee matter of a hot bath, for a start. And after that, weel no, I don't know that you're old enough to hear any more."

Jake looked at Molly tenderly. She had fallen asleep in a chair. He woke her to tell her the good news. "It's fine. They're coming in. Molly, I think it's time you took me home."

"This is home," said his wife, stretching.

"No, it isn't. When I called Aunty Flo before the wedding, she told me the Larkin house was ready for us to move into and we should go there straight away."

"That seems years ago."

"It sure does. Is it far? Could you help me get this set of wheels down the hill and acr oss the bridge? I don't fancy a swim in Dancer's Creek."

"Why? Why now?"

"Firstly, you haven't noticed, but our bed has already gone and, secondly, I think Fergus and Flo might like to be alone. Dingo said the old boy has left some unfinished business."

"Oh," said Molly.

Jake grinned. "Oh, indeed, and that reminds me, we've a little unfinished business of our own. But it will have to wait. The only thing I need is bed and Molly Morgan in my arms."

Chapter 23

Irish ran her fingers down Jake's spine. "No, you haven't put your discs out again. What's causing the pain is a damn great bruise right across your bum. When you dived for the pram, you flipped back hard onto the edge of the kerb. I saw you. Don't you remember?"

"I'm trying to forget," said her patient, groaning as she massaged embrocation into his skin.

"Just take it easy for a few days. But I was pretty impressed by the way you moved. I thought you couldn't get your legs coordinated."

"So did I, but they turned back to jelly afterward."

"Oh, you'll soon be chasing Molly round the bedroom."

"No, I won't," said Jake. "She refuses to run away!"

Irish laughed and told him to get dressed. She joined Molly and the twins in the garden. The babies were exploring their new terrain. Dingo had deserted his fiancée. He'd been drafted to escort Flatterjohn back to the city.

"That'll teach Larry not to go waltzing off on honeymoon!" he'd said. "He'll be spitting that he wasn't in at the death."

The boss had reminded him that it was no joke. "Flo could have died," he'd said.

Dingo, crestfallen, had suddenly grinned. "I bet Flatterjohn thought his days were numbered. Did you see what Fergus did with that hot marmalade?"

Irish, when the details of the interrogation had been made known to her, had gone rather green. "I hope Fergus didn't bottle that batch."

"I think Wee Bryan put it on the compost heap. He said it was only fit for tomatoes after it had been in contact with what he called a human cane toad."

"The bastard won't be sitting down for a while."

*

Aunty Flo stayed in bed for two days after her ordeal. Fergus the Conqueror turned into a surprisingly gentle nursemaid. He cooked and cleaned and spent most of his free time, after the daily bake, in trying to piece together the fragments of the pig collection.

Bud took time out from the saddlery to repairing the bullet holes in the timberwork. Dot, running the shop and cafe, did roaring business. Everyone came in to hear the latest gossip about the biggest drama in Dancer's Creek since the days of the bushranger. There was a media invasion.

Jake, turned by the press into 'the war hero, the only American to fight in East Timor,' was disgusted. Fergus became a 'verra dour Scot'. He was saying nothing that might lead to his being charged with assault of Flatterjohn. Wee Bryan overcame his shyness to tell the talking heads about the evil properties of tomatoes.

Aunty Flo did the frail old lady act very convincingly. She felt like it at the time. Dot did a moving piece about the ruined pig collection. It led to a public appeal for replacements. By the end of the week so many oinks had been donated that Bud had to open the fire station to house them. Aunty Flo perked up. "They'd make another great tourist attraction," she said. "I could open a Museum of Piggery."

Molly, while at first sharing Jake's dismay, consulted Peter Piper. Together they led the media through Dancer's Creek, explaining the grand vision, showing what had already been done at Tom Dancer's Mill. Rita opened The Homestead, furnished in grand colonial style, and laid on regional cheeses and wines...the media need such encouragement. They were shown Fergus up to his elbows in dough and Sharon and Janet making a new batch of rough cut for Marmalady. Molly walked them past the shop that was to become a mecca for old-fashioned home-made sweets, the boss and Bud let them film the first of Wee Bryan's onions going through the pickle plant. The blacksmith put on a demonstration and the quilters displayed their first masterpiece. The ABC stayed on for a few days longer, expanding the story into a documentary for national television. By the time it went to air, a month later, the tourist coaches were already coming into town. Molly the Marmalady was a media celebrity.

Jake sulked.

*

CNN picked up on the 'American War Hero' footage from its Australian counterpart and obtained the ABC's film. They spliced in scenes from the East Timor action, cut a shot of a landmine exploding from material covering the war in Kosovo, and visited Fingers Fingiano. Fingers, who took video of all his cases, for what he said was training purposes, was happy to co-operate. His reputation was enhanced by publicity. He let them have shots of Jake's operation and footage of his recovery, exercising in the pool and on the parallel bars between which he'd taken his first steps. The producers employed look-alikes to do a re-enactment of Jake leaping from the car and running to save the twins.

A TV crew was despatched to Bernadette to film Mom and Pop. Adelaide and Tom loaned them home videos taken at Christmas of Jake in Australian Army uniform on arrival and of him having fun with the children. The rehab hospital in Perth refused to cooperate. It still made a damn fine doco. There was talk of scripting it as a movie, with Tom Cruise playing the leading role.

The TV crew left a copy of the ABC program with Adelaide to show to Mom and Pop. When the family assembled in the home theatre they watched it in fascination.

"So that's Molly," said Mom. "Some lady. And aren't the twins cute? And that's Dancer's Creek. What do you think, Pop?"

"Same as you, I expect. It's time Jake brought his family home. We need them."

Jake, thankfully, was unaware that he had been 'outed'. Had he known of his moment of television glory, he would have done more than sulk. He would have puked.

*

Molly was uncomfortably aware that Jake was not happy. She worried that he had damaged his back more than he cared to admit and had made things worse when stopping the pushchair and its precious contents from meeting a watery fate. The spontaneity had gone from their love-making. Jake spent more time in his wheelchair than he had done at first and made little effort to do the exercises to strengthen his back. He was quiet and withdrawn.

He resisted prompting to play with the children. At first he had been happy to roll on the carpet and let Sandy and Shelley crawl all over him. His bubbling enthusiasm for fatherhood, his laughter and involvement faded. He took to wheeling himself to his bedroom and shutting the door, gazing blankly through the bedroom window at the garden.

Sympathy can be drawn very thin if drained persistently; patience can be stretched until it snaps. Molly, rushed off her feet with care of the twins and the demands of the business, was as taut as a violin string. Put the bow to her temper and she would have sounded vibrato and a high-pitched note at that. At such times she would put the twins in their pushchair and march them through the town to watch the builders, to visit workshops and to beg dough from Fergus so that they could get thoroughly messy rolling it on Aunty Flo's kitchen floor.

Aunty Flo, rejuvenated, was too full of her own new relationship to have noticed much amiss with Molly's. She was full of wedding plans and of the world cruise that Fergus had agreed would make a good way to spend a honeymoon, especially if it included a tour of Highland distilleries. She had found a young baker and his family to mind the shop. She had taught Dot how to cook sponges as light as a feather. She had obtained the lease of an old drapery store at the top end of town that would make a fine Piggery. Aunty Flo had even arranged for the local potter to make a line of Dancer's Creek pigs, stoneware money boxes of oinks wearing bakers' hats. Aunty Flo was no comfort whatsoever.

Larry and Dingo were unable to visit for weeks. Both were involved in preparing the cases against Nina Lavell and Gary Flatterjohn. Dingo rang to say the Director of Public Prosecutions was making sure he had cast iron evidence to ensure their convictions.

"Shouldn't be too much trouble. When we got Flatterjohn to Headquarters, the Chief had Nina brought in from the women's prison. We put them in a room together and left them. Lord, what a racket. By the time they'd had two rounds they were ready to dob one another in, even if it meant convicting themselves."

"Weren't you afraid they'd think up some story to cover for one another?" Molly sounded very dubious about the whole affair.

"No way. You see, Larry'd already got a confession from Nina, who obviously thought lover boy had tipped us off, and lover boy had been told we had the evidence that Nina had cleaned him out. The only thing we weren't sure of was which of them had shot Frank. It was Nina's gun that was used, but she wouldn't admit to pulling the trigger. She tried to tell us Frank shot himself."

"He might have done if she told him the baby was Flatterjohn's. If she goaded him about being really sterile and said she'd fooled him, he might have done."

"Don't ever think that, Molly. Your husband didn't commit suicide. He turned out to be a white guy after all...well, a dirty sort of white anyway. Flatterjohn shot him because Frank said he was going to the police."

Molly said nothing at first. Dingo wondered if she'd understood.

"Thank you," she whispered. "I knew he was a bastard, but at least he turned out to be a relatively honest bastard."

*

By the time Larry and Chantelle were able to take a break to stay with the Morgans, Jake and Molly were barely on speaking terms. There had been no argument, no heated exchange of views, not even a hint of what was bothering Jake. Larry, looking at his best man's surly face, could hardly recognise him as the ardent lover who had greeted Molly in the church with such obvious joy.

"Come on, man, let's go for a beer at the Federal," he said.

Jake nodded and started to wheel himself to the front door.

"Stuff that," said Larry. "I ain't got wheels. Get out of there and walk. If we both end up legless, we'll get Chantelle to fetch the car to us."

"My sticks," said Jake. "Where are my sticks?"

"Bugger them too. Lean on me, old pal. Lean on me."

"Great," said Chantelle as the door closed behind them. "What's eating him? You could feel the atmosphere as soon as we walked in."

"If I knew, I could do something about it, but he won't talk to me. You knew something was wrong before you came, didn't you?"

"We dropped in at the Piper's place before we got here. The boss and Rita told us. They haven't liked to interfere, Molly. They said you were best left alone to work it out, but they were worried because Jake had become so withdrawn. Maybe he's got clinical depression."

"You mean he's having a breakdown of some sort?"

"Perhaps. It's not unusual for men who've been in battle, Molly. Jake's battle continued long after he left East Timor. After he was blown up he was at war with his own body. Maybe the shock of the danger you and the twins were in was the last straw."

"But maybe it's something else. Maybe he doesn't like being married. After Jen left him, he said once he never again wanted the responsibility of a family. Or maybe he's angry because I won't go back to America with him."

"He's asked that of you?"

"I signed the application for a visa but I can't leave here before Aunty Flo's wedding. And I can't leave Australia until I've given evidence in the trials of Nina and Gary Flatterjohn. He knows that."

"He may know it, but does he believe it? You know how irrational men can be sometimes. Maybe he thinks you're making excuses. Maybe he thinks you don't want to go with him, that you're sending messages for him to go alone and leave you here, in Australia. You do want to be with him, don't you?"

"To be blunt, Chantelle, I'm even wondering about that. I love that man to the point of desperation but I don't know if I can take much more of this silence, this rejection. I had enough rejection from Frank to know what that feels like. If Jake's turning into a grouch, he can get stuffed."

*

"We must be the first mates who've ever staggered to a pub," said Larry. "We've staggered from a few, but we've not gone in like it before. Get a grip on yourself, man."

"Up yours," said Jake, between clenched teeth.

"Okay, what's biting you?" Larry put a jug of beer on the table in front of them. "Don't you scowl at me, cobber. I know you too damn well for you to pull the crap on me. What's wrong?"

"Money," said Jake, looking darkly at his drink. "Effing money."

"I'll drink to that. If you ain't got it, you're in trouble. If you've got it, you wonder when you're going to lose it. You got any?"

"Not a brass razoo, mate. By the time I finished paying the bills the Army didn't pick up, all I'm left with is a disability pension."

"Keeps you in beer."

Jake looked gravely at Larry. "You work, Chantelle works. Molly works. I sit at home and watch the bloody babies."

"What stops you working?"

"I'm disabled."

"No, you're not. You've got two good hands, a good brain, a duff back but your legs work when you want them to. You're the one who's keeping you stuck in a wheelchair."

"I don't fit in here. I don't belong. If I was back home, helping Pop, I'd know I was doing something worthwhile."

"And helping Molly isn't worthwhile?"

"Hell, Larry. I can't expect her to pay me. I want to be able to bring in enough money to support her and the kids. I want to put the roof over our heads and the food on our table. If I ran the family business, I could draw a wage. But I'm damned if I'll be a kept man."

"Is that what this is all about? Molly's got the money and you haven't? You damn fool. What happened to we, us, together? You married Molly. You wanted to be her partner. Didn't you want to share her life as well as the bloody bed?"

"She's a bleeding millionaire, man. She's rolling in it. And I'm an effing pauper!"

"Poor bloody you. You want to divorce her and take half her property?"

"You utter sod!"

"You dummy. You fat head. You're mad!" Larry got to his feet and glared down at Jake. "I know what it is. You're jealous of Molly!"

Jake shot out of his chair and planted his fist in Larry's face.

Larry hit him back. They traded punches until the barman dragged them apart and called the cellar-boy to help him throw the pair out. The friends were left in the place that was the traditional cooling off place for fighting men from the Federal. The horse trough.

Larry looked at Jake, who had a black eye and a cut on his brow. Jake looked at Larry's bloody nose and torn shirt. Then they shook hands and started to laugh.

Larry hoisted himself from the cold water and heaved Jake out. They steadied themselves for a minute, leaning on one another, dripping.

"Race you home," said Jake, starting to jog painfully along the road to Twogood Street.

*

"Money?" said Molly blankly. "What do you want money for?" The barrier once down, Jake was on a talking jag. He and Larry had rolled through the door, soaking wet, still joshing one another.

Chantelle had done the bullying, getting them into a hot shower and dry clothes, then sitting them down in armchairs, each with a bottle and a baby.

"You running dry, Moll?" asked Jake.

"Yes," she snapped. "I've been so miserable that ..." She couldn't go on. She ran into her room and slammed the door. She sat on the bed and cried and laughed and cried some more.

"Oh ho," said Larry, "Touchy."

Chantelle said it all, very loudly and very firmly. She left them to it while she laid the table for supper. It was nothing fancy, just chicken and salad, fresh rolls, followed by fruit and cream.

Molly, showered and changed, powdered and prettied, got out her best glasses and opened a bottle of chardonnay.

"We may as well get tiddly as well," she said, handing the nurse a glass. "In vino veritas, truth in the wine."

The men were told to put the babies to bed, They made a lot of noise in doing so. They hushed one another loudly. Then they sang Sandy and Shelley a couple of songs more usually heard in the bar after a football match. The twins seemed to like them but escaped into sleep.

Over supper Larry passed on some good news. "You may not be called to give evidence, Moll. The latest information is that the precious pair are both going to plead guilty as charged. They'll be inside for years."

"And then they'll come out and live high on the money they rorted."

"No they won't. Nina and Gary squealed. Most of it's been located and is coming home sweetly to the Government coffers. The investors will get some of it back, if not all."

"How did you manage that?"

"We sent in the big battalions. We told Gary Flatterjohn's wife we were going to confiscate the house, the Rolls, the furs, the jewellery and every last cent in their bank account. Then we let her visit him."

"Nasty."

"Effective."

"Talking of money," Jake began.

Molly threw up her hands in distress. "I hope you're not looking at me, Jake Morgan. I haven't got any money."

"Jake said you're rolling in it," Larry observed. "He thinks you're a millionairess. He's feeling like a kept man!"

"Damn fool," said Molly. "Jake, I invested half of Hariman Hamid's money in the Dancer's Creek Cooperative and I put the rest in trust accounts for Shelley and Sandy. I bought this house with what I got from Frank and Nina and put my mother's money into an annuity in case I couldn't work when I was a single parent."

"What about the $200,000 you were going to give Gary Flatterjohn?"

"I wouldn't give that little shit the time of day. Aunty Flo and

I talked it over just after he made the first threats. Apart from a top layer, that safe deposit box was full of cut up newspaper."

"He'd have killed you if he'd opened it."

"Aunty Flo and I knew the risk. We figured he thought women so stupid that he wouldn't suspect me of pulling a scam on him."

"After what Nina did to him?" Larry could hardly believe what he was hearing.

"Then where is that money?" Jake couldn't leave it alone. He was like a dog with a well-chewed boot.

Molly went red. "To tell the truth, Jake, I sent it to your Mom. I asked her to start looking for a house for us in Bernadette."

"Why? We could live with Mom and Pop. They've got a huge place."

"And why did my last marriage finally fall to pieces?" Molly grinned at him. "When I had to share the same roof with a mother-in-law. Hermione Anstruther was the last straw. Your Mom may be a doll, Jake, but I'm damned if I'll live with her."

"You'll come back to the States with me?"

"Yes, but not until after the wedding. In the meantime, I've wages to pay at Marmalady, there's insurance and money for the rates, and the car needs servicing. We're living off what's left of my redundancy pay and, if you don't get off your butt and find work, we'll be down to my lucky lottery money." She pointed to the framed notes hanging on the dining room wall. "Yes, all thirty six dollars and forty cents of it."

Chapter 24

Learning the way the cooperative ran kept Jake busy. Peter Piper welcomed his application for a job with delight. "I've been waiting for you to get your act together, lad. He leans on Molly too much, I said, but Rita told me to give you time to get well. You've finished with that wheelchair?"

"I use it to take out the garbage bins. If I want wheels, I've got the pushchair."

"Yes, I've seen you doing your daily exercise with the twins. Fairly belting along the road. Your back coming good?"

"As good as it'll ever be. It doesn't stop me doing most things."

"I'll bet. Molly looks like a contented cat, purring nicely these days."

"So where do I start? I've never thought I'd end up with a desk job."

"Desk job? Hell, man, you won't spend much time behind a desk. We've got a secretary and bookkeeper for that. You'll need to know that side of things, but you'll be supervising the redevelopment, meeting investors, speaking to the tourist industry, liaising with the shire council, lobbying the government for grants, drawing up heritage and environmental plans. You'll be acting as referee between different people wanting to use the same premises and finding new shops for the ones who get their noses put out. Strewth, Jake, you'll be lucky if you sit down long enough to read a newspaper."

"Did Molly know what she was doing when she started this scheme?" Jake was staggered by the breadth of it, the amount of business activity that was taking place, the number of people who were involved. He'd shut his mind to most of it before. It was something Molly and the boss were doing, something that occupied the minds of Dot and Bud, who'd been made manager of the pickling plant.

He'd dismissed Aunty Flo's Museum of Piggery as a joke until he saw the shelves and display cases in the old drapery and saw the china pigs, the ivory, carved jade, Limoges porcelain, the Beatrix Potter models of Pigling Bland and Little Pig Robinson. There was an entire case of Miss Piggy toys in every size, a shelf of leather oinks made of patchwork, a room full of plastic porkers and posters everywhere. The retail area was stocked with piggy banks and soft piglet toys made by a group of housewives. Behind the showroom was a yard in which Aunty Flo intended to keep a couple of miniature trotters for children to play with.

"Kids will love this place," he mused.

"And its not finished yet," said the boss. "Flo's going to bring back a whole load more from her round the world trip. She wants pigs from every country they go to. And those that aren't on her itinerary, why, she's written to their governments asking them to donate to her project."

Molly, relieved to have the pressure taken off her shoulders, got down to a long-deferred project. The Marmalady Cook Book was made ready for the printers. She planned at first to sell it only in Dancer's Creek, but the publishers predicted a huge market. Molly was asked to tell the story of Dancer's Creek as a preface, it having been pointed out to her that it could draw visitors from across the country. The Country Women's Association, true to their promise, had asked members to send her unusual recipes. These had to be tested and photographs taken of the products. When the proofs were passed, the publishers suggested she do a companion book, Piccalilli.

The boss was delighted; it would seal his reputation as a Pickle King. Then the women from the sweet shop group floated the idea of Lollipop, a book of confectionery. Fergus said, "Och the noo. Canna we do Loaves for Lovers?" Wee Bryan was very critical of a proposal for Tomato-a-gogo, but went hard on Potato-Potato.

"Stop," said Molly. "I can't do all this. We need a committee." So she set one up. Dancer's Creek Books was launched, purely to meet the local trade. It led to another enterprise. The bank moved into new premises near the supermarket and its old facade was restored. It was to become a gourmet's paradise, a bookshop specialising in cookery, herbs and cottage gardens. Molly warned the bank manager that, if Dancer's Creek became one of the rural and suburban closures so popular with the industry, bent on cutting costs to reward shareholders with an even greater share of their gross profits, she would start a community bank.

Jake wrote to his father. "Hope you're hanging in there, Pop, because there's no way I can come home for the present. I'm getting to grips with this project and there's a hundred and one things to do before the grand opening. The tourists are starting to come but many of the shops and workshops won't be open to the public until then. Marmalady and Bushranger Pickles are starting to get export orders. Tom Dancer's Bread is being sold at fancy restaurants in Perth. The next thing is to start planning an olive oil crusher; there's hectares of grazing being put down to plantations of the damn things."

And Pop wrote back and said, "When you're on a good thing, stick to it, son."

Mom sent pictures of Bernadette and realtor descriptions of houses she thought Molly might like. "This one's a steal," she said. "It's only two streets away from our place and it's got a garden that's unreal. There's a swimming pool but it's properly fenced, and a lovely entertainment area with shade for the children to play in. The kitchen's done out in American oak and the floors are cherry. I know it's a bit more than you wanted to pay, but Pop will chip in to help you out."

"Take it," said Jake. "It's near the school and the drug store. It's a deceased estate and is going furnished. The old lady who lived there had a good eye for antiques. You like antiques,

Moll?"

"I'm sold. Why didn't you tell me Bernadette was such a pretty town? I thought we were going to live in suburbia. It's got a real country feel."

"You'll like it," he promised.

"What about the weather? Will I need my fur coat?"

"Lady, if you're talking about your mink, you're not going out wearing that. But we'll pack it anyway. I've got very special memories of that coat and I know where it belongs. In the bedroom."

"You want another memory, Jake?" Molly held out her arms to him.

"Mm. I just feel like sliding into something soft," said Jake, picking her up and carrying her to their room.

*

Aunty Flo and Fergus had a glorious wedding, with a garden reception at Tom Dancer's homestead, catered for as the bridal gift of Peter and Rita Piper. The three-tier wedding cake was made by the groom and iced by the bride. Fergus wore the kilt and all the fancy Highland trimmings. Wee Bryan, the best man, had refused to wear formal dress. His funeral suit would have to do, he said gloomily.

Molly was matron of honour and Jake gave Aunty Flo away. The twins, toddling either side of their mother, were page and flower girl. Shelley ate her posy. Sandy started crying and had to be handed to Chantelle to be pacified. Irish and her new husband looked at the antics with trepidation. Irish was very pregnant. Dingo wondered how he'd cope with a fractious toddler. Larry grinned and whispered in Chantelle's ear. She looked at him with a merry smile. They also had one on the way but had not yet told Dingo and Irish. It would be another cause for celebration that night.

Molly also had reason to pop the corks on the bubbly. She was not pregnant. She'd seen to that, even though she'd not told Jake. She felt guilty, remembering how furious she'd been with Frank about the vasectomy. Though, of course, that had all been a red herring. He could hardly have told her about something that hadn't happened, she mused. Her little operation, done in day surgery, was carried out under doctor's orders. There was no way she could risk another child, he'd said. Molly said Jake would have to settle for his pigeon pair. There was no doubt that it made a difference to their love-making, having the fear of conception removed.

No, what Molly was worried about was money. She'd had such an unpleasant experience of Jake's resentment of wealth he had not earned for them, that she could not bear to tell him of her windfall. Frank, having been proven innocent of fraud in the Lavell-Flatterjohn scam, had never changed his will. As next of kin she had inherited, not only his substantial investments, but also the residue of the estate of his mother. She'd sunk it all into the co-operative.

Following Aunty Flo and Fergus down the aisle, she was uneasily aware that the newly-weds were well past their three score years and ten. She knew that the Dancer's Creek property would also be hers one day. She was a rich bitch again, but knew that money had less value than love.

*

By the time the bride and groom returned from their honeymoon, with three crates of assorted pigs, the Grand Opening was upon them. The Premier was to cut the ribbon across the bridge to Main Street. There was a folk festival on the sports ground, a jazz combo in Bushranger Pickles. The original school classroom, which had been used as a sports store for years, had been restored to its prime, with battered double desks with inkwells, chalk boards and slates, with cap and gown for the teacher and all the students in period costume. In fact, all the residents had taken to the idea. It had been decided by referendum that all involved in the front-of-house business of the tourist trade would dress the part. Walk through Dancer's Creek on any day of the week, and the ones in modern dress would be visitors.

By the Centenary of Federation 1901-2001, the Premier promised, there would be a by-pass around Main Street, leading to tourist car parks near the supermarket. The shire council had been granted funds to build a ring road so that residents could drive to their homes, but soon the only traffic on Main Street would be horse-drawn buggies, early model charabancs and vintage cars.

*

The packing was finished. Most boxes had already been collected by the removalists. Dot and Bud had bought the house and Jake was happy to have some ready capital to add to his money from the Army. As he said, they'd have to buy a car in Bernadette and he wanted to repay his Pop what had been loaned them. The twins were staying with Aunty Flo for the night. All that was left in the house on Twogood Street was a couple of garden chairs and a card table, and the bed, which Dot and Bud were to have. They were also leaving the washing machine, drier and appliances that would not operate on USA voltage. The good linen had gone. Molly had made up the bed with old sheets and blankets which Dot promised to wash and send to the Salvation Army, to be given to the destitute.

They dined with Fergus and Aunty Flo and, by moonlight, strolled through the quiet streets to their home. It was warm in the lounge. The pot-belly stove was burning. Molly sat on the floor beside it, thankfully that the rag rug had not yet been thrown out. Jake lit candles for atmosphere.

"Wait there," he said. "I want to say goodbye to our first home in a fitting fashion."

He returned with an armful of spare sheets that Molly had already bagged for the Salvos. He spread them on the rug and suggested Molly get her gear off. She chuckled and complied.

She could hear him in the kitchen, rattling about in the refrigerator, warming something up in the microwave. Jake came towards her, naked and beautiful, bearing a small jug.

"I read about this couple who made love with cream and chocolate sauce," he said. "I've always had a hankering to see what you would taste like with lemon curd."

Later, exhausted, replete, he picked her up and carried her into the shower. In bed at last he held her close and loved her once again.

"You're just as lovely without the fancy topping," he said. "God, I love you, Molly Morgan."

*

It was not until the flight had taken off that Molly remembered they had left the sticky sheets in front of the fire.

"What ever will Dot think?" she said, glancing over Shelley's head to Jake, who had an excited Sandy bouncing on his lap.

"I know just what she'll think. I left a second jar of curd in the refrigerator with instructions to Bud on how to serve it."

Molly got the giggles. They settled the twins for a sleep and turned into one another's arms.

They had not tired of the embrace when an idle thought drifted into Molly's head. "Jake, you know, you've never told me what the family business is. What does your Pop do? Does he run a funeral parlour or something. You keep avoiding the issue."

He looked at her solemnly. "Well, I was kind of afraid you'd run out on me, Molly my love. He grows citrus fruit. Tonnes and tonnes of bloody oranges, and lemons, and grapefruit. He wants to diversify from juice into guess what?"

"Marmalade?"

"Too right. And my Mom's already called the first meeting of the Bernadette Revival Co-operative. I knew you'd be over the moon."

"I could kill you, Jake Morgan. I could effing well kill you!"

Then, since he looked like a whipped and saddened puppy, she kissed him again and they hugged until her ribs hurt.

The steward, pushing the drinks trolley along the aisle, smiled. It wasn't that it was unusual to see public exhibitions of passion. He'd seen it all among the stars of stage and screen who usually travelled first class, often with other people's significant others. It was just unusual to see a Mom and Pop expressing such open affection. So he coughed to draw their attention, waving the jug of drink and a pair of champagne glasses.

"Orange?" he said, and wondered why they laughed.

Molly wondered how Jake would react if he found out she had made a clean sweep of her Dancer's Creek investments, first selling her interest in Marmalady to Dot, who would become a partner with Fergus and Aunty Flo. Next had come the offer from Hariman Hamid, who had invested in a mango plantation in Broome, but had been unable to find good markets. He had visited Peter Piper with a proposition. He wanted to dip his finger in the Dancer's Creek Cooperative and start a chutney factory. Peter Piper said shares were fully subscribed but he might be able to talk Molly Morgan into selling Hariman her interest.

Molly had refused at first. She'd wanted to retain her holding for Dancer's Creek was part of her life.

"I'm prepared to be generous," Hariman had said, his eyes twinkling behind the John Lennon frames. "You hold one thousand thousand-dollar shares, I understand? I'll buy you out with a twenty per cent profit."

Molly looked severely at the Indonesian businessman, who was already unscrewing the top of his fountain pen and opening his chequebook. She recalled that it had been an Indonesian-made bomb that had nearly crippled her darling Jake; that her husband would always have pain in his back from that brush with death.

"Fair enough," she said at last. "Forget the percentage but

write it in American dollars!"

Mr Hamid's eyebrows shot up and his glasses nearly slid off the end of his nose. "But that's extortionate," he protested.

Molly shrugged. "Take it or leave it."

"You wouldn't like to become my business manager, I suppose?" he said, blotting the cheque before handing it to her. "Shall we go and see your accommodating bank manager? He will convert this to a banker's draft, I'm sure."

"I take the job offer as a compliment," Molly said, smiling.

She had intended to transfer the money to an account in Bernadette, a long-term account in her name only. If Jake never learned of it, she would be happy. He could put the bread and butter on the table; she would always know there was enough marmalade in the bank for a rainy day. She looked at her darling man, who was nodding off to sleep after a luxurious in-flight dinner. No, she was doing this all wrong. Marriage was not a place for secrets, for thinking of self, but for building an open and loving partnership. Too bad if Jake did not like the money. It would be transferred to his name and he could worry over it. She took the banker's draft from her handbag and shook his shoulder, then stroked his cheek and kissed him softly on the temple.

"Jake," she whispered, "There's something I really must show you!" She held the draft in front of him and laughed as his jaw dropped and his eyes rounded.

"One million dollars US?" he gasped. "Holy spitting mackerels!"

"Beats thirty six dollars and forty cents," said Molly. "Better than winning the lottery!"

*

The End

About the author

Wendy Evans is a Welsh nut who, brought up in an Air Force family, travelled widely in UK.

After scholarship studies in English language and literature, geography, art and comparative religion, she attended the University of Wales, where she took a BSc in geography, geology, economics, and biology.

She taught in UK and Germany while married to an RAF officer, with whom she had three children, working as an artist during the vegetable years. They migrated to Australia and spent 14 years in the Pilbara iron ore mines where she worked as a mine geologist and geological cartographic artist. She ran art and drama classes, community organizations, wrote and staged revues and plays, ran a community coffee shop and became the entertainment manager for large social club, staging top international acts.

Wendy wrote for the West Australian (state daily) and its North West paper for eight years, as well as free-lancing for four other daily, Sunday and regional papers. She had a late child and started writing stories during that period, winning several awards, and writing folk music for WA's 150th celebrations, a major musical narrative, now on CD, and a musical drama for the National Folk Festival.

When the Evans's returned to city life she became a full time journalist, winning major awards, writing humorous and satirical columns syndicated across 13 papers. She wrote the Community Newspaper style-book and trained its cadets. As a member of the National Speakers Association she was in demand by community groups for talks on the importance of recording family history and ways to use the media.

***

Wendy passed away in 2008 with almost 20 unpublished novels completed - her works are being published by her daughters, Leigh, Suzanne and Michelle. She is still greatly missed by friends and family.

If you enjoyed this book, please take the time to recommend it to other purchasers with a review or star rating via your retailer.

www.ingramcontent.com/pod-product-compliance
Lightning Source LLC
Chambersburg PA
CBHW051421170626
46809CB00006B/2266